### "I got a call about Fiona last night."

Hugh shoved away from the shelf so quickly that Ellen took a step backward. "She called you?" he asked sharply.

"No, it was someone to do with the play she's in. He...he called to ask how she was." Ellen felt perilously close to tears. She faced the bookshelf and started pushing volumes into any vacant space.

Suddenly she felt Hugh's hand on the back of her neck, and his gentle rubbing brought every nerve to trembling life. "It's okay," he said softly. "Relax, Ellen."

"I—I didn't know what to say...how to explain I didn't know how Fiona was—or where she was. Then he told me someone had phoned last week to say Fiona was ill and wouldn't be working for a while." Ellen paused, took a deep breath. "So you see," she continued brightly, "Fiona's picked up a flu or something. I expect she's with a friend who's looking after her."

"You believe that?"

"No," she admitted, barely holding back a sob, then buried her face in her hands.

## ABOUT THE AUTHOR

Stella Cameron, author of the immensely
popular *All that Sparkles*, chose her native
Britain as the setting for her second Intrigue,
*Some Die Telling*. Surprisingly, she found
writing dialogue for her English hero the
trickiest part. "I've been over here so long
that I talk American," Stella explained. "But
it's funny—I'd never noticed until now."
Stella makes her home in Bellevue,
Washington, with her husband and
three children.

### Books by Stella Cameron

**HARLEQUIN INTRIGUE**
50–ALL THAT SPARKLES

**HARLEQUIN SUPERROMANCE**
185–MOONTIDE

**HARLEQUIN AMERICAN ROMANCE**
153–SHADOWS
195–NO STRANGER
226–SECOND TO NONE

# Some Die Telling

## Stella Cameron

# *Harlequin Books*

TORONTO • NEW YORK • LONDON
AMSTERDAM • PARIS • SYDNEY • HAMBURG
STOCKHOLM • ATHENS • TOKYO • MILAN

For my friend Louise Hendrickson

Harlequin Intrigue edition published February 1988

ISBN 0-373-22083-9

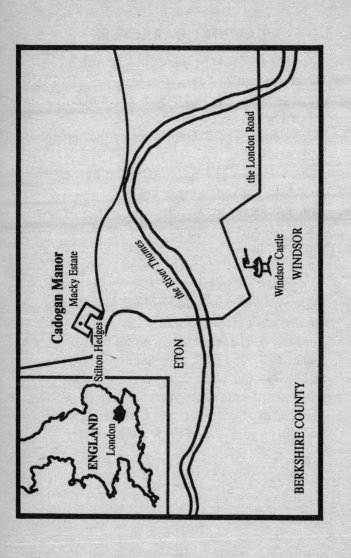

# CAST OF CHARACTERS

*Ellen Shaw*—Was she falling in love with a dangerous man?

*Hugh Weston*—He had a temper...and it seemed he'd been Fiona's lover.

*Fiona Shaw*—She'd disappeared by the time the body was found.

*Millie Weston*—The authorities decided she must have been smoking in bed.

*Simon Macky*—He was Fiona's fiancé; why wasn't he more concerned about her whereabouts?

*Xavier Macky*—He was master of Cadogan manor, but not by right.

*Violet Macky*—She'd do anything to make sure Simon didn't marry Fiona.

*Ross Ivers*—He ate weaker men for breakfast...and liked a woman for lunch.

*Jo Macky*—She was blinded in the fire that killed her parents many years ago.

*Ned Loder*—He'd worked at Cadogan Manor for many a year...and knew all its secrets.

Fiona. Hugh stared unseeingly at the heap of frayed leather book spines before him. Fiona, who had walked in from the street in the middle of a summer's afternoon and asked for employment. Chance or design?

There had been too much for him to absorb in the past few days. His mind probably wasn't connecting rationally. But the thoughts kept clicking over, a day-by-day, blow-by-blow sequence of events that had happened since Fiona Shaw breezed into his world. Many of those events had seemed unimportant—until now.

After only a few weeks of working for him, Fiona had asked if he was interested in sponsoring her sister for a work permit in England. Ellen, Fiona had assured him, was an expert on antique books, Hugh's own obsession, and Ellen also had the skills he needed in a bookstore manager. Ellen would slip easily into the nitty-gritty of running the business and give him all the time he needed for the main love of his life—hunting down the rare volumes his special clients paid him so well to find. Fiona herself, who had come to England with a touring theater company, had chosen to stay on in London and already had a small part in a new local production. The sisters would live together, but Ellen needed a sponsor who could offer her employment in her unusual field. Hugh was the perfect answer to the Shaws's problem. And they were perfect for him, Fiona had insisted.

And he'd bought the whole package, been convinced his so-called act of philanthropy would fill his own needs and realize the dream of a woman he didn't know but whose interests he understood because they were his own. Then in one week, the past seven days, the neat plan had begun to fall apart. A few minutes ago, when he'd placed the call to Fiona's flat in St. John's Wood, he hadn't really expected to discover that Ellen had arrived from America. But she had. So why couldn't he stuff his unfounded suspicions back into whatever hole they'd crawled from and be grateful?

Ellen was here. That had to prove that his doubts about Fiona were hogwash.

The tapping of his cat's claws on polished wooden floors distracted him. Vladimir leaped onto the desk, climbed on top of the pile of books and turned her marmalade back on Hugh. Her tail swung slowly to and fro, chopping the book titles into moving fragments.

Too many questions. He tried to will his mind into neutral and failed.

Surely the Shaw sisters would prove to be only minor pieces in the unwelcome chess game his life had just become. Currently the game seemed at stalemate.

"What are we going to do, old girl?" Hugh gripped the edge of the desk and pulled his chair closer until he could stroke Vladimir's thick fur. Hairs sprayed through a band of thin sunlight from the window. Winter might have been approaching, but this purring female who had, as a tiny kitten, been passed off as a male, managed to shed in all seasons. "Do you think I'm making something out of nothing?" God, he wished someone could convince him he was on the wrong track.

The cat stood precariously on the books and arched her back. Casting Hugh a disdainful yellow-eyed glare, she leaped to the floor.

"You've got it, Vladimir," Hugh remarked. "That was a foolish question on my part. It's up to me to find out if I'm right. No one else gives a damn—yet."

# Chapter One

Fiona had always been unpredictable, Ellen thought, but never this unpredictable. The crowd spewing from Hampstead underground station jostled her until she reached the steep High Street sidewalk. How could her sister have urged her to come to England, helped her to make all the arrangements, then simply not been there when she arrived or left any message at the flat they were to share? The sick dread that had been building approached panic for an instant. Fiona had made absolutely no contact in the two days since Ellen's plane touched down at Heathrow airport. Ellen had taken a cab to St. John's Wood and let herself into the flat with the key her sister had left under the doormat. In that two days her mood swang wildly between fear that something awful had happened to Fiona, and anger at the probability that her sister was repeating her old behavior patterns. Since they'd been children, Ellen had covered for Fiona's bizarre tendency to disappear, initially for hours and later for days. Usually she returned penitent, grateful for Ellen's loyalty and full of excuses for the sudden absence.

This time the excuse would have to be really something.

A chill wind sent a few yellowing leaves scurrying up from the ground, and she shivered. This threatened to be an October that single-mindedly heralded winter with no reminders of the summer past. Ellen took a calming breath and made her way to the curb to get her bearings. Where was Fiona? The last time she'd taken off, really taken off, had been after a scrape with the police. But she hadn't been guilty of anything, except knowing that her boyfriend was up to something illegal. Surely this absence wasn't anything like that one.

Wind, the wind that seemed to blow endlessly in this city of a thousand races, tossed Ellen's hair across her face and bore with it the sooty smell from the deep tube train shaft she'd just left.

Hugh Weston's place was on Flask Walk. "Left from the station, then first left," he'd said. "And we're on the left." She'd expected him to laugh at that, but he hadn't. He'd sounded a little somber on the phone but pleasant enough, very English in a clipped BBC announcer way. When he'd first identified himself she had asked tentatively if he was aware of any plans Fiona might have had to be away for a few days. He'd come back sharply with, "That was my main reason for calling. She hasn't been in for a week and she hasn't contacted me. I don't expect that kind of behavior from my staff. You're supposed to come to the shop this afternoon. May I expect you?"

She couldn't afford not to be expected by Hugh Weston. She'd given up her boring but steady job as a librarian in Boston, sold what furniture she had and backed out of the lease on her apartment to come here. And she could only stay in London if she was employed by this "perfect boss" Fiona had miraculously produced. But Fiona should be here to smooth the way, damn it.

Ellen shoved her long blond hair inside the collar of her raincoat and strode purposefully around the corner to Flask Walk. The street name was printed in black letters on white plates attached to walls on each side of the road. Below the name, in red, was the district code—NW3. She didn't want to miss the pleasure of experiencing all these new things, and she wouldn't. Fiona was probably with the mysterious fiancé she'd mentioned and then promptly ordered Ellen not to discuss with anyone, until the time was right. Whatever that meant. Still, she should have been at the airport . . . Ellen walked on determinedly. This interview with Hugh Weston was important, and thanks to Fiona, it was also likely to be difficult. It certainly couldn't be avoided. *Make it through this,* Ellen told herself, *then decide what to do about Fiona.*

Two teenagers resplendent in studded black leather, headsets clamped across the pink-and-yellow-striped stubble that covered their skulls, dodged back and forth to block her path. Ellen smiled grimly and passed between them. She'd been warned that fashions were wilder here, that she would see trends that might not appear in the States for a year or so. She knew the prediction was true, and she wished some of the concoctions she saw on passing bodies could remain permanently on the European side of the Atlantic.

She made her way down a narrow shop-lined hill. Her raincoat slapped her brown leather boots and she narrowed her eyes against the cold bite in the air. Fiona was impossible. The main selling point for this venture had been the talk of an upcoming marriage between Fiona and a man whose identity she promised to disclose when Ellen arrived in England. And Ellen had fallen for the ploy. As long as she could remember she and Fiona had joined forces against the world, filled the spaces in each other's lives that their preoccupied and elderly parents had been unable, or unwilling to fill. Even when they were parted for long spells, the tie was there. Ellen had been aching to meet this man of her sister's. When she did decide to show up, they would have a long talk about responsibility. Hugh Weston's mention of a week's absence had really rattled Ellen. That meant Fiona had probably known she wouldn't be there to meet

Ellen even before Ellen left for England. A short telephone call could have saved all this uncertainty.

Flask Walk widened where it crossed Back Lane, also on the left. Then came Flask Close, a little courtyard surrounded by crowded buildings that looked as if they needed to elbow one another aside for more space. And, too soon, Ellen saw two swinging signs, one behind the other, suspended above two doors. The first sign read Experienced Books, and through leaded windows she made out floor-to-ceiling rows of crammed bookshelves. The second sign said Fine Vines on one line, with Wine Bar in smaller letters below, but she didn't go far enough to look inside. Books were her territory, the older the better, the more the better.

She pushed open the door with one hand and pulled her hair free of her coat with the other. Her job here might be an already accomplished fact, but she regarded this first meeting with her new boss as an interview and intended to make a good impression.

A bell above the door jangled fiercely, startling Ellen, and she closed the door behind her with exaggerated care.

Several minutes later she was still waiting in front of the antique brass cash register. The shop was silent and filled with her favorite scent—that of old dusty books.

"Hello," she tried timidly, then a little louder, "Hello! Anybody here?"

Her voice was an intrusion. A "sssh" rose to her lips, a holdover from the library, and she hunched her shoulders sheepishly. Her heart thudded a little harder. On the wall, a big round clock with huge black numbers made an abrupt whirring noise. Ellen took a step backward and looked around. "Hello," she called. Maybe Hugh had asked her to come tomorrow afternoon. Nothing was as it should have been.

Something soft slunk around her legs and she yelped, only to look down into the upturned face of the biggest yellow-and-white-striped cat she'd ever seen.

She smiled and hunkered down to stroke the animal. If she weren't a sensible, mature, twenty-seven-year-old woman she'd say this place was spooky. The cat set up a purring noise similar to a chain saw missing a few cutters.

Hugh had heard the bell. He'd left the door unlocked. It was Wednesday, when the shop was closed for the afternoon, so the bell must have meant Ellen Shaw had arrived.

He finished copying a list of order numbers and left the study. At the bottom of the stairs leading from his flat to the bookstore he opened his mouth to greet the woman stroking Vladimir, then he changed his mind. Instead, he leaned against the doorjamb and watched her.

The likeness was uncanny. They weren't identical twins, but if he hadn't known Ellen existed, he'd have assumed this woman was Fiona. The same long blond hair, very shiny and slightly wavy, although Ellen's was longer than Fiona's. The same arched brows and small nose. She was smiling at the cat and he would bet she had a deep dimple beside her mouth.

Vladimir was putting on her irresistibly charming act. Not unusual, except that she rarely wasted it on women. She'd never honored Fiona with more than a dismissive flip of the tail.

"You're gorgeous, cat," Ellen Shaw said. "Are you in charge around here?"

"She thinks so," Hugh said. He kept his hands in the pockets of his old khaki pants with the frayed hems and approached Ellen. "You must be Ellen."

The woman stood up immediately but he noted that she showed no awkwardness. She did hesitate fractionally before shaking the hand he extended.

"That's me. Ellen Shaw. And you must be Hugh."

"Guilty," Hugh admitted. There *was* a difference between the two women. Several differences. Where Fiona's eyes were blue, Ellen's were a dark compelling brown. And Ellen was much taller than Fiona, and thinner, almost thinner than he liked, he decided. The dimple was there.

"I'm glad you called the flat," she said. "I wasn't quite sure what to do."

Another discrepancy between the twins. Although they had a similar air of enthusiasm, this one had a little reticence mixed in. Fiona had probably never heard of the word reticence.

"Didn't Fiona tell you I expected to meet you today?" he asked.

"She wrote me about it."

He frowned. "That's something, I suppose." He must be cautious about what he said. A careless comment could ruin any chance he had of finding out if his hazy suspicions about Fiona were founded. "Let's go into the bar. We could have some tea and sit and talk."

She glanced around. "Is it always this quiet in the afternoon?"

He pointed at the sign on the door. On their side it read Open. "I suppose you didn't notice that. We close on Wednesday afternoons to compensate the staff for having to work all day on Saturdays. The bar will be open again tonight, of course. I understand most stores in America are open seven days a week. We're headed in that direction in this country, but some of us are holdouts."

Ellen hadn't noticed the Closed sign when she'd come in. She wanted to say she had too much on her mind to register much of anything, but she simply made a polite noise and followed Hugh Weston up a single step and through an archway into a room that smelled of aged wine and old wood. He waved her into a seat at the scarred round table. "Tea okay?" he asked without checking his long stride.

"Fine," she said, though she would have preferred coffee. He skirted the dozen or so tables that made the small room seem even smaller and went behind a high bar that ran along one wall.

The man wasn't what she'd expected. He wasn't effusive nor was he cold, but straightforward. Fiona had said she liked him and Ellen thought she'd quickly feel the same way. And he was attractive.

"Milk and sugar?"

She took a second to realize he was talking to her. He had a wonderful voice, deep and clear. "No thanks." He was more than attractive. Almost handsome in a strong unaffected way. She liked his curly brown hair, which was a little too long and strayed over the open collar of his rumpled checked shirt. And a cleft in his chin, a full mouth that turned up at the corners, his straight, slightly sharp nose, all appealed to her. So did his eyes. They were more gold than brown, almost amber, and warmer than she would have expected from his short, to-the-point telephone voice.

He approached, concentrating on not spilling the tea. Early thirties, Ellen calculated. About six feet, broad shouldered and solid. More and more to like and she did want to feel good around this man.

"Are you hungry?" he asked. "We always have a lot of good cheeses and breads, and fruit."

"Thanks, but no. I ate lunch." She smiled as he slid the teacups carefully onto the table and dropped into a chair opposite hers. He really was a good-looking man. What, she wondered, was he doing rattling around on his own? Fiona had said he was single.

He caught Ellen's eye and she quickly reached for her tea. Being single didn't mean a man lived like a monk. There was probably some spectacular female already firmly entrenched in his life. Ellen unbelted and unbuttoned her raincoat and slipped it off. Hugh Weston's private business was nothing to do with her. What she needed most from him was the security he had already offered by agreeing to guarantee her a job—and maybe a little insight into what Fiona had been up to lately. Apart from Hugh there was no one in London she could turn to for help.

When she looked up from her tea he was studying her with disconcerting intensity. He set his cup back on the table, then said abruptly, "I want you to get started tomorrow. You didn't have any trouble finding this place, did you?"

Ellen set down her cup, too. "No," she said slowly. "But Fiona—"

"Good. We open at nine, but there's a good hour's work needed before that each day. I only have one full-time assistant in the bookshop and a student who comes in on Saturdays. I need to be freed up and that's where you come in. You'll take my place in the shop as much as possible. Ed Butters does everything for me here in the bar and he's going to miss Fiona, particularly at the moment. Business is picking up. We may have to find someone to take her place until she decides to show up. *If* she decides to show up."

If she decides to show up? The panic came gnawing back. "Fiona won't be gone long. I'm sure of it."

He looked dubious. "If you say so. Do you feel you have the qualifications to manage the shop?"

If he hadn't been convinced that she was capable, why had he agreed to sponsor her? He was confusing her, frightening her. "Yes, absolutely. I'll do a very good job for you." She must pull herself together and pin him down, make him understand she needed some support, at least until Fiona made contact.

"Is eight o'clock a good starting time for you?"

"Yes, but—"

"Good. At first I want you to concentrate on familiarizing yourself with the routine. And getting to know our regular customers."

She nodded. Could he be so insensitive as to think she wasn't concerned about her sister? He was behaving as if Fiona had been dismissed, had become a nonperson.

"How many years were you at the library?"

"Three." But he already knew that, didn't he? Her hair stuck to her neck and she lifted it free.

"What was your position there?"

"Reference librarian," Ellen said, barely managing to keep her voice level. He was leaning back in his chair but his posture suggested tensed muscle ready to move...to pounce?

"How did you get interested in antique books?"

Ellen stared. He had the answers to all these questions. From the forms she'd had to fill out and what Fiona had told him, he must know almost as much about Ellen Shaw as she knew herself. "I had an uncle who was an auctioneer. Books were his thing. First I started going along when they were cataloging private libraries that were coming up for sale. Then I gradually started helping. It all grew from there. I've still got a lot to learn."

"You'll never learn it all," he said shortly.

He was baiting her. He had to be, but why? The temptation to ask if he thought he did know it all was almost overwhelming. Ellen felt a twinge of antagonism.

He laughed and the pleasant deep sound surprised her. "Don't look so irritated. I didn't mean to sound critical. I merely meant the subject is bottomless. That's one of the things I love about old books. There will always be more surprises, more volumes we thought didn't exist."

Ellen laughed, too. "I'm transparent, I'm afraid. I can't hide what I think." Fiona had always teasingly warned her not to play poker because whatever she felt showed on her face.

Hugh was regarding her silently again and she shifted uneasily in her seat.

"I'm going to have to put a pretty heavy burden on you without too much guidance at first," he said. His unwavering stare unnerved Ellen.

"Don't worry about that. I enjoy challenge." She wanted to look away but couldn't. "Fiona—"

"I won't be here as much as I should be, and normally would be, but I expect Fiona's explained all that to you."

Why did she get the impression he'd rehearsed what he intended to say? "I haven't really—"

"I'm the only relative and there's a lot to do at a time like this. I didn't realize how much. Lawyers and funeral directors and all those people are pretty foreign to me, thank God. I'd like to keep it that way."

Ellen stared at him blankly. "I'm sorry," she said. "I'm afraid you think I know something I don't. Don't you remember my asking you on the phone if you knew where Fiona might be?"

He leaned forward so suddenly that Ellen flinched. "You mean you don't know where she is either?"

She swallowed. The anxiety returned. "No."

"Good Lord. I assumed you were making some kind of excuse for her not coming to work."

"I'm sorry I wasn't clear. I was asking you if you knew where she was because I don't." Her eyes stung and she blinked.

"But she knew you were arriving. You mean you haven't seen her since you got to London?"

"No, I haven't."

"But she left a note or message, surely?"

"No."

"How did you get into her flat?"

The neck of her woolen turtleneck felt as if it had turned into a tightening band of rubber. "She always leaves a key under the mat," she almost whispered.

He shook his head, and one raised dark eyebrow suggested disbelief. "You've been at her flat for two days. Fiona hasn't been there. You don't know where she is and you haven't *done* anything about it?"

A butterfly being pinned to a board must feel like this. "I didn't know who to... I didn't know what to do. Fiona has a history of deciding to duck out for a while. I expected her to turn up at any minute."

"But she hasn't?"

"I told you that. And the landlady is useless. I did ask her if she knew where Fiona was, and all the woman was interested in was making sure she'd get her next month's rent."

"I didn't realize Fiona was unreliable." His expression was vaguely satisfied, as if she had confirmed some suspicion he'd had.

Ellen bristled. "Not unreliable, exactly. Just a bit of a free spirit." If she didn't know better, she might think Hugh Weston disliked Fiona. But why would he help with Fiona's sister's visa and work permit if that was the case?

He pulled in his bottom lip with strong square teeth. "Mmm. She chose an interesting time to become a free spirit."

"Yes," Ellen said. He was right about that. "I thought she'd be hopping up and down with excitement at the airport when I arrived."

"That's not what I meant, although I agree with you that she should have been there to meet you. My problem is that my grandmother died a week ago and I've got a lot of cleaning up to do. Legal stuff. I don't need extra pressure."

Instantly Ellen felt selfish and inadequate. "Oh, dear. I didn't know." She stood up, then sat down again. "I haven't spoken to Fiona since early last week. I'm very sorry. Just tell me what I can do here. Really, I've had a lot of experience with books, and I'm good with accounts and I can be a pretty mean troubleshooter."

She closed her mouth. He was watching her again, weighing her.

"You'll have to be all of those things," he said flatly.

There wasn't even a suggestion of warmth in him anymore. But he had just lost someone who had probably meant a great deal to him. She must try not to react without considering what was going on in his life. "Will any other members of your family help with...with your grandmother's formalities?" She had no experience with such things.

"There isn't anyone. I thought I said that. She only had me."

Ellen softened toward him. He was really saying that he and his grandmother had only had each other. "Was she ill a long time?"

"No," he said tonelessly. "Let's start going over a few things. The system's old-fashioned. Everything's cataloged on file cards. Or we try to keep it all cataloged. A lot of the business is special requests and I deal with those."

He was avoiding the subject of his grandmother, Ellen thought, and wished she could think of a way to reach out and support him. "Don't worry about a thing, really. Just point me in the right directions and if I have problems I've got a tongue."

"Good."

She could feel the tight hold he was keeping on his emotions. "Can I do anything to help with the other things you've got to do...for your grandmother?"

"No, thank you." He'd turned sideways so that his profile was a clear outline against the dim light in the room. The corner of his mouth was drawn down and his square jaw was lifted slightly. "Fiona has done this before, you said? Dropped out of sight, I mean?"

"Well . . . not quite like this, I suppose." Not when Ellen was totally relying on her. "But she does have a tendency to cut out if she's under some sort of pressure."

"Did she seem as if she was under pressure?"

Ellen's stomach tightened. "I didn't think so."

"Neither did I. Why do you think she might do this now?"

She wished he would stop asking questions she couldn't answer. "I don't know. I'm sure if she knew you were going through all this she'd be here. Did you tell her your grandmother was ill?"

"My grandmother wasn't ill. She was burned to death in a house fire. Accidental, they said."

WHEN ELLEN ARRIVED BACK in Fiona's basement flat, the clock on the stove showed six o'clock.

She felt like a piece of time-share bubble gum—totally used up. A grilling session, she thought, tossing her coat over the back of a kitchen chair. Hugh Weston had conducted a grilling session as if she were on trial, not a prospective employee. He'd asked her what had seemed like a million questions about her background, her parents, her childhood, her goals. And with every question he'd added a little hook to include Fiona. She didn't know where the man was coming from. Everything he'd asked he must have already known.

Ellen trailed into the living room and flopped onto the hard overstuffed couch with its covering of some indeterminate fabric that still bore the outlines of faded cabbage roses. When she'd first let herself into the evenly divided box of small rooms it had seemed cheerful, a careless hodgepodge of colors and clutter typical of Fiona. The place depressed her now. She saw only how threadbare and mismatched everything was. The missing ingredient, the dash needed to bring everything alive, was Fiona. Ellen's throat stiffened painfully. If only Fiona would come back.

Above the flat stretched the three narrow floors of what had once been a beautiful Regency house. Ellen felt the presence of the people up in the other rooms—the landlady on the ground floor who thumped loudly with a broom handle at the slightest noise from below, and the serious-faced young couple on the two remaining floors. Knowing life was continuing all around her as if nothing was wrong intensified Ellen's sense of helplessness.

But something was very wrong.

Once she'd recovered from Hugh's announcement about his grandmother and sensed that he had not, in fact, been particularly close to the woman, she'd tried to concentrate on the instructions he poured out. But in between the instructions had come the interrogation, the strange little queries. "Does Fiona's flat seem lived in?" Yes, she'd told him. "Are you sure she didn't leave a message or try to reach you?" Yes, she was sure. "Has she ever been gone this long before?" And at that she'd hesitated. For several years she and Fiona had seen very little of each other because Fiona had been traveling. "Well, has she?" Hugh had pressed and Ellen had been forced to say she didn't know.

Was Hugh afraid something had happened to Fiona? Ellen buried her face in her hands. *She* was afraid something had happened. What other reason could there be?

Had Fiona become involved with someone criminal the way she had years ago? Then she'd been mostly an innocent pawn, the one who got invited to all the parties while her boyfriend tagged along. He'd tagged along and he'd stolen, small things at first, but gradually more and more until he'd been caught using a credit card that wasn't his and the whole truth came out. Fiona had been questioned by the police for a day and released. She'd taken off for a few days, then returned, but she'd never forgotten the incident or stopped being afraid of the kind of authority that could shut her away.

The phone rang and Ellen heard herself cry out. There had been no noise here since she'd arrived, except the occasional bang of the broom handle from upstairs. Another ring. She scrambled to pick up the receiver of the old black instrument.

She closed her eyes and prayed to hear Fiona. "Hello."

"Fiona?"

Her skin turned clammy. "No. This is her sister. Who is this, please?"

There was a short silence, then the man said, "I didn't know she had a sister. This is Len Widdy. We were wondering if she's feeling any better."

"Better?" Ellen repeated weakly.

"She isn't? Damn. I suppose that's why you're there. I don't know how long we can hold her part."

Comprehension came to Ellen. The man was someone from the play Fiona was in. And he seemed to think she was ill. "When did you last talk to Fiona?" she asked tensely. This could be the lead she was looking for.

A burst of music on the other end of the line made Ellen hold the receiver away for an instant.

When the noise subsided Len Widdy said, "A friend of hers called a week ago yesterday. He said she was in bed with the flu. He said he was taking care of her."

## Chapter Two

Hugh crammed the empty TV dinner container into the rubbish bin on the narrow porch outside the kitchen door. He braced his weight on the railing and looked down onto the cobbled lane that ran behind the row of buildings. Each property had a second-story flat very much like his and most were occupied by the owners of the shops below.

At the bottom of the steps to the courtyard he'd planted snapdragons in the sawed halves of a whiskey barrel. The blooms were gone now, the stems leggy and drooping. He liked gardening. It occupied his mind in a way that calmed him. One of the only things he'd missed when he left his grandmother's house in Maida Vale, a nearby London district, to study at Oxford had been his quiet hours in her little garden. He wished he could miss his grandmother, wished he could feel hurt at the loss, but although she had always been kind she hadn't loved him. After he'd stopped needing her as any child needs an adult—to rely on—there had been nothing left but the habit of living in the same house.

Now she was dead.

He was alone, but then he'd always been alone, hadn't he? The woman who had brought him up with quiet distant patience had never kissed or held him, had told him nothing of his parents except that his mother hadn't been sure which of the men in her life was his father and that she had deserted Hugh when he was little more than a baby. That had been all. His mother was never discussed and his early curiosity had gradually faded.

And now the coroners were finished with their dry reports, their dreary sheets of facts. Millie Weston, his last connection to mortal roots, had become a dehydrated life in easily filed form.

He screwed up his eyes. A silvery band hung above the patchwork of rooftops on the other side of a high wall, a dull strip of foil stitching earthly things to an encroaching night sky. Fiona Shaw's flat was in a basement with a little square of garden at the back. She, too, he knew, planted flowers in tubs, by the front door as well as outside the windows of her little bedroom. Ellen might be outside now, looking at the sky. He wished she were watching it here, with him. The idea that he thought of her that way made him uncomfortable. The woman was a stranger, might even prove to be a dangerous stranger.

He could see her clearly in his mind, her dark eyes so convincingly troubled, the habit she had of pushing back the mass of thick hair, the suggestion of a tremor at the corners of her full mouth when he'd deliberately pushed her about Fiona. She had seemed genuine. All the answers matched what he knew. But he hadn't dared ask any of the questions he'd really wanted to ask. A waiting game lay ahead, waiting and watching... and hoping. Only now he wasn't quite sure what he hoped for.

Tonight he wished he didn't have to be alone. Even practiced loners needed someone from time to time. The lid of the dustbin was askew. He thumped it down on his way back inside.

The last thing he felt like doing was spending the evening in the wine bar, but Ed would need his help and keeping busy wouldn't be such a bad idea.

A pall of cigarette smoke met him as he reached the bookshop, and the blast of Ed's favorite music, Dixieland. During the day, when the shop was open at the same time as the bar, the connecting door was closed and no music could be heard. At night Ed and his group of nightly regulars enjoyed their intimate jam sessions and the door was opened for ventilation.

"Hello, Hugh!"

"How you doing, Hugh?"

The bar customers called out their usual greetings. He knew that most of them regarded him as an oddity they'd chosen to adopt and champion. Students who lived in rented rooms around the area, an assortment of couples who considered Hampstead trendy, even the handful of would-be writers who congregated nightly to discuss masterpieces "in progress" but evidently never quite ready for submission, none of them had anything in common with him.

He made his way toward the counter, smiling, slapping backs, laughing at jokes he didn't fully hear. Ed Butters looked up from washing glasses in the minute steel sink tucked into a corner. "Evening, Hugh. Am I glad to see you." He wiped the back of a beefy forearm over his sweating face. "Things are really hopping tonight. I had an idea, though. Do you think Jean-Claude would be interested in a few extra hours' work?"

Jean-Claude was a language student from Paris who was spending a year in London to perfect his English conversation. He was the part-time help Hugh had hired for the bookshop on Saturdays.

Hugh rolled up his sleeves to take Ed's place at the sink. Customers were lined up at the counter good-naturedly demanding service. "You see to them," Hugh said. The bar had been a gimmick at first, an experiment to see if they could pull in more book customers. Now he made bigger money here than next door, but he was no bartender, even though he did know his wines.

Ed passed behind him, his red face and bald scalp shining. "What do you think about Jean-Claude?"

"What would he do?" They needed Fiona, or someone like her. She could do anything necessary.

"What you're doing. Wash glasses. Wipe tables... Maybe we could even make a barman out of him." Ed winked a pale eye at Hugh, a grin spreading his bushy mustache. They both knew Hugh detested pouring wine for people who didn't know a Vouvray from a Pinot Noir and who more often than not ordered a glass of some generic parsnip creation put out by a local brewer. He'd never tasted the stuff but it smelled poisonous.

When Ed came back to put two meat pies into a small microwave, Hugh said, "We could try Jean-Claude. He needs the money. But I can't see him with his hands in dishwater."

Ed shrugged and grabbed a towel. "He could give it a go. We're going to have to find someone full-time for nights soon. And someone to fill in for Fiona in the daytime, too. You've got a regular little gold mine here, mate. Might as well make the best of it." His cockney accent sometimes grated on Hugh. It did tonight. But everything grated on him tonight.

"Well," Ed went on, "what do you think?"

"I'll talk to Jean-Claude. He can't help in the daytime, though."

"When is Fiona coming back?"

Hugh didn't want to talk about Fiona, or think about her. "I don't know," he said shortly. "When she's ready, I suppose." Talking to someone about what he really thought might be a relief, but he couldn't until he had more to go on.

"She still didn't call?" Ed shook his head and didn't wait for Hugh to reply. "Strange, I call it, you two being, well, you two being friends and all. It's not like her."

"How do you know?" Hugh said before he could stop himself. "I mean, how can either of us know if it's like her. What *do* we know about her?"

The buzzer went off on the microwave. Ed gave Hugh a puzzled look before he took out the pies and went to serve the customers.

"You hired her," Ed said when he returned. "And you liked her from the start. You said she was just what we needed."

Hugh concentrated on the continuous stream of dirty glasses. "She is. Forget what I said. I'm not coping as well as usual."

"'Course you're not," Ed said, his voice loaded with genuine sympathy. "Losing someone's a strain. Too bad, I'd call it, the old lady going like that. Have they finished with the investigations and—"

"Not now, okay, Ed?" The police had finished, all right. Or they thought they had.

Ed punched his arm lightly, awkwardly. "I never was the soul of tact, or so the wife says. Sorry. But don't you worry about any of this. We'll manage. I could look around for a bit of help myself. I'd run whoever I found past you—"

"Do that," Hugh cut in quickly. The main thing was to keep everything running smoothly and his small existing staff happy while he did what he had to do—find out what really happened the evening his grandmother died.

"Right," Ed said, visibly pleased. "Did that sister of Fiona's show up? The one who's a librarian?"

The noise of the bar and Ed's probing were getting to him. "Yes. She came this afternoon. You'll meet her tomorrow."

"Well." Ed gave another of his broad grins. "She must know what our Fiona's up to. Didn't she say?"

Our Fiona. He must get out of here and think. "We were busy talking about her job."

Ed scratched his head. "I'd have asked anyway. Never mind, I'll have a word with her tomorrow. Don't you worry."

"No!" Hugh said, then he lowered his voice. "I don't know what's going on there, Ed, but I don't think we should push."

The man's expression clearly conveyed that he didn't understand what Hugh meant. Hugh wasn't sure himself, except instinct told him to tread carefully with Ellen Shaw where Fiona was concerned.

"If you say so." Ed gave him another bemused glance and turned away.

Despite the din and the increasing crush as the evening wore on, the hours until closing time passed with agonizing slowness for Hugh.

When he finally trudged back up to his flat, he'd made up his mind they would find more help for Ed and soon.

He collected the notebook and pen he'd left on the kitchen table and carried them into the sitting room. The tawny leather furniture he usually enjoyed looked uninviting. So did the artificial brightness of the electric fire. He poured a stiff Scotch and went to his bedroom.

Stretched out on his bed, the glass balanced on his chest, he held the notebook above his head and read what he'd written. Days and dates, starting with Tuesday of the previous week, and after each date a few words. All the words should add up to something, a cure for his doubts or a formula telling him how to proceed, if he should proceed at all.

Early on that Tuesday evening his grandmother, Millie Weston, had died in a fire at her home in Maida Vale. Neighbors reported first sighting the blaze in the region of her bedroom, and by the time the fire brigade arrived the house was fully engulfed. Before they could attempt to go in, there was a series of explosions and the firemen had been called back. Then the whole area was cleared, as fear grew of an underground explosion in the gas mains. The mains did blow and not only Millie Weston's house, but houses on both sides of the road were demolished.

The next note Hugh had made, for the same day, read:

Almost from day we met, Fiona asked personal questions. She got me to introduce her to my grandmother, then visited her several times. Insisted she liked her. Always found that strange. The Tuesday of the fire she insisted on doing an errand for me, going to Maida Vale to check up on things the way I usually did every Tuesday. Fiona said she knew I was too busy and she'd enjoy going. Haven't seen her since.

He read the statement several times, then turned the page. Wednesday had been a round of interviews with the police and fire investigators. Two more days had passed, then the verdict was handed down. Hugh had written it out verbatim:

Accidental death by burning. The seventy-eight-year-old victim was probably smoking in bed, fell asleep and the mattress smoldered, eventually leading to involvement of the old pipe system in a gas fire, then nearby mains. What scattered human remains have been recovered will be released to the deceased's only known relative, Hugh Weston, for disposal.

"Damn it all, I don't believe it!" He dropped the notebook and barely grabbed his glass before it tipped.

Millie Weston hadn't smoked in years and he didn't accept the investigators' theory that she could have taken it up again in secret. He also didn't accept that she'd gone to bed early—the fire started around seven—because she'd been a night owl as long as he could remember. And the suggestion that she might have been sick didn't work. He'd spoken to her in the afternoon and she'd been fine, more cheerful than usual and chattering about looking forward to having a visitor. It was the first time he'd heard her sound enthusiastic about Fiona.

The police examiners' story didn't ring true; nor could he fully believe the insane theories building in his brain. If only Fiona would show up with a plausible excuse for her absence. He might still wonder exactly what had happened to his grandmother, but he would stop inventing heinous crimes perpetrated by a beautiful young woman who couldn't possibly have any reason for hurting anyone, a woman surely incapable of killing anyone.

Killing. His head ached. Why had Fiona been so interested in Millie Weston? Why would she insist she enjoyed visiting an uncommunicative, sometimes testy old lady? Then there was the way she'd come to work for him in the first place. He hadn't advertised, yet there she'd been that day back in June, persuading him she was exactly what he needed, had to have. And she'd pulled it off with such ease. It didn't make sense that she'd chosen his business by chance, and from the new inquiries he'd made in recent days, she hadn't applied to any other shops in the immediate area.

Vladimir chose that moment to put in an appearance. The satisfied look and the hint of cool air she brought with her made Hugh wonder if he was about to be presented with one of the mice she sometimes found outside and laid in broken little heaps by the kitchen door.

He patted the bed beside him, and she jumped up and immediately settled in a suffocating collar across his neck. Hugh blew away a hair that settled on his mouth.

There had been all those questions Fiona had asked, the personal questions so cleverly couched that he didn't think about them until this past week. She'd found out more about him than anyone else ever had, and she'd managed it so smoothly.

He knew where he was heading in his mind—Ellen Shaw. Where did she fit in? Where did she fit in with what was going on with Fiona? He couldn't buy the story that the two sisters hadn't made contact since Ellen arrived, unless Fiona had got cold feet over something she'd done and dropped from sight until she felt safe. Could Ellen have been fully aware of some plan of Fiona's all along? And had she subsequently come to England to help finish what had been set in motion?

"Off, Vladimir," Hugh ordered the cat. When she was on the floor and stalking imperiously away, Hugh sat up briefly, then fell flat across the bed, his arms spread wide.

The next quick picture he made in his head was of Ellen when she'd taken off her coat in the bar. Yes, she was very slim, almost fragile in build, yet somehow soft and supple and very feminine. She'd assessed him, too, more carefully than she probably realized, he knew. And between them had passed that fantastic sexual spark that needed no words. The first seconds of intense attraction that left a man throbbing to touch, to know more. Well, certainly in one sense he would know more, he decided. That she would learn her job easily was obvious, but he had to know her better if she was going to take on a position of trust.

He balled his fists. Who was he fooling? Trust be damned. She turned him on in a way he hadn't felt for too long. This was a total mess. He should have nothing to do with her until his fears were put to rest. She shouldn't work

# Chapter Three

Cecily Horton seemed perfectly happy with the idea that Ellen was to become her manager. "You don't know how long I've begged Mr. Weston to find someone like you," she said, puffing slightly as she stepped from the bottom of a ladder and slid it to the next row of books. "He's got so much to do with all his acquisitions, and of course, now..." She let the sentence trail off while she rolled her watery blue eyes heavenward.

For the past forty minutes, since she'd arrived for her first day's work at Experienced Books, Ellen had trailed behind the trim gray-haired woman, listening to a stream of useful information. Concentration was hard. Fiona, her face, her name, the constant uncertainty about her safety took most of Ellen's attention. "How long has Hugh been in business?" she asked.

Cecily started another climb toward the ceiling. "Since shortly after he left Oxford, I think. He did tell me his grandmother, God rest her soul, cosigned for the mortgage because he didn't have a penny. Mr. Weston is honest, open about things. Everyone likes him."

Ellen stopped herself from saying she wasn't surprised but she wished she understood him a little better. "How long ago did he leave Oxford?"

The woman's face turned down toward Ellen and they exchanged smiles. Cecily leaned on the ladder. "He's thirty-one, is that what you wanted to know?"

Heat rushed into Ellen's face. "I guess." She laughed.

"You look a lot like your sister," the woman said, "but that's where the similarity ends, isn't it?"

Ellen wasn't sure what she meant. "A lot of people mistake us for each other, but in fact we aren't identical."

"I wasn't thinking so much about appearance," Cecily Horton said, settling herself more comfortably on the rungs. "You're both lovely. And Fiona's special. But she never thinks before she speaks, the way you do." She spoke frankly, comfortably, with no attempt at softening what she said.

Ellen decided she liked the openness. "Fiona isn't famous for her tact, if that's what you mean." It felt good to talk about Fiona; it relieved the tension, the sense of abandonment.

"I never met a young woman with more questions." Cecily's blue eyes crinkled at the corners and took on a distant expression. "She asks anything and everything. Mr. Weston thinks the world of her. I think he'd do anything for Fiona."

"You could have fool—I'm glad." Ellen recovered just in time. From what she'd observed of Hugh Weston's feelings for Fiona she'd have said he didn't care about her one way or the other.

"Oh, yes. They talk for hours, those two. She can really make him laugh." The smile disappeared, to be replaced by a deeply thoughtful frown. "There was a time when I thought they might become more than friends. Ed still believes they are, but...oh, I don't know. I do know she's good for him. That man doesn't enjoy life enough. Not that I expect him to be laughing much for a while."

Their eyes met in mutual understanding, but Ellen's brain was computing the information she'd just received. Fiona and Hugh were close, close enough to laugh and talk together for hours. Yet he behaved as if their relationship was almost less than casual employer-employee. He seemed very willing to think the worst of Fiona. And the possibility of their being anything more than friends was out of the question, since Fiona was engaged to someone else.

Ellen's stomach twisted as it so often had in the past few days. She changed the subject. "So Hugh's been here what? Nine years?"

"Oh, no. Not that long. He got a first, then went on at Oxford for a couple of years. English literature, I think. He's very bright."

"A first?"

"His degree," Cecily said. "What we call a first. The best, in other words."

"Figures," Ellen muttered.

She continued handing books up to Cecily, but her attention was trained on the open door to the stairs that led to Hugh's flat. Last night, after the call from the theater, she'd had to fight the need to contact him and tell him what she'd heard.

"This is all the poets," Cecily was saying. "We do a brisk trade in the Older Generation at the moment. Lots of William Blake and so on."

Ellen gave a theatrical sigh and recited: "'When my mother died I was very young,/ And my father sold me while yet my tongue,/ Could scarcely cry, 'weep! 'weep! 'weep! 'weep!'"

"'So your chimneys I sweep, and in soot I sleep.'"

Hugh had come noiselessly up behind her. She closed her eyes briefly against the bound of her heart and smiled at him over her shoulder. "Intense stuff."

He favored her with one of the unblinking stares she'd visualized again and again during her sleepless night. "I like intense stuff," he said quietly.

"So do I," she responded honestly, lifting her chin to return his look more directly. He must be taller than she'd estimated, well over six feet. She was five-foot-eight, but even in heels she felt short beside him.

"Mrs. Horton," Hugh said, resting a hand on the ladder, "if you'd like to brew some tea for us, I'll take over with Miss Shaw."

Ellen noted his formality with amusement.

Cecily Horton needed no further encouragement. She descended the ladder with surprising agility and bustled through to the empty wine bar.

"Fiona told me you were well versed in English and French literature, as well as the American stuff," Hugh commented.

He hadn't voluntarily mentioned Fiona before. Ellen almost poured out what she needed so desperately to say to someone—that she'd had a message about Fiona that might as well have been in an unbreakable code and that she was worried and didn't know what to do next. But if she did tell him, it might prove to be a mistake she couldn't afford to make, though she wasn't sure why. She managed a little laugh instead. "The 'American stuff' sounds condescending. Do you discount American writers?" He wasn't a man who would appreciate less than a direct approach. Even without Cecily's comment Ellen had felt that.

"Not at all. But we do have less call for the Americans than the others, obviously."

"Obviously. Don't worry, I can hold my own in most areas. If I hit a rough spot I'll holler."

"Holler?" The word sounded strange on his lips and they both laughed uncomfortably.

"Shout for help," she explained.

Ellen was holding a load of books. The ladder was behind her, Hugh in front, one of his shoulders against a bookshelf, the other arm closing her in as he still held the ladder.

She could smell the clean scent of his after-shave, see the pulse in his throat, dark hairs at the open neck of his shirt. The silence lasted too long. Ellen knew they both sensed it but she couldn't move, or speak. She didn't want to move.

"Has Mrs. H. been filling you in?" he asked evenly. His eyes were on her mouth. "She knows her stuff."

Ellen stirred, pulling in a breath. "We'll do fine together," she said. "She seems very kind and willing to work with me."

He smiled but his eyes remained watchful. "Good. That's what I was hoping. You'll make a good team. Mrs. Horton isn't interested in too much responsibility, but she'll back you up well."

Everything they said sounded like awkward inconsequential small talk. They were both fencing. Ellen decided to try a comment about Fiona. Hugh's reaction would tell her whether or not to go on.

"I got a call about Fiona last night."

Hugh shoved away from the shelf so sharply that Ellen involuntarily took a step backward, knocking her shoulder into the ladder.

"What did you hear?"

The hairs on the back of her neck prickled. Whatever she'd decided about his concern for Fiona had been wrong. Hugh Weston was very interested in her. "She hasn't been well. Flu or something."

He bent his head, came so close she saw the dark flecks in his golden eyes. "She called you?"

Ellen wished she could put down the books. Instead she held them tighter. "No. Someone else did."

He narrowed his eyes. "Someone else? Who?"

Talking it through wasn't going to help, Ellen realized. It would only dispel the fragile excuses she'd made, such as Fiona was probably with her fiancé; she'd had a fever, felt too ill to make contact. A dozen other theories had come and gone during the evening and the night. The truth was she had very little more information about Fiona's whereabouts than she'd had before the telephone call.

"Who called?"

The harshness of Hugh's tone snapped her head up. "Len. Len Widdy."

Hugh looked blank. "Who the hell is Len Widdy?"

"Someone to do with the play Fiona's in." Hugh hadn't mentioned Fiona's engagement. Her twin must have had some reason for not wanting him to know and Ellen wasn't about to betray the trust.

"What did he say?"

He felt much bigger than she, too big, and forceful. Whatever she said was going to sound ridiculous. She tried to shrug but only felt more closed in by him. "He just said that Fiona's had the flu."

Hugh frowned. "She's with this . . . Widdy, or whatever his name is?"

Why had she said anything? "No. He . . . he called to ask how she was."

"You've lost me." Hugh didn't move back but he put his hands in his pockets.

Ellen felt perilously close to tears. She faced the bookshelves in the cramped space available and started pushing the volumes she held into any vacant spot.

"Those are out of order."

She stopped and closed her eyes. "I'm sorry. This is impossible."

"Why don't you try explaining what's happened, slowly, step by step?"

"I don't..." Quickly, she pulled the books out again. "Look. I apologize for Fiona's behavior. As soon as possible one of us will give you a proper explanation. In the meantime, I appreciate you allowing me to get started here in your shop the way you have."

Suddenly his hand was on the back of her neck, rubbing gently, bringing every nerve in her body to trembling life. Instinctively she knew he wasn't a man who touched easily.

"It's okay," he said softly. "Relax, Ellen. Just tell me what the man said. Take your time."

Tears surged into her eyes and with them a wave of horror that she might break down. She cleared her throat, breathing deeply through her nose. "He asked how Fiona was. I didn't know what to say. Then he told me a friend of Fiona's had called him on Tuesday of last week to say she was ill and wouldn't be able to work for a while."

He dropped his hand and Ellen felt bereft. "I wish someone had called *me*," he remarked tightly.

*And me,* she wanted to say. "Even when she was a kid, Fiona always got sicker than anyone else when she picked something up. I expect she's with a friend who's looking after her."

"You believe that?"

Ellen turned on him. "What do you mean?"

He raised a hand as if to touch her face, but spread his fingers in the air instead. "Nothing, only that I can't think of a single excuse good enough for her not to have at least made contact with you yet."

He was right, but she wasn't going to say so. "She'll have a good reason when she does talk to me."

"I'm sure you're right," he said, while his face and voice betrayed that he thought the reverse. "But let's put that aside for now. Ellen, you aren't going to have any trouble here. I can already see that. But there are a lot of things we're going to need to go over."

"Yes," she said, determined not to show how miserable she felt. "I'm looking forward to the experience."

A thoughtful look entered his eyes. "I believe you are. Are you doing anything after work tomorrow evening?"

He knew she wasn't. "I don't have any plans," Ellen responded, keeping sarcasm out of her voice. Putting one foot in front of the other, going through the motions of life in a strange city and country were all she had to look forward to. In case he hadn't noticed, she was totally alone.

"That's good. At least—" he took the books from her "—I hope it's good. I'd like you to spend at least part of the evening with me. My bookkeeping methods are, um, unconventional, I suppose you might say. We should make sure you get a complete handle on everything as soon as possible."

Ellen waited, her heart speeding up, while he climbed the ladder and shelved the books. He rejoined her. "So, would you mind staying after work tomorrow? We'll go over a few things, but I promise to feed you first. I cook a fair TV dinner and the wine's good around here—if you like wine."

He looked...uncertain? Hopeful? She bowed her head for an instant. He looked young and, yes, he did seem uncertain.

"I like wine very much," Ellen said, smiling up at him. "And TV dinners."

After work, Ellen left the compartment of her home-bound underground train wishing Hugh had asked her to stay behind that evening instead of Friday. She didn't want to go back to the flat alone. The station at St. John's Wood was cleaner than the one in Hampstead, but quieter. This was a more residential area. When Ellen reached the street, instead of turning down Acacia Road she crossed Wellington and wound her way toward Abbey Road. She'd found it on a map Fiona had sent and had decided that when she got here she would go and see where the Beatles used to record.

Dusk joined gray sky and buildings to gray streets. By the time she found the sign for Abbey Road, streetlights had popped to life and puddled across the slabbed sidewalks, turning gray to dull pewter.

Ellen walked faster. The EMI studios of Beatles fame were in a large square building flanked by clones, and abruptly she turned away and crossed a black-and-white pedestrian walkway between its flashing orange warning beacons. Fiona should have been with her. These should have been some of the best times they'd ever spent, free and full of adventure.

Ellen broke into a trot, then a run.

Half an hour later she was still running, dimly aware of curious glances from passersby but not caring. Her breath came in choking gasps that seared her throat. All that mattered now was getting back and hiding in the little basement flat. At least it was a place to go. She passed Lords Cricket Ground and turned onto Wellington Road.

Almost there. If she had the guts she'd go to Hugh Weston tonight, spill the real depths of her fears and beg him for help. She didn't have the guts.

Black shadows knifed out from alleys between buildings now. In the long spaces between streetlights, the trees were alien giants, their dying leaves rustling overhead, crunching beneath her feet.

She heard her own sobs when she swung around the metal railing to the uneven steps leading down to Fiona's flat. A small flicker of hope died when she found the key still under the mat. She'd left it there each time she went out, hoping her sister would have returned before she got back.

The darkness inside had texture, and she put out a hand as if to ward it off. She couldn't go on. Tonight she'd call the police and report Fiona missing. Better still, she'd go to a police station and talk to someone. There was nothing to be gained by alerting her parents. They wouldn't understand or be able to help. They'd probably say what they'd always said: "Take care of it, Ellen. You know your sister's difficult." They had never figured out that when Fiona had first become difficult it had probably been in some vain attempt to get their attention. The breaths Ellen took didn't reach her lungs and she held her aching stomach.

She pushed the door behind her with an elbow and switched on a small lamp by the couch. Should she go to the police now? Fiona wouldn't want them involved. The phone was by the lamp. She touched it. Hugh would probably be at home. No. Calling him would only make things worse. He was her boss, not her psychiatrist. She couldn't risk alienating him even more than Fiona had already.

The door, swinging open again, let in a blast of cold air. And a man.

Ellen's hand went to her throat. She could make no sound come from her mouth. She stood in front of the weak lamplight and could hardly see his face.

"Sweetheart," he said, bowing and shaking his head. A glint caught the lenses of his glasses. "Thank God you're back. One more day of this holiday nonsense and I was going to fly to Paris and bring you home myself."

A second later Ellen was enclosed in strong camel-hair-clad arms and crushed against leather buttons.

"Please—" Her voice was an insubstantial croak. He held her so tightly she couldn't move.

A strong hand pressed her face against a silk tie. She smelled a pine after-shave. He tipped back her head and kissed her, opening her mouth, rocking her head fiercely from side to side.

Her fists against his chest were useless.

He kissed her cheeks, her eyes, and rested his chin on top of her head before he said, "I need you. Don't leave me again, Fiona."

The scream that had risen to her lips died. Ellen held her body stiff and waited, the deafening roar of her heart pounding in her eardrums.

They stood like that, locked together, for what felt like hours. The man smoothed her back steadily and, as he did, she felt the fear ebb. He wasn't going to hurt her.

"I'm not—"

"Why didn't you call as soon as you got back?" he interrupted.

The next feeling to assail Ellen was unexpected but welcome. It was a need to laugh, hysterically.

His grip had slackened and she pushed away. "I'm not Fiona."

# Chapter Four

He had a nice face. Not classically handsome, but pleasant and humorous—particularly when he laughed. And he was laughing now.

"I can't believe it. No one would believe it," he sputtered. "I barge in here and do my best Clark Gable act and all on the wrong woman. Damn, I'm sorry."

Ellen rested her hand on his arm. He still held her waist lightly. "Because you don't really give a damn?"

They both laughed.

"I thought you were Fiona."

"Yeah, I got that." She disengaged herself completely and went to turn on another light. "I'm Ellen."

"I worked that out, too. She's talked about you enough. What are you doing here?"

Ellen cocked her head. "Don't tell me she didn't tell you I was coming."

He pulled a paisley scarf from his neck and tossed it over the back of a little wooden chair. "She didn't." His laugh had died to a somewhat uncertain smile. His obviously expensive coat joined the scarf and he unbuttoned the jacket of a flawlessly tailored gray suit. He was at home here.

"Sit down," Ellen said.

"But she did tell you about me, I take it?" Behind glasses with light-colored rims, his dark eyes became troubled.

Ellen felt sorry for him. "Please, sit down," she urged and he perched on the edge of the couch. His build was athletic, not particularly tall, maybe five-eleven but all muscle. "I assume you're the man who's engaged to Fiona. But I don't know anything at all about you. She wanted to surprise me."

"Good Lord." He ran a hand through straight brown hair, took off his glasses and started searching through his pockets. "She's done more than surprise me." His smile was sheepish. "Sorry for the passionate greeting, really. You're a lot more like her than even she led me to believe. Taller, I suppose, and thinner..." A violent blush made him appear very young and Ellen wondered just how old he was. He leaned a little closer, squinting shortsightedly. "Your eyes are brown, aren't they? And your hair is longer, but apart from those things you're just about doubles, y'know."

"So we've always been told." She took off her raincoat and hung it in the closet behind the front door. Knowing his name would have been nice, but she wouldn't embarrass him further by asking. "I do know she's crazy about you," she said and controlled a smile at his visible pleasure.

"That's mutual." Everything about him spelled success—his expensive clothes, a heavy gold signet ring, the Rolex watch that glittered beneath one snowy shirt cuff. Only the flashes of uncertainty she sensed in him were at odds with the image he presented.

Ellen sat at the other end of the couch. She couldn't offer him a drink. There wasn't even a bottle of wine in the flat. "Coffee?" she said tentatively, then quickly added, "Or I expect you'd prefer tea."

"I don't drink tea."

"Oh."

"I don't care for anything at all, thanks."

She wanted to ask him what he'd meant about Fiona and Paris and vacations, but he was so patently uncomfortable that she decided to let him find his own way through this difficult encounter.

"I say," he almost shouted, "do you even know my name?"

"I'm afraid not." Ellen smiled and it felt good. "That sister of mine really does like a little drama."

"Oh, I say, that's too much." He put his glasses back on, leaped to his feet and offered her his hand. "Simon Macky. And I'm delighted to meet you. Absolutely delighted. So will my family be. Fiona and I are thinking of a Christmas wedding, and I know having you with her will make all the difference. You will be with us that long, won't you?"

"Absolutely." Her broad smile was difficult to banish. He was so touchingly sincere. "And I'm pleased to meet you, too."

He pumped her hand, then sat again. "Well." He cleared his throat. "When did you get in?"

"On Monday morning."

"Really." He frowned. "But you did know Fiona wouldn't be here, didn't you?"

Annoyance at her sister's irresponsibility seeped to the surface once more. "No, I didn't." She was so tired of going over this. "I've been very worried."

"Naturally. But you know what a wonderfully spontaneous woman she is." His fond smile showed how in love he was. "She cut out last Tuesday week. Some friend from the play invited her to go to France for a few days and she just took off. Came to the office, I think. I wasn't there, but a note was left with my assistant."

Someone from the play? Should she mention the call she'd received from Len Widdy, or would Simon disapprove of what had obviously been a lie to excuse Fiona's absence from her part? It would be good to know whom she was with. Should she call Widdy and ask if there had been a sudden flu epidemic in his group last week, and then find out who else was sick? "Did she say when she'd be back?" she asked Simon slowly.

The boyishly embarrassed look returned. "Well, actually the note was a bit vague. I checked my answering service while I was at my club this evening, but there was nothing from her. But I thought I'd stop by and see if she was here anyway."

Ellen's newly found relief was slowly shrinking. She had a wild urge to try to keep Simon with her as long as possible. He was tangible and alive and she didn't want to be alone here any longer. "So Fiona didn't give any hint of when we might expect her?"

"Well." He flipped a hand back and forth. "It's a bit iffy, I suppose. I did think she might be here tonight. But we're supposed to go down to Cadogan for the weekend and I'm sure she'll be back for that. So tomorrow, I assume. She's bound to be back by tomorrow night so we can leave early on Saturday morning.

Ellen took a few moments to absorb this. "What's Cadogan?" she asked, almost afraid to believe that he was right and she'd see Fiona the next day.

He spread blunt, well-manicured fingers on his thighs. "My family's place near Windsor. I live in town but I try to get down there on weekends. You'll come, too, of course."

"Oh, I don't think—"

"You must." He shifted closer, enthusiasm animating his face. "Wait till you meet Jo, my older sister. Our parents are both dead, but Xavier and Violet, our uncle and aunt, will be ecstatic to see you." His wry little grimace intrigued Ellen. "They're very old-world, I'm afraid, and much as they like Fiona I do think a little more family in evidence would please them, if you know what I mean."

Poor Fiona. Ellen tried valiantly for a reassuring smile as she said, "I sure do." She thought she had quite a good idea of what he meant. A picture of a stuffy tight-lipped couple exchanging glances at Fiona's less-than-conventional behavior froze the smile on Ellen's face.

"So you'll come?"

What was she supposed to do? Buy some tweeds and brogues, and maybe a shooting stick?

"Look, let me tell you a bit more about us," Simon went on. "Then you'll feel you've known us all your life."

Ellen doubted that but she nodded politely.

"We're farmers."

"Really?" She couldn't help a sweeping gaze over his beautiful suit. He didn't resemble any farmer she'd ever met.

"Yes, or mostly," Simon continued earnestly. "But we also have a brewery and that's my concern. I keep an eye on things there."

An instant image of Simon's Guccis tripping through dusty buildings that reeked of barley and hops threatened to became laughable. "You work at a brewery?" She supposed there could be separate offices.

"No, no. The brewery's in Hertfordshire. I hardly ever see the place. But it's a pretty big outfit. We do packaged foods, nuts and so on, in conjunction with beer and bulk wines. My offices are in the City. Gutter Lane. I'll take you around as soon as you're ready. We could have done it tomorrow but I'll be in meetings most of the day."

"It sounds very interesting," Ellen said. How strange that Fiona hadn't shared all of this. "Did you and Fiona meet recently?" she asked, suddenly inspired with a possible explanation.

He looked directly at her and she saw that he understood the true reason for her question. "No. She's been keeping her secret for a long time, I'm afraid. We met last March. At a party. We've seen each other almost every day since." A flush rose in his cheeks again. "I do love her very much. She's ... special. There's no one like Fiona."

Impulsively, Ellen reached for his hand and squeezed. Simon looked taken aback but returned the pressure.

By the time he left, she had agreed to make a threesome with him and Fiona on Saturday and visit his family.

Another sleepless night followed, this time because she was excited and apprehensive. Excited at the prospect of seeing Fiona the next day. Apprehensive about meeting the Mackys. And, most of all, excited and apprehensive and expectant as her evening alone with Hugh Weston approached.

"I EXPECT EVERYTHING SEEMS very different to you here in England," Hugh said as he ushered her up to his flat.

"A bit." Ellen waited for him on a narrow landing at the top of the stairs. Three closed doors lined one white wall. Two others stood slightly open on the opposite wall. Beside her a crooked, leaded-glass window overlooked the street. In the closest room she could see an old oak double bed and a nightstand piled high with books. Clothes were carelessly tossed over a wicker-backed chair.

"Come in, please." Hugh passed her and opened the closed door nearest to the front of the building. "This room's always cold. I'll put on the fire."

Ellen followed him, still uptight from waiting all day for him to put in an appearance. When she had arrived at the store that morning, running inside in her hurry to tell Hugh what she'd heard about Fiona, he had already left and remained out all day. Ellen had watched the shop door anxiously, afraid he wouldn't return by closing time at six and wondering what she should do if he didn't.

Every few hours throughout the day Ellen called Fiona's flat, but got no response. She made up her mind that if Hugh did come back and she did work with him for a while, she would find an excuse to keep calling in case Fiona arrived home before she did.

Then, as if on cue, Hugh had appeared a few minutes before six, while Cecily was putting on her coat and gathering her string shopping bag, which bulged with groceries.

Cecily had asked Ellen if she'd like to walk with her to the station. Hugh's calm statement that Ellen would be staying to have dinner with him had produced a double effect. Cecily Horton's eyes hadn't lowered in time to hide her curiosity, and Ellen, although unconcerned about what the woman might think, was annoyed at Hugh's peremptory manner.

She and Hugh were now inside a small combined sitting and dining room. He slid a plastic sack onto a table near a bay window. "Dinner," he said offhandedly and crossed to kneel in front of an electric fire. He turned a knob and bars of blue flame popped to life.

Ellen hovered just inside the door, her coat and purse in her hands. Was she attracted to this man because he was so untouchable? He went about whatever he had to do with a single-mindedness that closed out anyone around him. Now he remained in front of the fire, his back to her, rubbing his hands. His green canvas parka emphasized the breadth of his shoulders. Clothing definitely wasn't high on his list of important items. He had about him a clean, windswept, very masculine air, but it emanated from the man, not the almost carelessly casual clothes he wore.

"This is a nice room," she said uncertainly. "Cozy."

"I like it," he responded without looking at her.

She ventured farther into the room and ran a hand over the back of a couch covered in supple, brown leather. Two wingbacked chairs covered in similar leather flanked the fire. One had a worn footstool askew in front. A beautiful old rug, its soft umber and rose tones still distinct, lay over all the floor, leaving only a narrow surround of darkly glistening wood. Bookcases lined every available wall, and Ellen relaxed a little. One of the things that drew her to Hugh was their shared interests, or interest. Apart from his love of books she knew very little about him.

"Sit by the fire," Hugh said abruptly. "Here." He patted the chair to his right. When Ellen had done as he asked he shoved the footstool closer. "Use this. The shop's hard on the old plates of meat."

"Plates of meat?" Ellen laughed.

"Feet. Ed's influence. You'll have to spend an hour with Ed when you can. He's an education. Londoners, cockneys particularly, have a lingo all their own. You should learn it if you intend to stay here long."

*If she intended to stay?*

She hadn't been cold when she came into the room, but she was now. Was he changing his mind about wanting her here? The arrangement had been that if she worked out for him as an employee she'd stay in London indefinitely.

"I do intend to stay—as long as possible."

For the first time since he'd returned to the shop he looked exclusively at her. And he looked slowly, studying her face like an artist assessing angles and proportions. Then his attention moved to her hair, and she thought he smiled a little before carrying on downward to finish at the toes of her insubstantial flat black shoes.

Ellen didn't tend to blush, but when his eyes returned to hers, her face and neck were hot. She parted her lips to speak, but he glanced at her mouth and she forgot what she wanted to say.

"Do you like Chinese food?"

She stared at him blankly before she gathered enough composure to reply. "Yes. Why?"

"Because that's what I bought for our dinner. And I've got a bottle of plum wine if you'd prefer that to something traditional." He got up and collected the plastic bag.

He was quicksilver. No, he was a still surface, like a dark patch of smooth ocean, but with a riptide hiding below.

There was no way to know what he was really thinking, really capable of, and he changed without warning.

Ellen's instinct was to sit straighter in the chair. Instinct also warned her that he was probably trying to test her and expecting her reaction to be one of uncertainty each time he pulled one of his subtle mood changes. She slid down a little and plopped her feet onto the stool. The smile she settled on her face felt phony. "You promised me TV dinners," she said lightly. "And I don't like plum wine."

"You *don't* like Chinese food?"

It was his turn to look unsure and she almost laughed. "Are you a male chauvinist, Mr. Weston?" she asked, feigning shock. "Do you automatically assume the little woman will go along with whatever you choose as the order of the day?"

He stood, the bag dangling from one hand, watching her like a new specimen in his particular lab. "You're very direct."

"And you don't like that?"

He shrugged. "I didn't say I didn't like it. You surprised me, that's all."

"Mmm. The lesson is, never assume anything. And I do like Chinese food. In fact, I love it. I'll help you heat it."

"But not plum wine?" He watched warily as she got up and glanced around, looking for the kitchen.

"No."

"White Zinfandel? California?"

"Sounds great, but I wouldn't expect you to suggest anything from California. Where's the kitchen?"

"Back into the hall. Second door past this one. Why wouldn't I suggest anything Californian?"

"Because California's in America and things American don't seem to rate very high with you." Including American people, she thought, but closed her mouth firmly.

He followed her into the hall. "I never said I didn't like American things. Californian wines are gaining a lot of respect. Some of them show promise."

She waggled her head as she pushed open the door he indicated. "Show promise, huh? Do you ever hand out an unqualified compliment?"

Ellen gave the simple kitchen a quick once-over: an enameled sink with draining board attached to one side by clamps, a gas stove with legs and a tiny refrigerator on a tile-topped table. Every surface clean and uncluttered. She did find things different in England. She also found them very appealing.

"I think you're bright and knowledgeable," Hugh said behind her. "I'm glad I've met you. You're beautiful, too."

Her scalp tightened. Her palms, pressed together, became sticky and hot. She faced him slowly. His expression was impassive, as if he'd just told her it was raining. "Thank you," she muttered. "Thanks a lot."

"Not at all. We'd better find some dishes that can go in the oven."

Ellen watched him open and close cupboards attached to the wall above the sink. Maybe she should get her hearing checked. He gave no sign that he had just paid her a string of wonderful compliments.

"Do you mind taking these?" Before she could respond he dumped silverware into her hands.

Hugh didn't own two plates that matched, or glasses. And evidently he didn't care. They set the table while the food was in the oven, then he poured wine and showed her the view from a square porch outside the kitchen.

"The Bull and Bush is that way," he said, pointing. "Hampstead has some of the best-known pubs in the world. Spaniards, Jack Straw's Castle. They're a bit too touristy for me now."

"Have you lived here all your life?" she asked and instantly wished she'd kept her mouth shut. She knew he hadn't lived here that long. Fortunately, he had no idea that Cecily had told her.

"I grew up in Maida Vale," he said, one thumb jabbing in a generally westerly direction. "Then I studied at Oxford for a few years. Then here. This is home now. I don't think I'd want to live anywhere else. Where did you grow up?"

"In Boston," she said before she remembered he knew exactly where she'd grown up. Maybe he was just making conversation.

"You've never lived anywhere else?"

"No." She hadn't told him her news about Fiona yet. "I heard—"

"Where did you go to school?" The corner of his mouth was pulled down again in the way that sent a chill up her spine.

"Northeastern University in Boston."

"And Fiona went there, too?"

He was doing it again. Checking up on the Shaw story. "Fiona went to Emerson. She studied speech and drama."

"Oh, yes, of course she did. But you both graduated in the same year." His eyes narrowed while he pumped out his examination.

"I graduated a year before Fiona." Showing that he bothered her wouldn't help. "Six years ago. I was twenty-one. Fiona got through a year later."

"And she's been touring ever since."

"Not all the time, Hugh," Ellen said firmly. "Fiona should be back sometime tonight. In fact, if you don't mind, I'd like to try calling her."

He turned to her immediately and she couldn't read his thoughts. Again she noted his ability to wipe all expression from his features. He did miss a few beats before he said, "Be my guest. There's a phone in the sitting room."

"Thanks," she said and hurried out.

She listened to twelve rings before she hung up the phone and returned to the kitchen, where Hugh was taking dishes from the oven.

"No reply," he said without inflection.

He was infuriating. "Aren't you going to ask where she's been?" she said.

"I'm sure you'll tell me." With a dish in each hand, he passed her and went toward the sitting room.

Ellen took the remaining plate and followed. He left once more and returned with their glasses. "Sit down and eat before this stuff gets cold again."

Frustration threatened to choke her. "Fiona's been in Paris," she announced and sat down opposite him.

"Uh-huh." He sounded disinterested.

"Hugh," Ellen said impatiently, "aren't you glad to know where Fiona is? Mrs. Horton told me you and Fiona get along very well."

"Did she really? Subgum mein?"

"I beg your pardon?" She screwed up her eyes at him.

Hugh waved a spoon over a dish. "Do you want some of this?"

"Yes, I suppose so." Ellen slumped back in her chair while he served her a heaping plateful of food. She wasn't hungry but doubted he'd listen if she said so.

"There you are." He smiled at her and she noticed, with an unpleasant revolution of her stomach, that his eyes were hard and penetrating.

"Are you saying you don't get along with Fiona, Hugh?"

"I like her." He offered chopsticks but she shook her head and picked up a fork instead.

"Will you fire her when she gets back?"

"If she comes back I'll decide." A little muscle beside his mouth twitched. He wasn't as cool as he'd like her to believe. The detachment was an act for her benefit.

"I just told you she's been in Paris and she'll be back tonight."

"She's been in Paris getting over the flu?" He used chopsticks, easily disposing of one piece of food after another.

Exasperated, Ellen smacked her fork down on her plate. "Of course not. That was just a story she gave the theater company so she could be away for a few days."

Hugh put his chopsticks down with thoughtful care. "Run this by me, please. Fiona lied to the people at the theater, then went away to Paris."

"Yes . . . at least, that's what I think happened."

"You think? Isn't that what she told you?"

He was mixing her up. She swallowed some wine. "I haven't spoken to Fiona. But what I said seems logical."

"Excuse me," Hugh said as if he were speaking to an obtuse child, "but nothing about this seems logical. First, she's ill and being looked after by a friend. Only you don't know what friend. Then she's in Paris and the flu was a lie to get her there while she kept her job . . . or one of her jobs. Evidently she doesn't care enough about working here to send me any of these mysterious messages."

Ellen shook her head. "No, no, I know how it sounds, but it's not that way. Her fiancé told me she's in Paris."

Hugh had picked up his glass. Now he set it down.

Too late, Ellen thought. She had not intended to mention that Fiona was engaged, but it was too late. Hugh's raised brows said more than any words.

"You didn't know, did you?" Ellen said quickly. "No. I didn't think you did. She only told me after she'd persuaded me to come to England and I wasn't supposed to tell anyone. Fiona loves secrets. She always did. When we were children—"

"Ellen," Hugh interrupted softly. "Is this fiancé some-one you talked to on the phone, too, like Widdy, or what-ever his name is?"

The one bite of food she'd taken felt lodged in her throat. "Her fiancé's name is Simon Macky. He runs a brewery. His family are farmers in Hertfordshire." She paused, think-ing, reconstructing. "That's wrong. He does run a brewery and that's what's in Hertfordshire. But his offices are in London. Somewhere called Gutter Lane. And he came to see me last night." Triumph at having some facts to share gave her confidence. "Tomorrow we're going down to his family's place near Windsor. It's in a village called Stilton Hedges. This is all real."

Hugh had lost his appetite completely, not that he'd been particularly hungry before. Her face and voice exuded hon-esty and she was begging him to believe her story. "I'm sure it is all real." He was pretty damned sure it wasn't, but he could only wait and see.

His best bet was to lighten up on her and keep the lines of communication open. He smiled and saw the anxiety in her eyes soften. Why did she have to be so lovely?

"I'm going to talk to her about all this when she does show," Ellen said earnestly. "She really scared me and there's no excuse for the way she treated you."

No excuse that anyone was going to confess to readily, Hugh thought. "Go easy on her," he said, hoping he sounded jocular.

"No way." The great brown eyes had filmed over. "I'm angry."

Either Ellen was an even better actress than her sister, or she was relieved enough at his change of manner to feel like crying. *You're not home free yet, lady.* He took his wine-glass and looked into it, afraid she'd see his grim thoughts in his eyes. "Well, I expect you'll forget to be angry once you see her." He picked up his chopsticks again. "Eat your dinner. You probably should get home. You don't want her to beat you there."

"You said you had some things you wanted to go over with me."

"They'll wait until tomorrow."

She stared at him and the color left her face. "Oh, no. I forgot."

He understood immediately. "You accepted an invitation for tomorrow. That's okay. Go. We'll get to this on Monday."

"I can't do that." She set her napkin aside. "I'll just have to tell Simon and Fiona that tomorrow's not convenient."

"I insist," he said. "Go, and that's an order. And don't worry so much. I'm not going to fire Fiona, just tell her off—for ducking out and for not telling me about this fiancé."

"You're sure?"

"Sure."

Only a few more minutes passed before he closed the shop door behind her. "Damn it," he said aloud. "*Damn.*"

The bar was open and the usual cacophony poured forth, but he passed the entrance without pausing and leaped up the stairs two at a time. Jean-Claude had accepted the chance for earning extra money with evident delight and would be helping Ed tonight. Even if he weren't, Hugh couldn't have coped with all those laughing faces and with trying to behave as if everything was rosy.

He almost fell over Vladimir at the top of the stairs. The cat was stalking out of the bedroom. "Pest," he said absently. "Stay off my bed."

His office seemed the best place to go. He didn't want to be where he'd been with Ellen. Ellen. If only she was ugly, or dull, but she wasn't. She made him think thoughts he couldn't afford to think. Not about her. Not until he'd decided whether or not her reason for being here was different from the one he'd been told.

Vladimir made it into the office just before Hugh closed the door. She hurried to a corner and curled up with one wary eye open.

Hugh passed a hand over his face. He had an interesting choice to make. Either he could think of today as the day when his whole world had come down around him. Or he could say that today he'd received the best news of his life.

He paced in front of the desk. Ellen Shaw might seem open and desirable, but if his theory was correct, she intended him to see her that way. His theory? That was a laugh. His theory was a frustrating jumble of half-formed ideas that didn't fit together.

There had to be a mistake. He went behind the desk and sat heavily in his chair. Today he'd had an interview with a solicitor who had contacted him "on behalf of Mrs. Millicent Weston." His brain felt too big for his skull. Mrs. Millicent Weston, who had left her entire estate to a primary heir, her grandson, Hugh Weston. He'd gone for the appointment wishing he didn't have to waste the time on being told that he'd inherited a piece of ground the size of a swollen postage stamp with a pile of burned rubble on top. He'd expected to hear about insurance money. Big deal. The brightest possibility had been that the mortgage on the shop and bar could probably be paid off faster.

Morton Lister, of Lister, Lister and Lister had greeted him at the door of his office, bowing from the waist, smiling widely enough to show gold-capped molars. And while he'd grinned and fiddled with the watch chain looped across the straining pinstripes of his waistcoat, he'd muttered platitudes. "So sad. Such a terrible thing." And then he'd dropped his little bombshell.

Millicent had been touching in her concern for her grandson. A "boy" who hadn't had all he should have had.

Why Millicent had chosen to wait so long to help her dear
Hugh, the solicitor had no idea, but—and at this Mr. Lister
had spread his hands—now all that was going to be set right.
The lady had had an *extremely* substantial estate, most of
it invested in very solid stocks and bonds and this was to be
Hugh's.

Mr. Lister had seemed amazed when, fifteen minutes
later, Hugh had insisted he didn't want to go on with the
interview today. The plump and slightly sweating little man
had recovered quickly enough to say how much he'd look
forward to seeing Hugh as soon as he was ready to make
another appointment. Of course, in his present grief, it was
natural that all this was too much for Hugh.

"Oh, God." Hugh swept a forearm over the desk,
throwing stacks of papers and books into a jumble that shot
across the floor. If he had any sense he'd smile at the sickening Mr. Lister, take the money and run. Overnight Hugh
Weston had gone from struggling shopkeeper to filthy-rich
heir. He should be downstairs drinking to his good fortune.

He rested his head on crossed arms. None of it made any
sense. All the time he was growing up his grandmother had
been parsimonious. His shoes had been repaired and repaired, to the point where his toes were cramped into the
ends. She'd told him so many time she was a poor widow
he'd eventually stopped hearing. Her husband, a mill
worker from the north of England who died because of an
on-the-job accident, had left her with a small pension. The
pension and the income from a "little inheritance" she'd
never identified were all they had, and they had to be care-
ful if the money wasn't to run out.

Oxford? Grandmother had stoically accepted the school
reports stating that he was an exceptional student who
should be given the chance for a university education.
They'd manage somehow. And with his scholarship, a part-
time job and a small allowance from her, he'd made it. And

the mortgage on this business? She'd cosigned on the basis of her "small inheritance," but never offered him a penny in solid cash.

He thought back over this evening with Ellen. Getting through without falling apart and asking her what the hell she knew about this neat little surprise had taken every ounce of control he possessed.

He looked at the phone. *Please let her call and say Fiona's back.* While he thought it, he knew the call wouldn't come. Illness, a trip, a fiancé never before mentioned. All madness. Only one concrete fact remained the same. On the day Millie Weston died, Fiona Shaw had visited her.

Had Fiona somehow discovered that Millicent Weston was a very wealthy woman? Did she figure out some plan for getting her hands on the money? Would that plan have required his grandmother's death and, subsequently, the help of Ellen—perhaps to keep watch over him and report to Fiona, who was afraid to be around until the danger of discovery passed?

Either something very strange, more than strange—something deathly—was going on, or he'd been reading too many of the classic old mystery volumes he'd sought for his customers.

Hugh got up and kicked through the litter on the floor until he found his book of telephone numbers. He checked his watch. Nine-thirty. He dialed a number and waited until a woman's soft American voice answered.

"Ellen," he said. "This is Hugh. I wondered if Fiona was there yet."

She didn't answer for a long time and he closed his eyes.

"Not yet," she said finally and too brightly. "But she will be. Don't worry. She may be real late, but I'll make sure she gets in touch with you over the weekend if necessary."

"Yes, yes, you do that." He could hear her breathing. "Good night, Ellen."

He hung up. Fiona wouldn't contact him. She'd been the one to set everything in motion, and now Ellen was in place to finish the game. That had to be the answer. But how? Was he supposed to fall in love with her and then die? Craziness. Something out of a bad melodrama. But until he came up with a better theory it would have to do. Okay, he'd play the Shaw sisters' game—and he'd beat them at it.

His eyes felt painfully dry and scratchy. "You told Fiona, didn't you, Grandmother?" He looked unseeingly at the ceiling. "You told Fiona what you must have wanted to tell someone for years—that you were a very rich woman who'd pulled the wool over her stupid grandson's eyes so well that he never guessed. And telling her killed you. You loved me and you couldn't show it, except this way. Why didn't you ever say you loved me?"

He got up, went into the sitting room and pulled on his coat. Maybe if he went for a walk he'd calm down and get tired enough to sleep.

Nobody in the bar called out as he passed and let himself out by the shop door. His metal-tipped heels made sharp clicking sounds on the sidewalk. A wind had picked up and it bit into his face.

This should be easy. Let Ellen lead him for as long as it took him to catch her, and Fiona. Only there were a few drawbacks to that pat scheme. He didn't want to catch Ellen Shaw in some criminal plot. He wanted to find out he'd been wrong about her. He wanted, God help him, to feel her in his arms...and in his bed.

# Chapter Five

Hugh didn't believe what she had told him. He didn't believe Fiona was coming back.

Ellen sat on the couch with her arms tightly crossed. The slightest sound sent her rushing to the door, only to leave her more jumpy, when she opened it to nothingness, and more filled with foreboding.

What was it with Hugh? Could the reason for his quixotic moods, his antagonism, his apparent need to try to trip her up with his questions, be as simple as a feeling of betrayal because he'd considered Fiona a friend and she hadn't treated him like one? He was a loner, not a man with a bevy of buddies, unless his life was as dual-sided as his personality. If it was and there was a Hugh Weston, party-goer and playboy, he certainly kept him safely hidden in a closet while she was around.

She stretched out on the couch, pulling an ugly pink crocheted cushion behind her head. When she closed her eyes she could visualize Hugh clearly. He'd said he was glad they had met, that she was beautiful. A fluttery feeling came and she smiled. The man was a puzzle, but one potentially worth solving. Her best guess was that the reason he didn't have a woman in his life was that he was extremely hard to know. Ellen's smile became a grin. He was hard to know and she was tenacious. An interesting combination made more interesting by the distinct feeling that he'd like her to know him. Given time and opportunity she might be willing to oblige.

Drowsiness took over. If she dozed for a while, the waiting wouldn't seem so long.

A crash in the narrow forecourt outside the flat brought Ellen's eyes wide open. She bounded to open the door yet again, just in time to see a whirling mass of fur materialize into two cats who spit at each other before they disappeared into the darkness. The crash had been the sound of a clay pot breaking. Withered geraniums and soil now lay in a messy heap.

Ellen closed the door again and stood with both hands braced on the ocher-colored painted wood. She knew without looking at the clock that it was approaching ten. Tomorrow Simon Macky would arrive, brimming with his very British enthusiasm and expecting to spirit Ellen and Fiona away to his family's bosom. She imagined him, wherever he was now, preparing for the perfect weekend, during which Ellen would provide Fiona with an impression of the solid background he clearly wanted for his wife-to-be. So why hadn't Fiona shown up the way Simon had been so sure she would?

The time for waiting had passed—long passed. She had to do something. If Fiona had gone to Paris as Simon seemed so sure she had, she must have taken clothes, luggage. Hours ago, Ellen had considered and discarded the idea of checking for missing items. She couldn't put off the task any longer.

There were two bedrooms in the flat. The one at the back, Fiona's, overlooked an unkempt garden; the other, Ellen's, adjoined the sitting room. Ellen started her search in Fiona's room.

Within half an hour she gave up. How was she to know how many pairs of panties Fiona owned, or whether there was a nightgown missing?

Suitcases. She remembered seeing at least one in the coat closet. Rummaging behind coats and jackets and shoe boxes, she located a familiar piece of blue luggage and hauled it out. Inside nested a second, slightly smaller case. Satin pockets lining the sides of each yielded nothing but a few safety pins and a pack of gum.

Ellen sat on her heels and lifted her hair off her neck. Had there been another, even smaller case? She tried to reconstruct the last few minutes before she'd seen Fiona off at the airport for this trip to Europe. All she could remember clearly was that they'd hugged and kissed and cried a lot. The blue suitcases had already been checked in and she didn't know how many of them there had been.

Frustrated, she trailed back into Fiona's room and perched on the edge of the bed. Her eyes wandered over familiar treasures on the nightstand. A teddy bear music box that played "Always" in tinny notes. It had been a gift from an old boyfriend of Fiona's. The travel alarm their parents gave as an eighteenth-birthday present. Ellen still had a similar clock from the same occasion, but hers no longer worked. An empty bottle of White Shoulders, the very bottle they'd both used on the night of their senior prom, stood beside a picture of Ellen and Fiona taken that night. Ellen picked up the picture and peered closely at the two self-conscious young men who had escorted them. Rod Barnes had been her date. His blue cummerbund had matched her dress—and his eyes. Ellen gave another little smile, a wry one this time. She felt suddenly old.

She pulled out a narrow drawer in the nightstand, then stopped. There *was* something missing. There was a space on top of the nightstand where it should have been. With a glance at Fiona's mementos arranged in a rectangle, Ellen closed the drawer again. The red journal was gone.

Rapidly, she checked the drawers below, and every other drawer in the room. But there was only one place that Fiona ever kept the journal—on top of whatever piece of furniture stood beside her bed. It was a ritual, a secret joke between the two of them that they'd laughed over since childhood. No one else would understand the significance of that book.

The flat had become colder. She dragged the spread off Fiona's bed, draped it around herself and sat against the pillows. The red journal had been a decoy. Every year Fiona had bought a new one and taken a few minutes each day to scrawl something in her homegrown shorthand. The scribbling meant nothing. Her plan—and it had worked—was to keep their mother away from the real thing by convincing her that this *was* the real thing.

Gladys Shaw, an unwilling mother for the first and only time when she was in her early forties, had done her best to "guide" her daughters. Her guidance had taken the form of lengthy lectures on the evils of having anything approaching a good time. Their mother, the girls had disrespectfully and mutually decided at an early age, was a snoop bent on making sure fun wasn't a part of their lives.

So had begun the dummy journal. Unlike the real journal that Fiona kept in her purse and that went everywhere with her, this one always sat next to her bed.

The heavy dread built. Was the missing decoy journal a sign? If it was, the only person Fiona could have hoped to alert was Ellen.

That was it. She fought free of the bedspread and dashed into the sitting room. Fiona had removed that journal to let Ellen know something was wrong, and it had taken her days to even notice the book wasn't there.

With shaky fingers, she lifted the telephone directory from the floor beside the couch and hunted for the police listings. Even if the absence of the journal meant nothing, the absence of Fiona definitely did, and there was no longer any way Ellen could wait to do something about it.

She dialed the first two digits for the local constabulary and hesitated. Simon had left her the telephone number of his flat. He would probably want to be here when the police came. Ellen depressed the cradle and pulled Simon's card from beneath the lamp base.

He answered at the first ring. "Fiona?"

Ellen covered her mouth. He was as jumpy as she was. "Simon, this is Ellen Shaw. Please listen to me before you say anything." She remained standing, consciously willing herself to be calm. "Fiona isn't here and I don't think she's going to be. I don't believe she would do this . . . to either of us."

"Do what?" he asked but without conviction.

"You know what I mean. She should have been here to meet me when I arrived from the States, or, at the very least, got in touch with me so I wouldn't worry. You're worried, too, admit it."

His long sigh gave her his answer.

"I'm calling the police," she said.

"No," he said sharply. "No, Ellen. Please don't do that, not until we talk some more."

"What good will that do? She's spontaneous as you put it, but she isn't sadistic, and what this is doing to me is sadistic. I'm going out of my mind."

"Listen to me," he responded soothingly. "You haven't been around Fiona for a while. A lot has happened in her life. Look, I'm coming over. I can be there in no time. My place is in Mayfair, not far from Park Lane. At this time of night the traffic won't be bad."

"I don't think I should wait—"

"I do. Will you at least discuss this with me before you do something we may all regret?"

Reluctantly Ellen agreed. He sounded so sincere and there was no doubt that he was as concerned for Fiona as she was, so it made sense to wait for him and join forces in whatever was to be done.

Forty minutes went by before she heard the soft purr of a powerful engine drawing to the curb outside. Ellen waited for a knock at the door, which she'd left unlocked, but Simon let himself in and she was struck afresh with the strangeness of Fiona's not letting her know, long ago, that she was in love and planning to marry.

"Sorry," Simon murmured, pulling off black leather gloves and stuffing them into the pockets of a dark cashmere overcoat. "It took me a bit longer than I expected. Some sort of do at the Dorchester and the Lane was jammed."

Hugh's comment about cockneys having a lingo all their own came to mind. Simon and his kind also had a lingo of their own, she decided. Had she not been so anxious about Fiona she might have smiled. Instead she took a moment to study Simon when he straightened. Ellen was surprised at his evening clothes. If she'd had any doubt as to what Fiona might find attractive about him that doubt evaporated. She didn't know what Simon Macky's other attributes were, but he knew how to dress. He looked terrific.

Their eyes met. The hint of uncertainty was there in him again. He glanced down at himself. "I had a business dinner this evening and it went long. You caught me just as I got back. I didn't think I should take the time to change."

"No," she agreed shortly. She intended to have her way with what she'd decided to do. "I've looked up the number for the closest police station. They may refer us somewhere else, but it's a place to start."

"Ellen, listen," Simon said insistently, "I do understand how you feel."

She picked up the directory and sat close to the phone with the book on her lap. "Good. Then we're in agreement. What do you think I should say?"

"Nothing. Not yet, anyway." He moved to sit beside her. He patted her hand awkwardly, then took it in both of his. "We've got to be sensible. Fiona would be embarrassed if we called the police. I know exactly what's happened and, believe me, there's no need to worry. By all means, be upset with her when she does get back—I shall be, too—but don't make things so hard for her that she retreats."

Ellen looked at his serious face. "Retreats?" Was he insecure about Fiona's love for him?

"Goes away completely. She's in France, I tell you. And by now she's feeling horribly guilty, about you and about me and probably about the play. But she's undoubtedly having a good time. Fiona always has a good time wherever she goes." He sounded wistful, as if he envied Fiona's ability to turn any situation, no matter how dull, into a positive experience.

"She wouldn't stay away without calling or writing. I've known her all my life, Simon. We've done our share of fighting, but we're still close, and she was excited about my coming. She wouldn't abandon me like this."

He let go of her hand. "A lot's happened to her since you two were together. Me, for one thing. She's got loads on her mind, loads of adjustments to make. The more I think about it, the more convinced I am that she's using this time to catch her breath."

Ellen shook her head. "I can't buy that."

Simon got up and wandered behind her. He drummed his fingers on the wooden trim of the couch. "Okay. Let's put it this way. *I'm* asking you to give Fiona a little more time to show up or contact us."

Her palms stuck to the thin pages of the directory. "Why are you insisting on this?" she asked unsteadily. "We both know there's a problem. Do you want us to wait till she gets more in danger... or more dead?"

Simon inhaled and let the breath out noisily. As soon as she'd voiced her true fears, Ellen's skin felt clammy and her insides trembled. Now that she'd allowed herself to really face the possibility that Fiona could be dead, it became the only conclusion that made any sense.

"She isn't dead." Simon moved rapidly, returning to his place beside Ellen. "I'm right. She'll come back when she's ready to cope with the worry she's caused. She's impetuous. She does things without thinking about the consequences, and then she shies away from sorting out the mess."

"I don't know," Ellen said. "I just don't know. What am I supposed to do next if I don't go to the police?"

"That's easy," Simon announced with a falsely bright smile. "Tomorrow we'll carry on down to Cadogan as planned. They're all looking forward to meeting you."

"I can't do it, Simon. Not until I know Fiona's okay."

"Certainly you can do it." Simon shook her shoulder gently. "You're making too much of this. A couple of days in the country is exactly what you need."

She laughed nervously. "And how will you explain why Fiona's not with us?"

"Leave that to me. Wait and see. Very soon we'll all be laughing about this. We'll both give Fiona a good—"

A knock on the door stopped him.

Ellen clutched at Simon's arm. Her heart took a giant leap. "It's open," she whispered, then she stood up and shouted, "Come in."

When the door swung open, Simon was on his feet and striding forward.

He halted abruptly as Hugh Weston walked into the room.

Ellen stared from one man to the other. "Hugh. What is it?" His hair was wind-tossed, his old canvas jacket unzipped and hanging crookedly. "Did you hear something from Fiona?"

Hugh looked at Simon while he spoke to her. "No. But I did some thinking after you left earlier. We didn't cover as much ground as we should have. I was going to ask if we could talk some more, but . . ." He let the sentence trail off, his attention firmly fixed on Simon.

"I was just leaving," Simon murmured, casting Ellen a curious glance. "I take it you two are friends."

"Yes," Ellen said simply.

"Well, then. I'll see you in the morning as planned."

He was putting on his coat when she finally regained her composure. Hugh hadn't known anything about Simon, but surely Fiona had told Simon she had a part-time job with Hugh. "Simon," she said, putting a restraining hand on his wrist, "I don't think you've met Hugh."

Simon paused in the act of putting on his coat, then shrugged it all the way on. "Simon Macky," he said, offering Hugh his hand.

"Ah," Hugh said, running an appraising eye over Simon. "The fiancé." He shook Simon's hand briskly and briefly.

Ellen clasped her hands together. Whatever Hugh felt for Simon at the moment, it wasn't instant attraction.

"Hugh only just found out Fiona was engaged," Ellen explained. "She has a lot of us to answer to when she gets back."

Simon buttoned his coat slowly. "And why does she have to answer to Hugh?" He reached for his gloves. "I'm afraid I'm at a disadvantage. I don't think I caught your last name, Hugh."

"Weston," Hugh said. "I'm sure Fiona's told you about her job in Hampstead. She works for me, and we're all wondering when she'll decide she's had enough of her unscheduled holiday."

One black glove fell to the floor and Hugh bent to retrieve it. Simon's back was to Ellen as the glove was handed over but she had a clear view of Hugh's face. He stared intently at Simon, glanced past his shoulder at Ellen, then back again.

"Good night, Ellen." Simon didn't look at her. He brushed by Hugh and left the flat.

An awkward silence closed in around them. Hugh wondered if he should leave, too. The truth was that he shouldn't have come here in the first place. A muffled sound made him turn back from the closed door and look at Ellen.

She stood in the same spot, her hands still at her sides, but tears slipped from the corners of her eyes.

"Ellen," he began, then didn't know what to say next. The last time he'd been anywhere near a crying female, he'd been botching an explanation of why he wasn't ready to get married until he'd finished at Oxford. He hadn't known what to say then, either, and ever since he'd been too busy for involvements that might lead to similar experiences.

"I'm sorry," Ellen said, and choked. "I never cry. This is ridiculous."

"Um, can I . . . did something happen to upset you?"

She spread a forefinger and thumb across her brow, hiding her eyes. "I was going to call the police, but Simon thinks we should wait."

Hugh took a step toward her. This wasn't a put-on. She was truly upset. "You were going to call the police about what?"

"Fiona." When she raised her head he saw agony and confusion in her eyes, and his own gut contracted sharply.

"You didn't believe that story about her being in Paris, did you?" she asked.

He shrugged helplessly. Whatever he said was only likely to make her more miserable.

"I don't believe it," she said. "I think something awful's happened to her. She wouldn't do this to me. She wouldn't, Hugh. You know her. You like her—even if you won't admit it because you're angry with her. You know she's a kind person."

She spoke rapidly, a wrenching sob coming every time she took a breath. He felt a trembling inside, an inadequacy and a longing to reach out. He'd made a mistake in his calculations somewhere. Not about Fiona. His suspicions there hadn't changed. But this woman was no criminal.

"I don't know what to do," she continued. "Simon wants me to wait longer before I call the police, but I'm so afraid. What if she needs help right now? She could be...she could wind up dead if I wait, if she's not already."

Hugh did what he realized he'd wanted to do since he met Ellen. He took her gently in his arms and pressed her face to his chest. "Shh," he whispered. "Shh, Ellen. You aren't alone. I'll help you." He closed his eyes. She felt so soft, so insubstantial. "We'll work this through together."

Another sob jerked her against him and he held her tighter, stroking her back and shoulders, then crossing his arms around her and tangling the fingers of one hand in her hair. The tenderness she aroused in him was foreign and incredibly sweet. Muscles in his jaw worked. He had never felt what he was feeling now.

Ellen had kept her hands between them, flattened on his chest. Now she slid them up around his neck and raised her face until he felt the dampness of her tears against his neck. If he lowered his face a fraction, he could kiss her. He opened his eyes and stared over her head.

"Simon still hasn't heard anything from Fiona?" he asked, already knowing the answer.

"No." Her voice was muffled.

*And he won't,* Hugh thought. What the hell was going on? Ellen might be confused but he was more confused. He'd swear the frosty Simon Macky, who'd clearly disliked him on sight, hadn't known that Fiona worked at the bar. Why would a woman choose to compartmentalize her life, unless she had something to hide?

He pulled back a little to look into Ellen's face. "Why does Simon think you should wait any longer?"

Her eyelashes glistened, reflected in her eyes. "He's still sure she's in France. He says this is like her—to be having such a good time she lets her responsibilities go until she's in a mess and dreads sorting everything out." Her full mouth came together in a tremulous line.

Before he realized what he was doing, he smoothed her tumbled hair back. The hair was as soft as he'd imagined it would be. "You don't agree with him?"

"I don't know what I think anymore, Hugh. I just want Fiona to walk through that door."

So did Hugh. "It might be a good idea to at least alert the police," he said uncertainly. In this he was reacting partly out of selfishness. A little official scrutiny—something to draw the attention he had no hope in hell of generating himself—could help his cause. If the police started looking for Fiona, and found her, a lot of missing pieces might start to fall into place.

Ellen was staring into his eyes. At that moment he hated Fiona Shaw, hated her for using him, but hated her more for putting her gentle sister through this for whatever her self-serving purposes were. He longed to tell Ellen to stop worrying, that her dear Fiona would show when she was ready. He longed to share his own concerns.

"It's late," he managed at last. "You should go to bed and try to sleep. Think about what you want to do next."

She nodded and the tears started again. "I will. Simon wants me to go ahead with the plans for the weekend and spend it with his family. Maybe I'll do that. Getting away from here may be what I need."

*Don't go,* he wanted to say. *Stay here with me.* He didn't want her to go anywhere, least of all with Simon Macky. He breathed in hard through his nose. Another unfamiliar feeling hit. Jealousy. Jealousy that Simon Macky, not he, would be with Ellen this weekend. But he mustn't let her know how he felt about her, not as long as he suspected Fiona of causing his grandmother's death.

"I'd better get home." Stepping away took all the determination he had. "If I run I might catch the last tube."

He opened the door, then looked back. She hadn't moved. Her pale face tugged at his insides afresh. "Call if you need someone to talk to," he said with a smile that threatened to crack his face. Quickly, keeping one hand on the doorknob, he reached out and pulled her close. He kissed her lightly on the lips, then pressed her cheek to his. "It'll be okay. Get some sleep."

Ellen heard the door close behind him before she opened her eyes again. She pressed her fingers to her mouth. The scent and feel of him lingered, clean, born of the wind, spontaneous and honest.

Hours later she was in bed but still awake. Please, she prayed, let Simon be right about Fiona and let me be able to know Hugh. Really know him.

## Chapter Six

"This can't be it," Ellen whispered, awed. "It's fantastic. A castle."

"Not exactly." Simon laughed and pulled his black Aston Martin to a stop in front of tall wrought-iron gates. "That's the back of the house." He rested his chin atop his hands on the steering wheel. "I've loved this place ever since... I've always loved it."

Ellen could see a formal pool ringed with pyramid-shaped topiary. From the gate, the pale gravel drive swept to the pool, divided and joined again in front of a balustraded terrace that ran the length of a Victorian half-timbered mansion.

She glanced sideways at Simon. He'd kept the conversation light during the drive from London, jocularly referring to Fiona's flamboyance and reinforcing his insistence that she would be back soon. He wasn't smiling now. His attention was trained on the house with what looked like speculative single-mindedness. The preoccupation in his stare disquieted Ellen. He seemed to have forgotten she was there.

"It's a beautiful house," she said. "It must be old."

"Not so old," he remarked. "Late 1800s."

"By North American standards, that's old. What does Fiona think of it?" Visualizing her zany sister in these intimidating surroundings took imagination.

He stirred and sat up, sliding his hands around the wheel. "She loves it, too. By the way, don't mention her job in Hampstead to my uncle and aunt, okay? Or to Jo."

"But—"

"Please." Simon turned toward her. "They don't approve of Fiona being on the stage. My uncle and aunt, I mean. Jo thinks it's great. But I don't want them to know Fiona works in some sort of shop."

Ellen frowned. "It's not 'some sort of shop,' Simon. It's a very good used-book store specializing in antique volumes. And Hugh Weston is very knowledgeable."

His expression had closed and his lips formed a grim line. "What good Fiona is there I can't imagine. I didn't realize she knew that much about books."

Ellen frowned. Simon really hadn't known Fiona worked for Hugh. If he had he'd have known she worked in the bar and wouldn't have made the mistake of thinking she dealt with books. No wonder he'd been so cool to Hugh last night. Simon had received more than his share of shocks recently.

"Simon," Ellen said gently. "There's a wine bar adjoining the book shop. Fiona works a few days a week in the bar. I'm the one who works with books."

He braced his elbow on the back of the seat and rammed his fingers into his hair. "Fiona works in a bar?"

"Yes. And she arranged for Hugh to sponsor my work permit in England because old books are my specialty."

"You're a reference librarian in Boston."

She felt sorry for him. "I *was*, Simon. There was no outlet in the States for what I really wanted to do, so coming here to this job seemed perfect. That and being near Fiona again."

Simon had stopped listening. "Oh, my God," he said slowly. "What was she thinking of? My family can't hear about this. They can't, do you understand?"

"Because they're snobs?" Ellen retorted and immediately regretted the comment. "I'm sorry. Of course I won't tell your family about the bar, if that's what you prefer. But they're likely to ask how long I intend to stay and I'm not ashamed—"

Simon's hand, closing on her wrist, hurt. "Of course you're not ashamed, but would you please not mention Weston?"

Ellen looked at him blankly. "Why?"

A sheen of sweat showed on his brow. He let go of her wrist and made a fist against his mouth. "I'm afraid, that's why," he said finally. "Somehow one of us might slip, tie Fiona in. You know how that goes. You might forget and say she got you the job, then all the questions would start."

Anger wasn't a natural emotion to Ellen, but she felt it rising now. "What exactly *would* you like me to say, Simon? When I agreed to come down here to Cadogan I had no idea I'd be expected to put on some sort of front, pretend I'm something I'm not."

He looked uncomfortable. "I've offended you. I didn't mean to. But I didn't know Fiona had this other job and I can't understand it. Has she...did she...did she talk to you about why she took this particular position?"

"Oh, Simon. No, she didn't, and I'm sorry she hasn't told you about it, but she's independent. We both know that. She probably needed extra money and didn't want to admit as much to you."

"Mmm." He narrowed one eye and Ellen felt he was looking through her, rather than at her.

Her stomach made unpleasant little jumps. "Don't worry about this, okay?" she said, but his eyes still didn't focus. "Simon, if the subject comes up, I've got a job in a bookshop. Period. There's no need to say any more. I just don't want to lie, all right?''

He took a deep breath like a man waking out of a long sleep. "Thanks," he said vaguely. "Do that. We'd better get on. We've still got several miles to go."

Ellen shook her head, uncomprehending. "Cadogan's right there."

"As I already mentioned, that's the back of the house. The estate's U-shaped. It covers several hundred acres, and Stilton Hedges, the village, is tucked into the middle of the U. Aunt Violet would fillet me if I didn't bring you to the front door, m'dear. And we have to motor through the village and around to the other side of the property to reach the main drive. That'll take a while yet."

She sat back and folded her hands in her lap. As far as she could tell, Simon and Fiona had nothing in common. Fiona the free spirit, the champion of underdogs, and this very socially conscious man came from different worlds. How they could ever mesh, she had no idea.

They'd just driven past the town of Windsor, with its dominating fortress embedded at the heart. "Windsor Castle's just as magnificent as I thought it would be," she said, making conversation. "Bigger, if anything." The castle stood on a hill, somewhat distant now, but still clearly visible with its great gray towers and battlements. About the walls, the forests had turned to autumn reds and golds, and made a flamboyant skirt.

Simon straightened his arms and locked his elbows. "We get used to looking at the place from here. All of this—" he nodded to an endless stone wall above which she could see only trees "—is part of the estate. A lot of our workers live in cottages spread out over the place."

Ellen laughed. "I don't suppose you can imagine how foreign all this seems to me."

"I think I can. Fiona took a while to be comfortable with everything."

Ellen doubted Fiona could ever be comfortable with everything, as Simon put it. "You said your family were farmers," she returned. "Do they do all that inside there?"

"Oh, no." He laughed as if she'd made a huge joke. "Although the stables are here, of course. My family are crazy about horses." He made a wry face.

"You don't like horses?" Ellen asked, surprised.

"No. Never did, much to good old Uncle Xavier's chagrin. My sister loves the things, though. Jo's not here today, by the way. She's staying with friends, but you'll meet her first thing in the morning."

First thing in the morning sounded a decade away to Ellen, and she wondered how she would get through what promised to be a boring round of being polite to people she probably wouldn't like. More to the point, she didn't expect them to like her.

She thought of Hugh and automatically closed her eyes. His particular scent came back, and the firm but gentle pressure of his arms around her, the way he'd kissed her so sweetly, so kindly before he left last night.

"Are you tired?"

Simon's question startled her and she opened her eyes. "Just thinking. Tell me what else you do here."

"Raise sheep. On the hills over there. Look in any direction and you'll see Macky sheep. There are tenant farms, too, and we do a fair amount with crops and pigs and so on at the outskirts of the estate itself. We turn here."

He swung onto Datchet Lane and traveled a mile or so before following a sign for Stilton Hedges. They had driven away from the wall surrounding Cadogan. Ellen felt overwhelmed by the size of the place.

Stilton Hedges was a tiny quaint village. Life apparently revolved around a leaning whitewashed pub called The

Horse and Carriage. Sun washed the worn sidewalks and played on the craggy faces of locals, faces reddened by years of exposure to the weather. Next to the pub, a combination post office, wool shop and newsagent was the largest business on what was evidently the village's only paved street. Simon drove too fast for the rough and narrow road, and Ellen clung to the edges of her seat. She was disappointed when they headed away from the village again before she'd had a chance to do more than glance at it quickly.

"Only a mile from here," Simon said. A faint flush had risen in his face and Ellen took it as excitement. He did love his home. "They're a bit stuffy, I'm afraid. Violet and Xavier, that is. But you'll soon get used to them."

She doubted that. Twin gate houses flanked the front entrance. They drove for a couple of minutes before she saw tall red chimneys and multiple red roofs. As they drew closer she noticed how unusual the half-timbering on the house was, the wood applied in curving, rather than straight, lines.

Much too soon, Simon swept to a halt in front of a massive double front door, its brick portico overhung with wisteria. "Here we are," he said with a satisfied smile. "Uh-oh. Reception committee's out in full force."

The doors were open and a knot of people stood on the steps. Ellen felt like a player in a "Masterpiece Theater" production. A country version of "Upstairs Downstairs." Simon introduced her first to his aloof uncle, who gave no doubt that he wished he were somewhere else. Ellen searched for a likeness between Xavier and Simon but found none. The older man, probably nearing sixty, was tall and gaunt with dark hair only beginning to gray at the temples. His eyes were his best feature. Although appraising, they were a pleasant tawny color and suggested they could be warm if he ever relaxed.

Violet Macky, a striking intimidating woman, managed a skillful inventory of Ellen's appearance while they shook hands. Violet wore her raven-black hair parted in the middle and curving in a smooth straight style to her well-defined jaw. Her name suited her. She had intensely violet eyes on which she lavished too much makeup for Ellen's taste.

A line of servants were introduced, then Ellen, feeling self-conscious, was led into a hall dominated by high dark wooden arches and painted leaded windows.

"Violet," she heard Simon say, "Fiona couldn't get away this weekend. She's busy with the play. But she was as sure as I am that you'd want to get to know Ellen."

"Quite." Xavier replied first and then promptly excused himself. "I want to see you in my office, Simon. We've got a lot to go over. Ivers should be down by lunch if he got my message."

"Ross is coming?" The bewilderment in Simon's voice made Ellen eye him sharply. He was wringing his driving gloves between his hands. "You didn't tell me that. I haven't heard from him in days. He's been off on one of his mental health breaks."

"When we heard you were coming, your uncle wrote and asked him down, Simon," Violet interrupted. "We couldn't reach him on the phone but his man said he'd be back this morning. We want him here. That should be good enough for you."

Simon bowed his head for an instant. "Ross Ivers is supposed to be my assistant. My right-hand man. Don't you think you should have cleared it with me if he was going to be in on our conference?"

"No," Xavier said peremptorily. "Violet, dear, would you take care of our guest? Simon and I should get down to work."

Something like panic hit Ellen when Violet agreed. With a gesture inviting Ellen to accompany her, Violet led her upstairs, a maid in black dress and white apron and cap following with her small overnight case.

"I hope this will be comfortable for you, Ellen. May I call you Ellen?" Violet said, not waiting for an answer and opening a door to the most charming bedroom Ellen had ever seen. She had little time to enjoy it, however, for pointing out the bathroom, Violet suggested Ellen might freshen up and then asked her—no, commanded, it seemed to Ellen—to meet her downstairs as soon as she was through.

A few minutes later Ellen was ushered into the lush little ground-floor drawing room, draped at its dominating bay window with green velvet. Green velvet cushions lined window seats, and droll oils of stern-faced men and women long dead hung on extravagantly patterned paper-covered walls.

"Do sit down, Ellen."

Ellen chose a place by the window where she could at least see the outdoors and freedom.

"Tea?" Even as she spoke, Violet pulled a gold-tasseled rope hanging beside the white marble fireplace.

The unreality of the place seemed to wipe all coherent thought from Ellen's mind.

A maid appeared, took Violet's offhand instructions and left silently.

"Now, let's get comfortable. There's simply lots I want to ask you."

Another inquisition. For Fiona's sake she'd be charming to this woman—but only for Fiona's sake.

An hour later, with Violet still sitting close beside her on the window seat, Ellen glanced longingly through the window and for one insane moment considered opening one and climbing out. She'd drunk weak tea out of fragile Limoges cups that made her hands feel bony and too large and groaned silently each time Violet insisted on a refill from a blindingly polished silver pot. Little cookies sprinkled with glittery sugar had been frequently waved in front of her. The one she felt obliged to take had fractured at the first bite and sent a shower of crumbs over her skirt.

"What did you say your father does?" Violet asked. Ellen was beginning to forget which questions she was being asked for the second time.

"He's retired," she said wearily, then added, "He was a schoolteacher."

"Really." Violet made "really" sound like "oh, dear."

"And you're a librarian." That question had been asked before, at least twice, and Violet was definitely underscoring her view that librarians were people to be pitied.

"I'm a bookseller now," Ellen said defiantly. "Used books actually," she added with a sense of satisfaction. She wasn't about to elaborate on what that meant. Let the woman think she sold tatty old paperbacks for a few pennies to people who couldn't afford new books.

"That is a pretty frock, dear," Violet remarked, shifting topics without pause. "Did you buy it in London?"

Ellen almost reached back to make sure the label of her inexpensive blue woolen dress wasn't showing. "It's from the States. A factory outlet where they sell things cheaply if there's a flaw or something. Or sometimes because they get big consignments of clothes that just didn't sell in regular stores." She shouldn't be doing this, but the horrified expression on Violet's smooth face was worth the small wickedness.

Violet recovered quickly. "How very clever of you, and thrifty. It sounds like something Fiona would have done."

In other words, they were both impossible. "Simon loves this house, doesn't he?" Ellen said, deciding she'd better change the subject and try to salvage at least some of what she'd promised to do to help Simon and Fiona.

"It's a wonderful house," Violet said as if Simon hadn't been mentioned. She immediately launched into a lecture about the influence of the Pre-Raphaelite Brotherhood on the place, about William Morris and countless painters and artisans Ellen knew only as names. Ellen saw, with a kind of growing tension, that Violet's hands fluttered, that her eyes took on a feverish light as she talked. Things, priceless things, were her consuming passion.

Ellen waited for a pause. It came as Violet gazed at the wallpaper with something close to reverence on her face, after she'd explained in a hushed voice, "William Morris, of course."

"Do you and Mr., ah, do you and Xavier have any children, Violet?"

"No." Violet twisted a huge emerald on her ring finger. "After Xavier's brother and his wife died we were too busy making a home for their children. Then it seemed too late, somehow."

Why, Ellen wondered, couldn't she be touched by the moisture that glistened on those dark lashes?

"That was wonderful of you. But it must be gratifying to see Simon's dedication." A thought struck suddenly. "How old is Simon?"

Violet looked up sharply. "Thirty-one. Why?"

"Oh, nothing. It's none of my business, of course. I was just thinking that Simon will take over the estate one day. Isn't it a bit unusual in this country for property not to pass from father to son?"

Violet's carmine lips pressed together hard for an instant. "When Simon's father died, Simon was two. Xavier took over." She lowered her voice and laid a cold white hand on Ellen's wrist. "Frankly, my dear, Simon took a long time to settle down. It was decided that the best course was for Xavier to keep control throughout his lifetime."

Ellen thought for a moment. "And Simon agreed to that? He didn't mind?"

"Not at all. He has all he wants and very little of the headaches that go with all of this." Violet spread her hands.

"Too much power in Simon's hands, much as we all love him, could be a very bad thing."

"But he will have to take over eventually," Ellen went on with the sense that she was pushing into water too deep for her.

"All that's been taken care of," Violet murmured with an air of closing the subject. "I hate to think of it, but if Xavier goes first, I'm more than capable of taking charge."

End of discussion, Ellen thought. Poor Simon. This uncle and aunt of his clearly liked the power that had come to them and they weren't about to let it go. And poor Fiona. How would she fit into this world so different from her own middle-class arena?

They sat unspeaking for a while. "Fiona liked it here," Violet said abruptly and with a bright smile, "although she never liked to dress for dinner. She enjoyed the horses, I must say. She and Jo went riding several times."

Ellen nodded and made a polite noise. Another new vision of her sister. Apart from riding a donkey on some vaguely remembered beach during a rare summer holiday, Ellen couldn't think of a time when either she or Fiona had been on horseback.

"Violet!" The door swung open and a big blond smoothly handsome man strode in. "There you are. I wanted to talk to you before—"

He noticed Ellen who was somewhat obscured by a velvet drape. "Good God! What . . . ?" His face paled and he grabbed the back of a chair.

Violet got up in a flurry of gored tweed and moved quickly between Ellen and the man. "Ross, this is Ellen Shaw, Fiona's twin. She's in England to visit Fiona. Isn't the likeness extraordinary?"

Ellen couldn't hear the man's reply.

"Where have you been?" Violet went on in a sugary voice totally unlike the one she'd used with Ellen. "I've been trying to get you for days and Simon says he hasn't seen you, either."

"I had some business to attend to." The man's voice was deep with a clipped quality similar to Hugh's. "I got Xavier's note this morning when I arrived at my rooms. He could have been a bit more explicit, don't you think?"

Violet didn't reply.

"I don't appreciate having plans made for me with no warning. Things haven't . . . Oh, I'll have it out with Xavier."

"Do you really think you should?"

"I think I'm the best judge of what I should do. And yes, I do think I should have it out with him. You know I don't like sudden changes. This should have been headed off."

"Ross," Violet said, a note of pleading in her voice, "we weren't to know. And if you wouldn't insist on popping off without warning you would have been told about the, ah, change, earlier."

The man made an impatient gesture. "Drop it. Does Simon know I'm going to be here?"

"He does now. Xavier told him."

Ellen moved uncomfortably on her seat. Evidently she'd been forgotten during this exchange, an exchange that meant nothing to her.

She heard Violet cough delicately and she glanced up. The man stared at Ellen for an instant before he came toward her. She felt his force and absolute confidence. "I'm Ross Ivers," he said. "I'm pleased to meet you. Fiona and Simon did mention you, but I had no idea you were coming to England."

Which made him just one of a whole group who hadn't known. "Fiona wanted me to be a surprise." She smiled but felt sick.

"Ross is Simon's assistant," Violet put in. "He's really almost a part of the family."

The idea of Simon's being this powerhouse of a man's boss seemed ludicrous. The Simons of this world, Ellen thought, were the stuff men like Ross Ivers normally gobbled up as hors d'oeuvres in their upward battle toward success.

Any further conversation was postponed by the announcement that lunch was served.

For the first time since her arrival at Cadogan, Ellen relaxed. Being with Simon again was a relief. The rapport between him and Ross pleased her and banished the fear that he was surrounded by people bent on manipulating him. Ross had a repertoire of jokes that filled any slight lag in conversation. Even Xavier unbent enough to smile at Ellen and ask how she was enjoying England so far.

After lunch, the three men excused themselves. "I'll be more in evidence this evening," Simon promised with a rueful smile. "Violet will look after you this afternoon."

The afternoon was spent in the village—Ellen's idea—and she promised herself she'd have many more such excursions to similar villages. Stilton Hedges still sported a round red postbox, a bright red telephone box, and in a wide spot in the middle of the road was a working water pump, which could in theory be used to draw water for horses and men riding through. Violet seemed to gain pleasure from Ellen's enthusiasm. Over scones and jam and Devonshire cream at a thatched-roofed tea shop, they laughed and talked more intimately than she would have thought possible. The subject of Fiona and Simon came up, and Ellen noticed a distinct lessening of tension in any comments Violet made about the pair.

The truce was short. Once back in her domain, Violet reverted to her former imperious self, and Ellen's uneasiness returned. At ten that evening when dinner was finished and the men closeted in the library for port and more business talk, Ellen admitted exhaustion to her hostess. Violet insisted upon accompanying her upstairs, and she found herself wondering how early she and Simon would be able to leave the next day.

Violet dismissed the maid and went about turning down the heavy rose-colored brocade spread on the four-poster bed. "Mmm. It's a little chilly in here. You shall have a fire. There's nothing like a fire."

Ellen couldn't think of a response and none seemed needed. Violet knelt before the white marble fireplace with its high mantel and intricate carving. She fussed with crumpled newspaper and wood, and the pile of coal on top before setting light to the paper. "There," she said softly, turning a flushed face to Ellen. "You can lie in bed and listen to the crackle—and watch the flame shadows on the walls. Lovely."

"Lovely," Ellen agreed.

Violet stood, brushing her hands together. "There are lots of wonderful stories about this room. It's said the original owner of the house used it for his, er, special lady friends." She moved aside some drapery on one wall and revealed an area of patched plaster. "This used to be a door. On the other side there's a dressing room and that's where the gentleman conducted his liaisons."

Ellen smiled. Violet's obvious delight at recounting stories about the house was contagious. "What did the mistress of the house think about that?"

Violet turned away and opened one of the diamond-paned windows. "Mistresses of houses have to be strong people if they want to keep control. If they lose it, they have only themselves to blame. Now, do you have everything you need?"

When the door closed behind her hostess, Ellen sat at a writing table near the open window. Leaves rustled in the trees outside and she could smell them rotting on the ground below.

Violet Macky was a strong mistress of this house. She would never lose control. The tiredness Ellen had felt earlier had gone, to be replaced by a nagging conviction that she'd missed something very important today, something she couldn't afford to miss.

She reconstructed every conversation, tried to recall the nuances of the exchanges. Nothing. There were some messages she'd picked up clearly. Simon was in an unenviable position here, and Violet definitely hadn't shown any eagerness to talk about Fiona. The wedding had never been mentioned once, nor what Fiona's place would then be in the family.

Ellen closed the window and picked up her nightgown, which had been draped on the bed. Obviously the maid had done her work. Ellen's small suitcase wasn't in evidence, and when she opened a closet she found what few clothes she'd brought hung inside. Toiletries were neatly set out in the small pink-and-white bathroom she'd used earlier.

She was a stranger here, just as Fiona must feel when she visited. The Mackys and Ross Ivers had made her feel welcome this afternoon and during the evening, but now that she was alone, Ellen felt totally isolated.

When she was ready for bed she slid between ivory satin sheets and watched the shadows of the dancing flames on the wall. Simon was here in the house somewhere, but he seemed to have no substance. If she went to him and tried to explain some of the uncomfortable thoughts and suggestions of thoughts that traveled unceasingly through her brain he wouldn't understand.

But there was someone on Ellen's mind who didn't feel like a straw in the wind. Hugh Weston in his simple flat in Hampstead felt very solid, even at this distance.

It was ten-thirty. He'd probably still be reading. Instantly she could picture him in one of his leather chairs, his feet on the old stool, Vladimir curled up in front of the electric fire that would never be tolerated at Cadogan, where the lady of the house would disdain anything other than the real thing.

She wanted to talk to Hugh, to hear his voice. An antique gilt phone stood on a table by the bed. She was tempted. Maybe if she told him some of the doubts she had, he'd be able to help her be more rational.

It was out of the question. She switched off the light and scooted a little lower on the hard mattress. She and Hugh were strangers. The kiss aside, his kindness aside, he had been doing what was natural to him—giving comfort to a damsel in distress. He owed her nothing, and if he knew the kind of thoughts she was having about him, the silly romantic notions, the desire to lean on him, he'd probably be amused.

Hugh Weston's business, his old books and wine, were all that mattered to him. And perhaps a woman Ellen hadn't met.

She was nothing to him but a potentially good employee, and she'd already caused him more trouble than was professionally good for her. Hugh as anything but an employer was an idea she'd better squash.

# Chapter Seven

If Morton Lister resented Hugh's asking for a Saturday morning appointment he hid his annoyance well.

"Delighted," he said, closing the door of his office behind Hugh. "Make yourself comfortable. Drink?"

"No, thanks," Hugh said. "I hope this isn't too inconvenient for you. Getting you into the office on the weekend."

"Not at all, old chap, not at all. Got me out of a do for the church. My wife's thing, don't you know. A bunch of women talking about their recipes for gooseberry tart." He shuddered and Hugh warmed to him a little. "Anyway, you saved me and I thank you for it."

The solicitor wore an aged tweed jacket with leather elbow patches and shiny twill trousers that sagged at the knees. Hugh settled into the chair he indicated and looked him over, deciding that the weekend version of the man was infinitely preferable to the weekday variety.

Lister sat in his swivel chair and tented his fingers over the cluttered desk. "So, Mr. Weston. You said you'd been thinking. I take it you're ready to go over your grandmother's will in detail now."

Hugh moved forward until one of his own elbows was also on the desk. "Yes. I'm afraid it all seemed too much the other day." He wanted to go over the will all right—and a few other things Mr. Lister might not expect to be asked. Hugh was relying on the element of surprise to get what he wanted from this interview. "I'm sure you understood my reticence when we first met," he said, deliberately making eye contact.

"Quite so. Quite so. But I'm glad you're up to dealing with things now." He rummaged in his pockets and produced a bulky key ring. "Please excuse me while I get the relevant documents."

Rather than sinking back in his chair, Hugh took advantage of Lister's absence to position himself even closer to the desk. Since he'd left Ellen the night before he'd spent hours planning what he hoped to get out of this meeting. Enough time had been wasted on feeling and reacting. Now he would think and only think, then react appropriately. Morton Lister had known Millie Weston as Hugh had never known her. Lister was Hugh's only hope of working backward in the mystery his grandmother had become. He needed to know her story from the beginning. Then, with luck, he'd have all the pieces he needed to put the puzzle of the end of her life together.

"Here we are." Lister returned, carrying a narrow metal box, which he cradled as if it were a baby.

When the box was between them on the desk, the solicitor produced another key ring and selected a very small key with which he unlocked a hasp. Without opening the lid all the way, he carefully slid out a bulky sheaf of folded papers.

Hugh tapped his fingers together. Was being ponderous a prerequisite for this man's occupation?

"Now," Lister began. He unfolded the papers, then set them on the desk in front of him while he took off his glasses and found another pair in a drawer. He put them on and smiled myopically at Hugh. "Can't stand these bifocals. Turn my stomach. My wife says I'm vain—don't want to show my age and all that. Poppycock, of course."

"Of course," Hugh said, praying for patience.

Lister flipped through the pages, making a series of "mmm" and "ah" sounds. Then he went back to the beginning. "It's all very straightforward," he said, taking off the glasses and waggling them between his fingers. "Everything Mrs. Weston had at the time of her death goes to you."

This was it. Now he had to say all the right things. Ask all the right questions. "Where exactly are my grandmother's funds kept?"

The glasses stopped swinging. "We will transfer all monies to you as soon as the formalities are taken care of."

Hugh settled a bland expression on his face. "Is there some reason I shouldn't know which bank she used?"

Lister cleared his throat. "Of course not. We took care of all your grandmother's affairs. Her assets are kept in the same bank we use—the Royal. We've been her executors for, let me see—" one pink hand passed back and forth over his mouth "—twenty or so years at least. Probably closer to thirty."

Almost as long as he'd been alive, Hugh thought absently. "So everything of my grandmother's was dealt with by you? My grandfather's pension as well?"

"That's right." Mr. Lister's blue eyes slid away from Hugh. "She preferred not to bother with these things."

"So you issued her the funds she lived on?"

"Yes."

"How substantial was the pension?" Best to work slowly toward what he really wanted to know.

"Mmm." Lister reached back into the box and pulled out a small green book. He turned pages, running his fingers down what looked to be columns of figures. "Negligible, really. It went up slightly over the years but not enough to make much difference to Mrs. Weston. Of course, this stopped with her death, so you don't need to concern yourself with paperwork. It's been dealt with."

"So where exactly did my grandmother get the *very substantial* estate you spoke of, Mr. Lister?"

The little man fidgeted with the papers in front of him. "You have to understand that this is a little unusual, Mr. Weston. And more than a little uncomfortable for me."

Hugh lifted his chin. "Would you care to elaborate?"

"Well." Lister coughed. "Mrs. Weston had a benefactor. But it was your grandmother's wish that this person's identity not be disclosed."

"My grandmother was..." Heat rose on Hugh's neck beneath his turtleneck sweater. Where was his famous control when he needed it? "My grandmother, Mr. Lister, was a simple woman who subsisted on very little. The pension—" he nodded at the green book "—came from whoever owned the mill in Lancaster where my grandfather was injured, correct?"

"Quite so."

"My grandfather died from his injuries, and my understanding has been that all my grandmother had was that pension. *All*, Mr. Lister. According to her, for the past fifty years she had that money and nothing else. Now you tell me she was loaded? And you also tell me I'm to inherit her large estate, which she accrued from some anonymous benefactor and you don't want me to ask who this person is, for God's sake?"

Mr. Lister let out a gusty sigh. "I didn't say I didn't want you to ask. Only that I'm bound not to tell you. I can say that in a way the ongoing, shall we say, contributions also resulted from the tragedy that befell your grandfather. In fact—" he leaned across the desk "—I don't think I'd be betraying a trust if I told you that someone who used to be associated with the mill felt that your grandfather's family deserved much more than this." He poked the green book. "This was a meager pittance. Totally unacceptable as recompense for your grandmother's loss."

Hugh thought for a moment. "So you're saying that someone decided to make my grandmother a charity project."

"I hardly think—"

"Forgive me," Hugh broke in quickly. "I didn't mean that the way it sounded. But I'm groping. I'd like a clear picture of how I've come to be a wealthy man when I've spent my life believing I'd never have a penny I didn't earn."

Lister found a crumpled handkerchief in his jacket pocket, polished his glasses, then wiped his puffy eyes. "Mr. Weston, I'm going to be as honest with you as I can. You must understand that I have my professional ethics to consider."

"I do understand." If they sat here until tomorrow, Hugh would get some facts.

"Very well. These are the details as your grandmother gave them to me. The present, ah, benefactor is a descendant of the original one. The original party was one of the owners of the mill. He left after the accident. Apparently, his concerns over safety had been ignored for years, and your grandfather's death was the last straw for him. He sold his interests and started the trust fund for Mrs. Weston. The, ah, descendant of that person is continuing what was the father's wish—that Mrs. Weston never have to worry about money for as long as she lives."

"Lived," Hugh corrected.

"Quite so. Since the payments are to continue I tend to forget—"

"Just a minute." Hugh held up a hand. "What do you mean, the payments are to continue? I don't need any more money and I'm certainly not taking it from someone I'm not allowed to know. Taking what my grandmother had already seems almost immoral."

Mr. Lister turned sideways in his chair. "Come, come now, Mr. Weston. Hardly immoral. And although the payments are to continue, they will not be coming to you. That's one of the details I wanted to make clear to you."

The import of what Lister said came slowly to Hugh. "Not to... Are these payments considerable?"

"Extremely so."

"All right. They don't come to me, so who do they go to?" A potent mix of trepidation and excitement tensed every muscle in his body. This could be it, the answer.

Lister was shifting papers around again.

"Who, Mr. Lister? Who did my grandmother bequeath these mysterious payments to? I assume this was her idea?"

"Most certainly." Lister pushed back his rounded shoulders like an offended chicken ruffling its feathers. "Mrs. Weston wished to do something for...this other person, and in so doing I assure you she showed great kindness and gratitude."

"Gratitude?" Hugh chewed the inside of his lip. "She was grateful enough to someone to leave her—or him—ongoing income that should keep this fortunate recipient on easy street for as long as... How long, Mr. Lister?"

Lister looked weary. "I can't divulge that, Mr. Weston. Let's just say that, that...the length of the agreement depends on an issue I can't discuss with you."

"And you can't, or won't tell me who this person is to whom my grandmother felt so grateful?"

"No."

"Or who it is that extends the funds?"

"No, Mr. Weston. But you are a very wealthy man. Isn't that enough?"

"It's too much, really, Mr. Lister. Overwhelming, in fact." The old coot wasn't giving an inch, but Hugh hadn't finished yet.

"Is there any other information you think I should have?" He'd give anything to get his hands on the papers in front of Lister. Just a few minutes and he might find the name of this elusive recipient of Millie Weston's gratitude.

"This is very difficult," Lister sighed. "But really, it doesn't affect you directly. Although your heirs..." He shook his head.

"I don't have any heirs," Hugh said shortly. "Could we please get this over with?"

"Yes. It was Mrs. Weston's instruction that should you predecease her, uh, other beneficiary, that person would inherit the amount of her estate at the time of her death."

Hugh blinked, uncomprehending. "I'm afraid you've lost me."

"I'm sorry. Let me make this clearer. Mrs. Weston's current assets come to you, completely. But, at the time of your death—should that occur prior to the death of the beneficiary who will be receiving the ongoing payments bequeathed by Mrs. Weston—your present inheritance will go to that person. Now, this would not encumber your own assets before the inheritance, or whatever profit or interest you realize as a result of the inheritance. Only the sum *as is* would be removed from your estate."

Hugh stared at the man. A sudden nausea overtook him and he gritted his teeth against the sensation.

"Are you all right, Mr. Weston?" Lister stood up and moved around to Hugh's side. "You look ill."

"I'm fine." As fine as a man could be when he'd just discovered that someone had an excellent reason for wanting him dead. He glanced at the papers on the desk, then up at Morton Lister. "This has all been a bit much. Do you suppose I could have that drink you mentioned earlier?"

"Of course, of course. Brandy?" He started for a drinks tray on a trolley against a paneled wall.

"No, no, I don't think so," Hugh said. He remembered seeing burners and a kettle in the office outside this one, the office where Lister's secretary worked. "Tea would be just the thing—if it's not too much trouble."

"My dear chap, it's no trouble at all. You sit there and get your bearings. I'm sorry about this, so sorry..." His voice continued in a mumbling stream as he left the room.

Hugh waited only a second before snatching up the wad of sheets Lister had left on his desk.

There were a dozen of them at least. Hugh turned them over as quickly and quietly as possible, reading headings, searching.

Then he found it.

His scalp prickled. Even the small hairs on his spine felt raised. He reorganized the papers slowly, with infinite care, and put them back the way Lister had left them.

"And all future payments into trust," the clause had read, "shall go not to Hugh Weston, but to Simon Jonathon Macky."

## Chapter Eight

A maid announced simply, "Agnes, ma'am. Mrs. Macky said for me to get you," and with that directed Ellen to the breakfast room.

Sunlight streamed through French doors onto a highly polished oval table and the dark curly hair of a woman who sat there eating.

Ellen hovered in the doorway and the woman lifted her head. "Good morning. Ellen, isn't it? Come in and help yourself to some breakfast. I'm Jo Macky and I'm so pleased you could come."

"Thank you," Ellen said, advancing. The woman's cheerful voice had held genuine welcome. "Simon told me you'd be back..." She swallowed, unable to continue. Scars webbed Jo Macky's closed eyelids and seamed shiny patches of mottled skin over her brow and right cheek. She was blind.

"Sit down, Ellen," Jo said and her smile brought an unself-conscious radiance to her features. "Obviously Simon didn't tell you I'm blind. Don't blame him for that. He's so used to me he forgets. And Fiona probably wouldn't think to say anything either, bless her. She's such a sweet girl. Simon's very lucky."

Embarrassed that her shock had been felt, Ellen moved slowly to sit in a chair beside Jo's. Simon should have warned her. And if Fiona hadn't been so set on her little se-crets . . .

"Please relax," Jo said. "And don't feel badly about your reaction."

This woman was extremely sensitive to atmosphere. "Thank you. I was surprised, I'm afraid." Looking at her more carefully, Ellen thought sadly that Jo was a lovely woman cruelly marred, but with no sign of self-pity.

The maid Agnes came into the room carrying a fresh pot of tea. Silently, she poured a cup for Ellen and refilled Jo's, then left the pot on the table.

"The kidneys are tasty this morning," Jo said as soon as the door closed again. "And the eggs, if you get to them before they're stone cold."

Ellen glanced around and saw a long heavy buffet laden with silver-domed serving dishes. She wasn't hungry, but she took her plate and went to lift a cover. "I don't think I've ever had kidneys for breakfast." She laughed uncertainly. Nor had she ever been confronted with so many choices for breakfast. "Are these tomatoes fried?"

Jo giggled and said, "Yes, they're fried. You aren't like Fiona, are you?"

Startled, Ellen turned toward her. "We're very alike, only my eyes are brown and my hair's longer, and I'm a bit thin . . . Oh, dear."

"No, no," Jo said quickly. "Stop that right now. No feeling awkward allowed. Of course you'd think I was talk-ing about appearance, particularly when you're twins. But I mean you and Fiona are very different in temperament. You're far more thoughtful, or perhaps tactful is the word. Fiona wades right in, says the first thing that pops into her mind. The first time she ate breakfast here you should have heard what she said about fried tomatoes, and kidneys and cold toast!" Jo laughed. "Incinerated, she called the toast. And why, she wanted to know, would we bother to get it hot only to stand it in 'metal thingies' until it was cold again?'' Unerringly, Jo picked up her tea and took a sip, then smiled broadly as she set down the cup. "Violet was here and for once I really wished I could see her face when Fiona called the silver toast racks 'metal thingies,' and said 'the damned bread fractures when you try to spread butter on it.'"

Ellen couldn't help chuckling. "Sounds like my sister. Tact was never her middle name. But I'm not feeling awkward, I promise."

"Good girl. You shouldn't be." Jo paused, then said, "Anyway, Fiona's the best thing to happen around here in my memory. She's certainly the best thing that ever happened to that stodgy brother of mine. The sooner they're married, the better. What did Violet say about Fiona?"

Ellen thought a moment. "Not a lot." How interesting that what Violet did and said was so important while Xavier was never mentioned. "She said that Fiona liked it here. And that she had never liked..." That was it! The something she couldn't quite remember last night.

"What?" Jo persisted. "What did she say Fiona doesn't like?"

"To dress for dinner," Ellen said absently, returning to her seat with only a few pieces of fruit on her plate and a piece of the cold toast Fiona had scorned.

"Ha!" Jo exclaimed. "She doesn't either. And she'll change some of those things around here, you mark my words. Fiona..."

Ellen hardly heard what Jo said. She laughed from time to time and murmured agreements, but her mind rehashed the previous day's conversations with Violet. Violet had spoken of Fiona's strong opinions, her determination: "Fiona never *liked* to dress for dinner. Fiona *liked* this place. Fiona *enjoyed* the horses. Fiona and Simon *got* along so well. Must *have been* the old 'opposites attract' thing, I suppose." All past, over, as if Violet had already decided

Fiona wouldn't come back here, wouldn't become a permanent part of Simon's life. The strawberry Ellen had put into her mouth turned to mush before she forced it down her throat. And Ross Ivers's reaction when he'd seen her? Shock. The only explanation for that must be that he'd mistaken her for Fiona who he, along with Violet and probably Xavier, had decided wouldn't be back. But how could they have been so certain? Had Simon told his uncle and aunt and Ross the truth about Fiona's unscheduled absence? Had they already relegated her to an episode in Macky history?

"You're very quiet."

She started guiltily. Jo's face was turned to hers and she looked puzzled. "I was listening," Ellen lied. "I love your accents here. There are so many different ones. Even you and Simon don't sound quite the same."

"Well, I guess Simon's elocution lessons really took."

"Elocution?" Ellen found concentration on what Jo was saying impossible. Why would Simon make a show of telling Xavier and Violet that Fiona couldn't make it down to Cadogan because she was working if he'd already told them the truth?

Dimly she heard Jo say, "Speech training. We all had it, of course. But Simon had rather a bad time as a little boy and went through a period when he wouldn't talk at all. Afterward he barely made sense and Violet had someone work with him especially hard—"

The door, sweeping open under Violet's hand, cut off whatever else Jo might have said. "Good morning, Ellen," she said dismissively and turned to Jo. "Jo, darling. The men are going to be tied up all morning and I've got an appointment in town—"

"On Sunday?" Jo interrupted. "Theater, Violet?"

"Um, yes. That and I promised I'd have lunch with Sybil."

Jo wrinkled her nose. "Poor you." She inclined her head toward Ellen. "But we'll have fun, won't we? We'll talk dresses and weddings. And I'll give you the grand tour of the grounds."

A glimmer of sunlight on Violet's dark hair, tossed back by a flick of her head, pulled Ellen's attention from Jo. She caught a hard glitter in Violet's vivid eyes just before it was concealed by the lowering of the woman's lashes.

"I'd love that, Jo," Ellen said, still watching Violet. Fiona wasn't wanted here, by anyone but Simon and Jo.

"Do you like to ride?" Jo asked. "Fiona does. We taught her."

"I don't ride," Ellen said. If only she could get away now, immediately, and go to the police. Fiona must be found. There'd been too much delay already.

Violet said nothing, simply observed.

"Well, we'll walk anyway. The gardens are still lovely," Jo said as if she could see the riot of waning colors on the grounds.

A frantic inner quaking hit Ellen. There was a kind of madness here, a wild dichotomy between surface and undercurrent.

"Don't overdo," Violet said suddenly. "Simon talked about getting away by midafternoon. Ellen—" she extended the pale right hand Ellen didn't want to touch "—it's been a pleasure to have you with us. Please come back soon."

The right words, in the right tone. "Thank you," Ellen murmured, aware of the passing of cool fingers over hers. Violet's black pumps clicked on shimmering wood. Fine gray wool swished over the lining of her full skirt and she left. A suggestion of expensive perfume remained.

Ellen brushed back her hair. Between now and her return to London she would decide what to say to the police.

"Are you going to eat any more?" Jo asked.

"Hmm?" Ellen looked at her plate unseeingly, slowly focusing on its ornate green-and-gold rim. "No. I'm full, thanks. In fact I can't think of anything better than getting outside right now." Outside where fresh air would dilute the sense of doom. The dark rooms in the house overpowered her.

They left by the front door. While Ellen accepted her raincoat from a silent butler, Jo, tall and slim when she stood, took a thick woolen sweater from a chair in the hall and pulled it on over her silk blouse and tweed skirt. She slipped an arm comfortably through Ellen's and they set off companionably into the gardens.

"Are you sure you wouldn't like to ride?" Jo asked after they'd toured the formal gardens where only a few hardy blooms remained on the hundreds of rose bushes.

"Absolutely sure," Ellen assured her. "I'm surprised you got Fiona on a horse."

"She took to it at once. We chose a nice quiet mare for her, of course."

We? "You and Simon? I thought he didn't like riding, either."

Jo sighed. "He doesn't. Ned Loder, our bailiff, always makes time to go out with me. He helped Fiona." She steered them toward a corner of the house. "I'll never understand the way Simon feels about horses. He loved them when he was little, but then . . . well, a lot changed for all of us."

What had changed? Ellen wondered. She wouldn't ask.

Heavy footsteps scrunched on the gravel behind them. Ellen looked over her shoulder and saw a husky middle-aged man in worn tweeds bearing down on them, his chin jutting purposefully.

"Ned?" Jo said, standing still. "Is that you?"

"Yes, miss." His sturdy bowed legs, encased in leather gaiters, covered ground rapidly. "They said you were out here. You won't be wanting to ride today, now. Too soggy underfoot."

Jo frowned. "We won't be riding, Ned. But it isn't soggy at all. There hasn't been a drop of rain for days."

"Heavy dew," the man responded stubbornly, his ruddy face set. Pale blue eyes flickered toward Ellen and were quickly averted. "You shouldn't be out here walking so long. You had a busy time yesterday with your trip to your friend's and all."

"We only just came out," Jo said patiently. "Would you like to walk with us, Ned? And would you like to meet Fiona's sister, Ellen? Ellen, this is Ned Loder, who's been with us as long as I can remember."

"Nice to meet you, Ned," Ellen said uncomfortably.

"Right. How do, miss." He touched the brim of a shapeless gray hat the same color as his hair and fell in beside them.

Conversation seemed impossible with this surly man ambling along, his beetling brows pulled into a solid line over his eyes.

"This is the kitchen garden," Jo said, pausing to point to her right. "The kitchens are over there." She pointed in the other direction.

"I think you should go back now, Miss Jo," Ned Loder said.

"Rubbish," Jo responded, irritation creeping into her tone. "You fuss over me too much. I'm as healthy as a horse. We'll make a circle around the house and then we will have had our exercise for the day."

Ellen wished Ned Loder would get lost. Clearly, Jo liked Fiona and it would feel good to talk to someone about her.

"The pool's around here." Jo kept Ellen moving briskly.

They turned another corner. This must have been the side of the house Simon showed her from the road.

"Miss," Ned said loudly, "I really think it's—"

"We're not going back, Ned. *You* go back if you want to. Ellen will look after me."

Ned grunted and continued trudging.

The grounds here weren't as well kept as they were elsewhere. Ivy grew, knotted and unchecked, over the balustrades along the terrace, and flower beds sported more weeds than flowers. Ellen surveyed the building and noticed what hadn't been obvious from the road: much of the central wing had either been rebuilt, or added later. The brick was newer and darker, and the timbering, although a good copy of that on the rest of the house, wasn't exactly the same.

"When was this done?" she asked, then added, "The new part of the house?"

"Years ago," Ned said so hurriedly that Ellen stared at him. He walked faster, almost rushing. "You should see these gardens in high summer. A regular sight they are. And the woods. Those woods are something to see, I can tell you. Miss Jo likes to ride out there in summer, don't you, miss? I keep a pretty fair flower patch around my cottage—"

"Ned," Jo broke in softly. "It's all right. I can talk about it all now. It's good for me. There's a bench around here somewhere. Let's sit down for a while."

"I don't think—"

"I do, Ned," Jo cut in firmly.

"If you say so," he said, tight-lipped. He took Jo's arm and guided her to an old iron bench. Jo sat and Ellen joined her, but Ned continued to stand.

"I used to find it hard to come around here," Jo said quietly. "I still don't go into this part of the house, but perhaps I'll get over that one day, although ladies in their forties probably don't make many big changes, I suppose."

"Miss—"

"Please, Ned. Ellen's going to be part of the family, so she ought to know. There was a fire, Ellen. That's why the central wing had to be rebuilt."

"Oh dear." Ellen swallowed, not looking at Jo. Of course the scars must be from burns.

"The fire started at night when we were all asleep. The family's rooms were here then because my mother preferred this side of the house. Quieter, she always said, more family feeling. Mother loved the terrace." She sounded wistful. "We used to eat there a lot, and afterward Mother would sit and watch us play down here."

Tears smarted in Ellen's eyes and she glanced at Ned, but he'd turned his back. "Don't talk about it if it hurts," she said to Jo.

"I don't talk about it often. And never to Simon. He's got some horrible pictures in his mind, I think, young as he was. Our mother and father died. And our sister. Jenny was a year older than me. Thirteen."

In the short silence that followed, Ellen saw Jo's mouth tighten and the sharp movement of her throat. There were no appropriate words.

Jo bowed her head. "Simon was the only one who wasn't hurt—physically anyway."

"I'm so sorry." The only possible platitude felt so empty. Ellen wanted desperately to ask what Jo meant by "physically anyway" in relation to Simon, but knew she mustn't pry.

Jo stirred, lifted her face to the sun and smiled. "That's why I'm so grateful he met Fiona. She changed him, y'know."

"What do you mean?"

Ned Loder's hands were clasped behind his back, and Ellen saw how he twined and untwined his fingers. This conversation disquieted him.

"I was burned," Jo said, reaching to rest a hand on Ellen's forearm. "The blindness seems terrible, I suppose. I'm used to it. But you can see burns. Blindness, too. Whereas the things that happen inside someone are hidden and people don't understand them as easily. Simon was never the same after what happened. It was all so strange."

When Jo fell silent, thinking, Ellen almost held her breath, willing the rest of the story out.

"I remember how my parents used to laugh at what a serious little boy Simon was. He started talking very early, and very well. But only when he felt like it. After... afterward, he wouldn't talk at all. I was in and out of hospital for a long time, and at first, whenever I was home he just clung to me, but he didn't say anything."

"Until the, um, speech training?"

"No, no. It wasn't like that. Suddenly he changed. Just changed completely. As if he were a different little boy. He wouldn't stop talking. Only we could hardly understand a word he said. Gibberish, all of it. I thought for a while he was unbalanced in some way. That's when the elocution teacher became a permanent fixture around here." Jo shuddered. "Poor old Simon. She really put him through his paces, but he did stop gabbling rubbish."

"He seems very poised to me," Ellen put in. She didn't add that she wondered why his poise left him in his uncle's and aunt's presence.

"Fiona's had a lot to do with that. He went into another funk when he was around nineteen or twenty and then he insisted on leaving home. Anyway, no need to go on about it all. I just wanted you to know about us and how I got like this." She touched her face. "It's always less awkward if you can be open."

"Thank you," Ellen said simply.

Jo stood up and offered her a hand. "For a long time I was afraid Simon would just drift away. Even the brewery job seemed like a convenient excuse the uncle and aunt could use with friends."

The uncle and aunt. Jo didn't like Violet and Xavier much more than she did, Ellen decided, although she made no comment.

With her hand still in Jo's, Ellen breathed the cool autumn air appreciatively. Ned took up his position beside Jo while they carried on with their lap around the house.

"You really do like Fiona, don't you?" Ellen asked when she could contain the question no longer. "You're glad Simon met her?"

Jo pulled them both to a halt. "I certainly do. You must be able to tell that. My brother means everything to me. He's been my world since I was twelve years old and I've worried about him most of that time. I was worried about him even a year ago when he didn't seem to care about anything but getting drunk. Then Fiona came along and he's a different man."

Ellen experienced again the sickening falling away inside. Mixed messages. What should she believe? If Fiona meant everything to Simon, why wasn't he more concerned about her absence?

"You do believe me?" Jo prompted.

"Yes, yes, I do."

"Good. It means so much to me that after everything, all the tough times, Simon is going to be the one to breathe new life into this family. You know, until Fiona came along, I was convinced we'd never really get over the past."

A small noise, half choke, half cough, escaped Ned Loder.

"Ah, Ned. Don't," Jo said and squeezed his arm. "Ned remembers what happened too well. He knew them all. My parents. Jenny. He's been my friend ever since. And Simon's. Ned was the only one outside the family that Violet trusted near Simon when he was so upset after the accident.''

Ellen met the man's troubled eyes. A deep flush suffused his weathered cheeks. She smiled at him but he bowed his head.

There had been too much suffering here. Ellen longed for everything to be as Jo hoped—mended by Fiona's magic quicksilver presence. The breeze became a wind and she shivered. The front door was in sight again and she lengthened her stride.

London. She must get back, get away from here where nothing was real. She must find Fiona.

"YOU'RE WRONG." Simon kept his eyes on the road but Ellen saw how tightly he gripped the wheel.

"Simon, I'm not. There's something wrong, desperately wrong, and we can't wait any longer.''

"She's like this, I tell you,'' he insisted, turning a corner too fast. The tires screeched. "Please be patient.''

Sweat broke out on her brow and spine. "I don't understand you. Look at you. You're as frantic as I am. Why don't you at least come to the police with me and find out if anyone . . . ? Oh, Simon, I'm so scared.''

He glanced sideways at her. They'd left Cadogan late and dusk was already drawing in. His face was half in shade, and the eerie light made mirrors of his lenses and cast dark shadows about his eyes and mouth.

"Do you hear what I'm saying, Simon? I'm scared, and unless you agree to go with me to the police I'm going alone, just as soon as you drop me off.'' They were already on the outskirts of St. John's Wood. Five more minutes and she'd be at Fiona's flat.

Simon pressed his teeth into his bottom lip. "Look, I'd better be honest with you. I didn't want to say this, but there doesn't seem to be any alternative.''

"What?" She turned to him, terror rising in her throat. "What is it?"

He hesitated, passing a hand over his hair. "I'm not completely surprised Fiona's taken off for a while."

Simon stopped for a traffic light and seemed to consider what to say next. Ellen waited tensely.

"You met my family. I'm not talking about Jo—you already know she's crazy about Fiona."

Anger rose slowly in Ellen. "But your aunt and uncle aren't so pleased about her?"

He drove on and turned at Queen Anne Terrace. "Here we are," he said, drawing to a stop in front of the narrow house.

"Finish what you've started, Simon."

"Okay. In a few words, no, Violet and Xavier aren't keen on Fiona. They wouldn't be keen on any woman who didn't come bearing solid gold connections or, at the very least, a title. Don't blame them too much, please. It's the way it is for some people."

The anger simmered now. "You're the same kind of people, aren't you?"

He rested his forehead on a fist. "No, I'm not. I love Fiona. I'd love her regardless of who or what she is. She needed time and space, Ellen. This trip to France was to get that. Please don't pile more pressure on her by running to the police and starting something that could scare her off completely."

Ellen sat quietly for a while. What he said made sense. It all fitted in with what she herself had felt at Cadogan, and she hated those people for not wanting her sister.

"Do you understand?" Simon asked quietly.

She felt like crying with frustration and hurt. "I guess I do."

"Thank you. If it'll make you feel better I'll have Ross Ivers put some feelers out tomorrow and see if he can track her down. I can trust him not to tell Violet and Xavier what's going on."

*Stand up to them,* Ellen yearned to tell him. *Be a man and take your place, the place where you belong—in charge.* She said, "All right. I'll go along with what you want—but for a week at the most. If we don't hear from Fiona, and I mean that I want to hear her voice, within a week from today, I go to the police. With or without you, Simon."

He stared at her for a moment, then got out of the car and came around to open her door. On the sidewalk, he refused her invitation to come in for coffee. He watched her take the key from beneath the mat and let herself into Fiona's flat. Within seconds, the Aston Martin's engine revved and she listened until the sound of the car faded.

The flat was chilly and full of the heavy silence Ellen had come to detest. She kept on her coat and went into her bedroom. The little room felt damp. Yellowing lines waved along brown and beige wallpaper as if water seeped from an unseen leak.

She didn't want to be here.

Ellen knelt in front of the two-bar gas fire and reached for its switch. Hugh. She wanted to be with Hugh. Longing washed unchecked through her. His face, the remembered strength of his brief embrace came fresh and achingly sweet into her mind. Should she call him, or go to him? The blue-red flames of the fire popped alive. Hugh would at least be kind. She closed her eyes against the emptiness. Kindness wasn't all she wanted from him. Right or wrong, logical or illogical, he drew her with some quality within him, and that quality wasn't simply born of her dependence upon him. His sexuality was part of that...quality, or whatever it was, and something else: a sense of rightness at the thought of being with him.

Her own laugh increased the empty feeling, the mixed-up loneliness. She didn't have the courage to go to him. If she did, what would she say? "I want to be with you. Help me figure out what to do about Fiona, and by the way, I could probably fall in love with you."

Oh, sure, she'd pick up the phone and tell Hugh exactly that. And then he'd remind her they were little more than strangers and suggest she get a good night's sleep, which would undoubtedly make her feel better in the morning.

"Always." The tinny notes of the old song jarred Ellen violently. A scraping thumping noise followed. For seconds she couldn't move. Then she looked over her shoulder toward the hall. The light there came from the living room.

When she stood, her legs trembled. Fiona's music box. As abruptly as the music had started, it stopped.

She rose instinctively to her toes and crept into the hall.

A sharp rap at the front door snapped her head around. She leaned against the wall, breathing through her mouth, long calming breaths.

The knock came again. She had to get her act together. The thumping noise she'd heard a few seconds earlier must have been from whoever was at the door; Fiona's old music box had been faulty for years and it had probably just gone off on its own.

"Coming," Ellen said, warmth seeping back into her rigid muscles.

She opened the door to be confronted by Simon, his hand raised to knock yet again. "I . . . are you okay?"

A smile settled on Ellen's lips. "Yes. A bit tired but okay."

"I didn't mean to be rude when I turned down the coffee. I could come in if you want me to."

Poor guy. He was going through his own misery. "It's not necessary, really. In fact, I was looking forward to going to bed."

He stepped backward, hesitated and came closer again. "All right. If you're sure. But call if you need me. Tomorrow I'll be in meetings all day, but I'll tell my secretary to let me know if you phone.''

She thanked him and watched as he climbed the steps to the walk. He waved before going to his car.

Alone inside the flat once more, Ellen crossed her arms. She felt chilled from standing in the doorway and started back toward her bedroom. In the hall she stopped, her head cocked. A small pinging sound. Then she heard something else, one more note from the music box.

Blood pounded in her ears. Slowly, on tiptoe again, she approached the open door of Fiona's bedroom. Yet another single note of music tinkled out.

Then silence. Silence and the yawning darkness inside the room.

Cold air, gradually gathering strength, slipped around Ellen's face and neck, moved her hair. Her skin tightened, and her spine.

The darkness had about it a solidness. She took a step into the room, holding her hand in front of her as if to ward off an obstacle.

"Fiona?" she whispered.

No reply. Increasing cold met her. Flimsy curtains billowed inward and pale moonlight cast the pattern of the window frame across the bed. The window was open. It had been closed when she left.

Breathing hurt. Ellen continued on tiptoe until she could turn on the bedside light.

The room was empty.

On the rug lay the music box and the empty bottle of White Shoulders.

Ellen slowly opened drawers and cupboards, then, more rapidly checked the room, the whole apartment. Nothing missing. Nothing to report to the police. Nothing concrete to get her the help she so desperately needed.

She returned to stare at the music box. When she picked it up she saw that one paw had snapped from the teddy bear's arm.

The breeze, colder and colder, penetrated her bones. But it hadn't been a breeze that knocked Fiona's precious things to the floor.

Someone had been here when she came home. Even as she'd entered the flat that person had still been here, listening, waiting, deciding what to do next. The intruder made up his mind and moved in the darkness, knocking the box off the nightstand as he did so. Then Simon's return had frightened him off.

Ellen's limbs shook uncontrollably now. She went to the window and dragged it shut.

## Chapter Nine

The draperies on the window in his sitting room were open.

Ellen stood on the sidewalk opposite Hugh's place and stared up at the yellow light behind the panes.

One o'clock in the morning. Finding the courage to come here had taken hours. She should at least have called the man first. But he'd have told her not to come, to calm down. *Help me.* She only wanted to ask him for help, to hear him say everything would be all right, to have him tell her she wasn't a fool to be worried but that everything would be all right.

She shouldn't have come. Ellen glanced up Flask Lane toward the High Street. Her taxi had bumped out of sight minutes ago. The wind was full, approaching a gale and laced with fine rain. Scraps of paper blew against the buildings. The city was asleep. All but Ellen...and Hugh. He was up there awake, too. She had only to ring the bell beside the bookshop door and she would see him.

Her shoes, damp inside, thunked on the uneven road. The center of the bell glowed. Ellen spread her hand on the wall beside it, craning her neck to look up. If the light went out she'd go home.

The light shone steadily.

She pressed the bell and heard its sawing buzz in the recesses of the building. Ellen's heart missed several beats, before it took off at a roaring gallop she could hear in her ears.

He wouldn't come, not at this time of night.

Through the glass door, she saw a glow slither down the stairs from Hugh's flat, then a long, wavering shadow. He came into the shop, peering, his head ducked as he tried to make out his visitor.

For an instant Ellen considered running away. Just running. Up to the High Street and the first taxi to come along. If she went now he'd think someone had played a prank and go back to his book, grumbling, but not knowing his visitor had been Ellen Shaw.

When he reached the door he stopped. Ellen's heart slammed at her throat. He braced a hand each side of the door and stared at her in the gloom. There was no doubt he knew who she was, yet he didn't throw open the door and sweep her inside.

The sound of the bolts snapping open came, and the handle turned. Then Hugh stood on the threshold, his arms crossed, his face obscured.

Ellen backed away. "I'm sorry if I woke you."

"You didn't."

He was angry at being disturbed. She had made a mistake coming here. Her attachment to him was foolish, made up of her dependence on him and her inability to make decisions that should be so simple. And he wasn't interested in her, probably didn't even like her.

"Do you want to come in?"

She felt ill enough to vomit. Cold sweat trickled down her back. "I've disturbed you. I should have called to ask if this was convenient—"

"I asked you if you wanted to come in. It's cold standing here."

He sounded...flat. Not really angry, not really anything, just flat.

All right, so she'd done the wrong thing in responding to instinct, but did he have to be so abrupt? "Look, Hugh. I came because I need someone to talk to and you seemed the right person. Obviously I was wrong about that. I'll get lost. Forget I came, okay?"

His hand, shooting out to grab her elbow, seemed to force the breath from her lungs. He pulled her into the dark shop and shut the door. "It's cold," he repeated. "Come on up and have a drink."

She still couldn't see his face clearly, only the shadows beneath his cheekbones, the glint of his teeth and eyes. "No, no," she said faintly. "I have disturbed you. I'll leave. Forgive me, please. I—"

"You're not going anywhere. You said you wanted to talk, so we'll talk. I didn't mean to put you off."

But he had put her off. And she didn't believe he wanted her here. "It can wait, Hugh. I was too hasty, as usual. It's the old worry—about Fiona—and I shouldn't be bothering you with my problems. Maybe tomorrow—"

"Damn it!"

Ellen jumped. He still held her elbow and his grip tightened. Tears sprang into her eyes and she blinked furiously. She would not be intimidated, not by this man or any other man.

Before she could make another attempt to leave he released her arm and rubbed his eyes. "I'm the one who should be apologizing. What a boor I must sound. Things are still a bit tense for me. I'd like you to come up, okay?" He glanced at her. "Okay?"

Ellen hesitated, then said, "Okay. But you must think I'm insensitive. I keep coming at you with my concerns when you've got your own."

"Could we talk upstairs, do you think?" His voice softened. "That drink sounds good, doesn't it? And maybe we can help each other unwind."

Ellen preceded him up the stairs. Why was her stomach still clenched? Why didn't the rapid change in his mood ring true?

In the low light of his sitting room Ellen felt again the subtle yet strong attraction he held for her. He moved about rapidly, taking her coat, picking up his own from one of the leather chairs and insisting she sit there. And she watched him, lithe, unconsciously powerful in his heavy turtleneck sweater and jeans. She'd never seen him in jeans before, or tennis shoes. Nor had she seen him in such dark clothes. He reminded her of the night, the best part of the night, with its intoxicating qualities that could sharpen the senses and bind the soul in its silken folds made of wind and small sounds, of scents swept free of the day.

"What would you like?" The navy sweater intensified the darkness of his hair, making it almost black.

Ellen breathed through her mouth. The trembling was there, low, in her womb. "White wine, I guess, if you have it." His eyes were a contrast, lighter, the color of fine amber.

"Coming up. Are you hungry?" His mouth was hypnotizing, the lower lip full, the corners dented upward, and the deep cleft in his chin . . .

"What is it, Ellen? Are you all right?"

No, she wasn't all right. She was frantic and at the same time he was doing things to her that had no place in this moment. "I'm fine. And I'm not hungry, thanks. Just the wine would be nice."

Hugh left the room and she heard the kitchen door bang open and shut. For the first time since she'd arrived, she noticed Vladimir eyeing her from her spot in front of the fire. The cat got up slowly and stretched. Tail twitching, she crossed to Ellen. "Hi, old lady," Ellen said and was rewarded with the touch of a cold nose on her hand.

When Hugh returned he handed Ellen a glass, set a cup and saucer beside the other chair and sat down. The cat jumped on his lap. "This animal of mine likes you," he remarked.

"I like her," was all Ellen could think of in response. As he had leaned over her, she'd smelled his clean musky scent, and something else. Night things again? He seemed to carry with him a trace of the wind and rain. She'd like to be out there with him, walking, arms entwined, with him.

Hugh stroked Vladimir and watched Ellen. She wasn't at ease. There was a distance in her eyes and in what she said. Whatever had brought her here tonight made her uncomfortable, and she was feeling her way through. He stroked Vladimir and watched Ellen. She sat on the edge of the chair as if ready to flee. Usually she wore boots. The light low pumps she wore now showed off narrow feet and ankles and long well-shaped legs all the way to the hem of her skirt, hiked slightly above her knees. Beautiful legs. He switched his attention to her face, but she concentrated on the wine in her glass.

"How was your weekend?" he asked.

She looked at him immediately and his insides clamped together. Did she have to be so damned lovely when she could also be the most dangerous human being ever to come into his life?

"It was okay," she said after a while. "How was yours?"

Cat and mouse. When would she make her move? How? If she did make a move? "My weekend was like all the others—routine." *Liar.* But when a man thought he was confronted by a master liar he could only answer in kind. "I did pick up a few first editions from an estate sale on Saturday afternoon." *Be excited,* he begged of her silently, *show what you should show. Ask questions about what books I bought.*

Ellen nodded absently and sipped her wine. She was in on it, he thought. She had to be. Simon Macky with Fiona Shaw and now Ellen planned to get their hands on Millie Weston's money, and he, Hugh, was the only remaining obstacle.

"Oh, yes. And I did something else exciting," he said. He wasn't good at these guessing games.

She looked up, unsmiling. "What?"

"Made a will. Should have done it years ago."

No reaction. Just an empty stare from hardly focused eyes. "On Saturday?" she said finally. "I didn't think lawyers worked on weekends."

"We call them solicitors here. I made special arrangements with the man who dealt with my grandmother's affairs."

"I see."

No, she didn't. The last thing she saw, or even guessed at, was what he'd discovered. If she had known she wouldn't be here tonight. She'd be helping Simon and Fiona rethink their next move.

"So, you're worried about Fiona. I thought she was in France. Didn't you have a good time meeting her future in-laws?"

"I'm not sure she's in France. I told you that before I left for the weekend."

"I think you worry too much." This smoke screen Simon, Fiona and Ellen were using to keep him intimately in contact with Ellen both bored and scared him.

"The Mackys don't like Fiona," Ellen said abruptly.

He looked at her through narrowed eyes. What kind of game was she playing? "She's marrying into the family. I'd say that sounded as if she's pretty well liked."

"By Simon. But he isn't *the family*." She made quote signs in the air. "His sister, Jo, likes her, too, but the others don't."

"Simon is the son and heir. Surely he'll take over from his father eventually. Fiona will be fine."

"You don't understand. *I* don't understand. The older Mackys aren't Simon's parents. They're his uncle and aunt. Simon should already be in charge of the estate because his father was the older brother. At least, that's the way I think it should be."

Why would she tell him this? Hugh wondered. Why would she tell him anything? He made a noncommittal noise.

"I think they've fixed it so all Simon gets is what they dole out to him. A flat in some fancy area and a token job at their brewery, but no real power, no control over his own life."

Hugh was starting to comprehend. The lady was probably telling the truth. And if she was, it would explain why Simon was in such a hurry to get his hands on the fat inheritance that would be his if Hugh wasn't around. "Why would he accept his uncle and aunt taking things over? If he wants control he can have it, can't he?"

"That's what I thought. But apparently he's had some emotional problems and it's been arranged that Xavier—he's Simon's uncle—will administer everything throughout his lifetime."

"What kind of emotional problems?" The last thing Hugh had expected was a story that handed him a cast-iron motive for Simon Macky to engineer two deaths—Millie Weston's and Hugh's own. But he mustn't forget Ellen didn't know what he'd found out. This little visit, the tearful revelation, could be calculated to soften and make sure he remained a sympathetic patsy.

She chewed thoughtfully at a fingernail and he picked up his cup to drink his tea. He didn't intend to cloud his brain with alcohol.

"I can't explain to you about Simon, because I don't really know," she said in a low voice. "He suffered some sort of mental trauma when his parents and one sister died in a fire. Not surprising. And, so the story goes, he's never wanted the responsibility of running everything. Only I don't believe it. I believe he's fed up to the teeth with being told what to do as if he were a kid. But that isn't why I came, or at least not the only reason . . ." She hesitated. "It's part of it. Oh, Hugh, I'm so mixed up."

A break in her voice made him look at her and his jaw stiffened. Tears slid from wide-open eyes and she held a trembling lower lip in her teeth.

He must not let down his guard. "Can you try to explain?" The gentleness in his own voice came naturally. He couldn't have spoken to her any other way at this moment.

She sniffed and fumbled in the pocket of her skirt for a handkerchief, which she held over her mouth. Her blond hair shimmered against the shoulders of her peach-colored blouse. "I think someone wants Fiona to stay gone." The words came on a great sob.

Hugh wrapped one fist in his other hand and willed himself to stay where he was. "Why?"

"Because . . . because . . ." She cried openly now, her small breasts rising hard against soft fabric. "Because she isn't what the Mackys want for Simon. She isn't important enough and she doesn't have the right connections."

This wasn't the way he'd expected the conversation to go. He didn't, couldn't, believe Ellen was putting on an act. But he had to. "Are you trying to tell me the Mackys have actually done something to keep Fiona away? What?"

"I don't know," she said. "But why isn't Simon more worried about her? Why doesn't he want me to go to the police?"

His stomach made a slow revolution. "You want to go to the police?"

"Yes," she murmured and he leaned closer. "I want to tell them she's missing. Simon says she's just gun-shy about the wedding and if I report her missing it'll upset her more." Her eyes pleaded with him. "Tell me what to do. Do you think I should go to the police?"

He didn't know what to think anymore. With difficulty he glanced away. She sounded sincere. She looked so damned sincere. But he knew what he knew and he couldn't afford an error in judgment. "Simon's probably right," he said, his throat hurting with the strain of not going to her. "Fiona's headstrong, but she's also vulnerable. And she likes to have a good time, we both know that. Calm down. She'll show up when she's ready." *Ready to enjoy the fruits of her efforts.* "She hasn't been gone that long anyway."

"Too...long," she replied with apparent effort. "And I think someone was in the flat when I got back tonight. I surprised him and he left through the window in Fiona's room. I know that window was closed before I left, but it was wide open and some of her things were knocked on the floor."

Hugh pushed down panic he dared not feel. "Now that's something you should have called the police about."

"I couldn't."

"Why, for God's sake?"

"Because nothing was taken. What would I say? That a window was open and a music box broken? They'd be nice, and then they'd tell me you can't report a noncrime."

But, Hugh thought grimly, she could tell them she hadn't heard from her sister, who should have been waiting for her the minute she arrived in London. She could tell them what she'd told him and at least see if they thought she should be concerned. Only she didn't have any intention of drawing that kind of attention to what was going on. And all of this, this deliberate playing on his sympathy by making him her confidant, could only be to soften him and make him a careless easy target.

"You're right. They wouldn't take you seriously. And I don't think they should." If only *he* could find a way to alert the police, or anyone who would help him work this chaos out. "Stop worrying. You probably left the window open and you've forgotten."

She blew her nose and wiped her face. "Yes, of course you're right. And I shouldn't have troubled you." She stood up and set down her glass. "Thanks for listening."

Ellen tipped up her chin. There was no help here. He didn't believe there was a problem. Nobody did, or would, until she had proof. And she wasn't getting anywhere on that front. "Good night, Hugh."

"Hell!" he shouted. His arm shot out, striking the table beside him. The smash of his cup and saucer hitting the hearth split the air, and she slapped a hand over her mouth. Fragments of china seemed to hang an instant before settling like hail on tile and rug.

"What . . . ?"

"Damn it! Damn it all!" Dull red seeped into his face and she could hear the rasp of his heavy breathing.

Shaken, Ellen turned away. She didn't see him move from the chair, didn't feel or smell him until his arms went around her waist as she bent to pick up her coat.

"All right," he said harshly, standing behind her and pulling her body against his. Her hair fell forward and she felt his mouth on the back of her neck. "You came here to accomplish something and you've done it."

"I don't know what you mean! Please let me go." Prying his hands loose was impossible; he only held on tighter, then quickly spun her to face him in his arms.

"I told you before how beautiful you are." With one hand, he smoothed back her hair. The lines of his face were tensed, his lips drawn back from clenched teeth.

Ellen started to speak, but instantly his mouth came down on hers. Her legs threatened to give out. She filled her hands with the rough wool of his sleeves.

His kiss was more an assault than anything. Hard, parting her lips, forcing her head from side to side, it invaded her.

Fuzziness rubbed the edges of her mind. She couldn't make space between them or wrench herself from his embrace.

As abruptly as he'd started to kiss her, he stopped, but continued to hold her body to his. "Damn you," he said hoarsely into her hair. His arms were crossed over her back now and his chin was clamped on top of her head. "What do you want from me, Ellen Shaw? Why don't you just come clean and tell me exactly what to expect?"

Ellen closed her eyes, squeezed them shut until tears came. She opened her mouth to breathe and heard the choking noise from her own throat.

"Ellen?" He shook her.

Weak, almost faint, she looped her hands behind his neck. "I don't know what you mean. I don't understand." He supported her now, and he trembled; she felt his steady trembling to her center and the gnawing ache began. She had no guidelines for this, no measure or experience to tell her what was happening. But she wanted him. No matter what this strange violent holding, touching meant, she wanted him.

"Open your eyes," he said so softly she instantly did as he instructed. "Look at me. I want to see into you. Maybe if I can see inside your head I'll know."

Anger. Sadness. Confusion. He showed them all. The rigid set of his face, the glistening sheen on his clouded eyes, his frown—what had she done to cause this? Did he feel for her something of what she felt for him, and did that bring him fear? This quiet reserved man, was he threatened by some new feeling she had evoked in him?

"Hell," he said half under his breath. And he kissed her again, sweetly, his mouth caressing hers, touching softly, repeatedly, as if to heal some hurt he might have brought her.

Ellen slowly threaded her shaking hands into his hair where it met the high neck of his sweater. She pressed closer and closer, her hips arching into his. He was aroused. The ache inside her burned, seared into her thighs. Their clothes were a wall she hated.

He lifted his head and looked at her. Carefully, like a man touching something fragile that might break, he smoothed her face, framed her face, stroked it with flattened palms and fingers. "Why?" he asked brokenly. His lashes were wet. With jerky fingers he made circles behind her ears while he kissed her again.

She watched his eyes close and tasted him. When her hands found the smooth skin at his sides beneath his sweater, he shuddered and thrust at her. The waist of his jeans was low and with the backs of her fingers she felt the rough texture of hair just beneath the band. *Love me,* she begged silently with her mind and body, and the ache became a pain she couldn't bear.

Hugh laid his cheek on hers and slipped his hands inside the neck of her blouse to knead her shoulders.

"Kiss me, Hugh," she whispered. "I want to be with you."

He became still, so still she held her breath. His sigh, when it came, tore at her. With the sigh, his hands stilled heavily on her shoulders, then slipped slowly down, the fingers curling along the edge of her collar until they rested fleetingly on the tops of her tingling breasts.

Then he turned away.

"Hugh?" Ellen caught at his arm. "What is it? What's wrong?" She stepped close, made a wide sweeping arc over his back with her hand and felt him jolt as if he'd received a blow.

"Hugh, please tell me—"

"Go." He spoke so low she strained to hear.

"But—"

"Ellen, don't..." His voice cracked. "Just leave, please."

THE BEIGE AND BROWN WALLPAPER in her bedroom blurred. Lines ran into lines. She hadn't undressed. She lay flat on the bed, her head turned to the wall.

No decision seemed possible. Nothing made sense. Her sister wasn't here, wasn't anywhere Ellen could discover, and no one cared. Not Simon, the man Fiona was to marry. Not Hugh, the man Ellen had been told liked Fiona so much.

He'd kissed her, held her, made her feel as no man had ever made her feel—voluptuous and abandoned, and desired. Then he'd spurned her, or simply changed his mind about wanting her. And he *had* wanted her for at least a while, as intensely as she'd wanted him. What had he meant when he said that if he could see inside her head maybe he'd know? Know what? That she was vulnerable and easily broken? That he had only to take her hand and lead and she'd follow wherever and as far as he wanted to go?

The terrible ache that demanded ease had gone. In her frantic rush from the flat and the shop and into the street, the pain had dulled beneath the wrenching in her throat. A taxi had mercifully appeared as soon as she'd reached the Hampstead High Street. Seated behind the driver she'd yearned to give the man anything but this address, but there was nowhere else to go.

Fiona hadn't been gone long, Hugh told her. Ellen worried too much. After all, she'd been told her sister was in France...

France?

Ellen sat up, swung her feet to the floor. France?

She remembered suddenly the shoe boxes in Fiona's closet. Fiona kept her shoes in their boxes, but Ellen recalled that Fiona had another use for them, as well.

Scrambling, stumbling over strips of rug in the hall, she dashed into Fiona's room and flung open the closet. Ellen pulled the boxes out, one after the other, tossing aside lids until she found what she was looking for. A box containing photographs and papers.

At first she picked up each item and checked. Then, her breath coming in short gasps, she dumped the box upside down and rummaged through the pile.

A tan bankbook slipped from between some pictures. Ellen seized it and checked the entries. The balance was small, but there had been no withdrawal made in more than a month. What had Fiona used for money when she left for her trip to France?

The shallow breaths hurt. Ellen pushed envelopes and folded sheets of paper back and forth, searching. And while she searched she prayed she wouldn't find what she was looking for.

One envelope didn't bend. She lifted it and slowly opened the flap.

From inside the envelope, Ellen pulled Fiona's passport.

# Chapter Ten

"No, Simon," Ellen said into the phone with as much patience as her screaming nerves allowed, "no more waiting. I'll repeat. I'm holding Fiona's passport in my hand. She couldn't have gone to Paris, or anywhere else outside this country without her passport. I'm going to the police. With or without you."

Deciding what to do after finding the passport had taken only minutes. She would act, and now. The possibility of Fiona's being in some legal mess remained, but that was a chance that must be taken.

"I'll be there," she heard Simon say before he hung up without continuing his efforts to dissuade her.

Ellen leafed through the telephone book, open on the couch, and dialed another number. She closed her eyes, willing her heart to be quiet.

"Yes."

At the sound of Hugh's voice, she swallowed hard. "This is Ellen—"

"Ellen, I'm—"

"No. Don't talk. Listen, please. Fiona's passport is here. You know what that means?"

He cleared his throat. "She can't be in France," he said slowly.

"Right. And I'm going to the police. I've already called Simon Macky. He doesn't want me to, but I don't care what anyone else wants anymore. I'm going. She may be in some sort of trouble. Kidnapped. Lost with amnesia. Worse. I don't know. I just thought I'd tell you."

He didn't answer.

"Well," she said more briskly than her tight vocal cords should have allowed, "as soon as Simon gets here I'll go. I've told him he can come if he likes, but I won't change my mind."

She heard him draw a long breath. "Do you want me to come, too?"

Ellen pinched the bridge of her nose. "That's up to you. You do employ her. And at the moment you're even more involved with... You're my sponsor, which means I have to keep you informed of what I'm doing for as long as I'm in England."

"You do want me to come, don't you?"

She shrugged. Why didn't she tell him no, no she didn't want him? Because she did? "I think it would be nice to have some show of solidarity for the police. They have to take me seriously."

"Mmm."

He was silent again. Ellen shook so badly it took both of her hands to hold the phone steady. "I must go, Hugh. Let's hope everything turns out okay." Brave words.

"Don't leave without me," he said abruptly. "If I find a cab quickly I can make it there in half an hour. But wait for me, you understand?"

"I understand."

The dial tone sounded again, and Ellen looked at the receiver for a moment before she replaced it.

She gathered her purse and went into the bathroom. The police would take an apparently calm and controlled woman more seriously than one who seemed hysterical.

She washed her face, applied a little makeup and brushed her hair. The worry in her eyes wasn't something she could erase with any kind of paint.

Quickly, hurrying now in case Simon or Hugh arrived sooner than expected, she kicked off her damp shoes and went back to her bedroom to find dry hose and pull on her boots.

She picked up her raincoat and stood with it bunched in her hands. Hugh had behaved so strangely. He had been the one to sponsor her, a total stranger, for a working permit in England. The only reason he'd done that was for Fiona. Fiona could charm any man, had always been able to charm any man. Just how much had she charmed Hugh Weston?

Cecily Horton at the book shop had said, "He thinks the world of her. He'd do anything for Fiona." Yet he behaved as if he didn't give a damn about her. Why, why?

And Ed Butters thought there was something more than friendship between them. Cecily had told Ellen that, too.

"Oh, my God." Ellen sank down on the edge of the bed. Were Hugh and Fiona lovers? She swallowed against welling nausea. That kind of closeness would explain why Hugh had been willing to do so much to help with her own entry into the country. It could also explain something else. No. She wouldn't think it.

Simon would be here any minute. Ellen trailed into the living room and sat where she would see approaching figures through the threadbare drapes at a single long window.

Fiona and Hugh. Lovers? Hugh had behaved as if he didn't know Fiona was engaged. Had he known? Had Fiona told him, then tried to extricate herself from their relationship? Ellen gnawed the inside of her lip. Hugh continued to act as if he didn't think there was any reason to be concerned over Fiona's absence. Could that be because he didn't want any attention drawn to himself? Could he be playing down Fiona's disappearance because if Ellen got close to the truth, whatever it was, he would be in some sort of danger?

Agitated, Ellen leaped up and put on her coat. She paced. Hugh's behavior earlier tonight. Unbalanced? That wild flare of temper when he'd smashed the cup. Then roughness turning to incredible aching tenderness. Then... She couldn't even describe how he'd made her feel next, how small and discarded and shamed.

He would play down Fiona's absence if he didn't want her found. Ellen fumbled to close the buttons on her coat. The pounding in her chest became stifling. He wouldn't want Fiona found if he'd killed her...

Abruptly, unable even to attempt buckling her belt, Ellen sat down. If Hugh had been in love with Fiona, deeply involved with her, and if he then discovered she was going to leave him for another man, would he have been capable of murdering her in some passionate rage he couldn't control? Tonight he'd given a firsthand demonstration of the quick fury he could unleash.

Uncertain what to do, she stood close to the door. After that first angry embrace, Hugh's body had sent its message—his desire to make love to her. Had the message been for Fiona? Ellen shoved her hands into her pockets. While Hugh kissed her, had he instead been kissing Fiona?

Light-headedness overtook her. If he had killed Fiona he could kill her, too. Wouldn't he do that if she presented a threat to the keeping of his secret? A silent scream rose into her throat.

The only person she could trust was herself. She was strong and she'd make a way out.

A sharp rap on the door rocked her nerves from head to toe. She dithered, pulling at her collar. A key turned in the lock and the door swung open.

"Ellen?" Simon entered and closed the door behind him. "Are you all right? You look awful."

She lifted her chin and attempted a smile. "I'm fine. A little shaken, that's all. Simon, don't argue about this anymore, okay?"

He spread his hands in a defeated motion. "I bow to your decision. But I still think you're wrong."

Ellen took Fiona's passport from her pocket. "Do you deny that Fiona couldn't get into France without this?"

"I s'pose not."

His hair was uncharacteristically ruffled and, under a sport coat, he wore a polo shirt and cotton pants too lightweight for the season. Ellen looked at him closely. His face was flushed and his eyes bloodshot. With something close to shock she realized he'd been drinking. Too much.

"Sit down," she said sharply. "We'll leave in a minute." Just what she needed, a drunken male to back her up with the police. Irrationally, considering what she'd just been thinking about him, she was glad Hugh would be with them. At least he would make a solid impression.

Simon perched on the edge of the sagging couch, his chin planted on his fists. He closed his eyes. Useless. The man was useless to her. Ellen took a deep breath, gathering her strength. Fiona loved Simon Macky and he loved her. This change Ellen saw in him could only be the result of worry over his fiancée, even if he did keep denying that he was concerned.

The shakiness she felt inside increased. Simon seemed to doze. She had the feeling that if she tiptoed away he would simply stretch out on the couch and sleep.

"Simon," she began. He grunted. "Simon, will you help me tell the police exactly what's happened?"

"Hmm?" He opened his eyes and squinted at her. "Nothing's happened as far as I can say. I told you that."

"Damn." She sat beside him and held his arm. "Don't keep this up. I don't understand you. Your fiancée has dropped out of sight without a word and—"

"No, no, Ellen. She did send word. At my office, but I wasn't there. I told you that. She left a message."

Ellen stared at him for an instant. "Good grief. I'd forgotten that. She left a note." She stood and leaned over to take him by the shoulders. "The note, Simon. Where's the note?"

"What?" He raised glazed eyes to hers.

"Where is the note Fiona left?" Ellen said. Her skin burned and turned cold by turns. "I want to see it."

"No note," Simon mumbled. "Just a message with my secretary who told me. I don't even know if Fiona delivered the message herself. I . . . I just don't know."

Ellen released him and slumped down again. "Shoot. I thought we might have something else to go on." Tears sprang into her eyes. Simon seemed to be less together with every moment, and she didn't know exactly what to do about him. He shouldn't come with her to the police.

More footsteps sounded on the concrete steps outside. Hugh came in. Simon couldn't have shut the door completely. "Good evening, or should I say good morning?" he said. "Evening, Macky."

Simon's instant metamorphosis astonished Ellen. He shoved back his hair and stood, straightening his jacket. The corners of his mouth drew down sharply.

"Evening, Weston." He nodded.

Hugh threatened him in some way. Ellen looked from one man to the other. Simon fumbled with the lower button on his jacket, shoving it through the hole.

The job, Ellen thought suddenly. Maybe Simon really was disturbed by the thought of his future wife working for Hugh in some occupation the Mackys would regard as menial.

"What's the plan?" Hugh asked after too long a pause. The two men were circling each other, assessing.

"We're leaving," Ellen put in hastily. "I'm going to take Fiona's passport—"

"You don't need me," Simon interrupted.

An awkward silence followed. Ellen sought Hugh's eyes, but he stared only at Simon. His steady appraisal held...hate? Ellen's stomach turned yet again. Was she looking at the hate of a betrayed lover? With every tiny building block of doubt and uncertainty, the conviction that Hugh and Fiona had been an item grew.

She stirred and let out the breath she'd unconsciously been holding. "I do need you, Simon." Despite Simon's drunkenness, being alone with Hugh was something she feared.

Simon walked past her without a glance. "No. I think not. Call me after you've spoken to the police. No point in overkill. The two of you will manage—if you insist on going ahead with this. But be warned." He opened the door. "I'll be very surprised if they take you seriously."

"The hell you will!" Hugh shouted as he grabbed Simon's arm. "What makes you so sure what the police will or won't think?"

A fluttering, like a thousand tiny moths, filled Ellen. She was seeing it again. That sudden irrational temper of Hugh's.

Simon tried to pull away but Hugh held fast. "What makes you so sure, Macky?" he repeated.

"I'd advise you to let go." Simon's voice gradually rose. "Now!"

"And if I don't?"

Thunderous banging came from above. The landlady. Ellen closed her eyes and said, "Stop it, please. Let Simon go, Hugh. He's right. This won't take all of us."

Hugh settled his mouth in a grim line, looking from Ellen to Simon. With one last twist of the coat sleeve he released his grip. "If you say so."

Without a word, Simon left and Ellen let out a whistling breath. "Why did you get so angry with him?"

"Forget it." Hugh's face was impassive again. "Ready to go?"

Ellen opened and closed her mouth, then pulled the passport from her pocket once more, as well as the bankbook. She held them toward him. Could she get away somehow, escape, while he looked at the books?

"Keep them," Hugh said peremptorily. "Let's just get this over with. I hope to God Macky's right about one thing—that we don't have anything to worry about."

"Yes," Ellen managed. She led the way into the forecourt and up the steps to the street.

Hugh was a pace behind her. She felt him, big, powerful. Outrunning him would be impossible. She glanced around and slowly, very slowly, a flicker of relief started in her brain. He didn't have a car. He couldn't spirit her off, and if he grabbed her on the street she could scream, and maybe be heard.

"I'll run ahead," Hugh said. "Come at your own pace. I'll see if I can grab a cab by the tube station. I didn't think to keep the one I had because I assumed Macky would have a car and drive. Okay?"

He'd started to trot away but then he stopped and waited. Ellen walked slowly toward him.

"Are you okay, Ellen? I'll walk with you if you'd prefer. Only—"

"No," she said, finally finding her voice. "Go ahead. You'll be quicker than me. I'll catch up."

He nodded and took off at a full sprint.

She'd been wrong. Ellen started to run after him. Relief brought blood singing into her ears. She'd been *wrong*. He did want to go to the police and he did want to help her. A man afraid of being found out in a crime wouldn't willingly go within miles of the police. Hugh was guilty of nothing but a quick temper, caution and a usually reserved nature, and perhaps a little discomfort with displaying passion. He would overcome that. They'd get through the bad times and then she'd help him overcome all his reservations, if that's what was meant to be.

"Wait up, Hugh!" she yelled, running faster. And she would run forever, if necessary.

# Chapter Eleven

Hugh helped Ellen out of her coat and handed it to her. "Are you going to be all right?" he asked. She'd hardly spoken on the way back to Fiona's flat from the police station.

"I don't know." Lamplight behind her turned blond hair into a pale halo. She didn't seem to know what to do next.

"Give me that." He took back the coat and hung it in the closet. "Things probably won't seem so bad in the morning. Which will be in about two hours." He laughed, but Ellen didn't. "Why don't you try to get some sleep. Cecily will open up in the morning and you can come in late."

"Yes," she responded woodenly.

He dug his hands into the pockets of his old leather bomber jacket. "Would you like me to stay awhile? Make some tea or something?"

Nothing.

Hugh pulled his lower lip between his teeth, then released it slowly. He couldn't leave her like this. He shut out the fact that he should leave, at once, without running the risk of getting close to her again.

"They didn't take us seriously," Ellen said suddenly. "That policeman, the big one, didn't care at all."

Hugh sighed. "Just because he didn't think there was anything to worry about doesn't mean he didn't care."

She shaded her eyes, bracing an elbow against the arm that gripped her ribs. "I hate being in this place," she murmured. "It doesn't feel as if Fiona ever lived here."

For a crazy moment he considered bundling her back into her coat and taking her to his flat. In the past few hours he'd decided one very important thing. It didn't help sort out the puzzle his life had become, but he was sure it was fact: Ellen knew nothing about what Simon and Fiona had done, or had in mind to do in future. He had begun to worry that she might be as much in danger as he. Not perhaps from Fiona, since she was her sister after all, but certainly from Macky—and maybe even from Fiona if the chips were down. How could two women look as alike as Fiona and Ellen Shaw yet be so different?

Ellen was talking. "The police don't know Fiona. How can they say that she sounds like the kind of woman who gets bored and moves on, or does something like this to break the monotony?" Her eyes filled with tears. "Or to get attention?"

He balled his fists in his pockets. If he took them out he would have to touch her. "I suppose they get a lot of stories like the one you told. And Fiona does have a history of dropping out of sight from time to time."

"But I showed them the passport and I said she'd told Simon she was in France."

"And they told us they believed she'd made up stories to cover for herself while she went somewhere quite different." But, if that were true, why hadn't Fiona contacted him to allay his suspicions? Because she didn't expect him to be a problem for long? And Ellen, why hadn't Fiona made certain Ellen wouldn't worry? Here, any answer eluded him.

"What did the officer mean about Simon? When I gave his name?"

Hugh scowled at the ceiling. That one had surprised him, too. "I don't know. Just that while he was stationed at the Mayfair precinct he knew of Simon."

"Does the Hampstead precinct know about you?" Tears had begun to course down her cheeks.

She wasn't a woman who could be fooled. "No, of course not. And the officer shouldn't have said what he did. I guess Simon doesn't always carry his drink too well. No great sin."

"But he must have been brought in drunk more than once for a policeman to remember him like that."

"I suppose so," Hugh said, suddenly weary. Damn Simon Macky. "Try to forget it." From the dawning expression on the officer's face at the mention of Simon's name, from the immediate loss of interest in the story Ellen had to tell, it looked as if Fiona's wonderful fiancé had plenty of dirt to keep under the rug.

"What do you think I should do next?"

Hugh met her eyes, such beautiful dark brown eyes in a pale finely boned face. "Do as the police suggested," he said, not feeling the conviction he tried to convey, "and give it a bit longer. They said they'd make inquiries and keep a look out for her. And they will check with the people she knows at the theater. That's about all we can expect from them." And, he thought, Fiona wouldn't surface until she was ready. He'd bet his last pound that she'd been spooked and gone underground to wait for the dust to settle just in case someone did put the pieces of what she'd done together.

Hugh was pretty sure his conclusions were close to the truth. At Simon Macky's instigation, Fiona had sought Hugh out, ingratiated herself with his grandmother, then wormed out the details of the will. Then, either alone or with help—Hugh suspected the latter—Millie Weston's death had been pulled off. How Simon knew anything about the will in the first place remained a mystery, but, given time, that too should come out.

Ellen stood by the window, one side of the faded curtain lifted in her hand. A somber dawn light was just beginning. The old window frame rattled in the wind and she flinched.

"Please, Ellen," he said, "let me make you some tea."

"I don't want any damned tea." She swung toward him, her mouth parted to show small even teeth. "You English think your rotten tea makes everything okay. That policeman said 'bodies' had a way of showing up. He said it like I wasn't telling him my sister was missing—my sister! *Bodies* have a way of showing up! Oh, God—"

Unable to stop himself, he grabbed her and wrapped her in his arms. Only when she made a small sound did he register that he must be squeezing the air out of her.

"He was trying to lighten things up. I know that sounds outrageous, and he certainly was being insensitive, but we English have a reputation for so-called dry humor."

Her arms slipped around his waist. "He said there were no unidentified candidates in the morgue right now," she said brokenly. "Those were the words he used. It made me feel sick."

Hugh closed his eyes and silently cursed the policeman.

"You need to go home, Hugh." Ellen withdrew her hands. Moisture made her lowered lashes slick. "Thanks for being with me tonight. I needed you and I won't be this kind of trouble again, I promise you."

*Oh, but you will, you will.* "I wanted to be with you." Now he not only had his own safety to worry about, but Ellen's. Macky wouldn't want her to continue nosing around his business.

"Will you be able to get a taxi at this hour? You could..." She looked up at him and brought her lips together.

*Stay,* Ellen longed to say. *Stay with me, please.*

As she looked into his eyes his expression changed, concern being replaced by a question. Without looking away, he unzipped his jacket and took it off.

He wrapped the jacket over one forearm, then folded his arms and bowed his head. "We haven't known each other long," he said, "so why do I feel as if you've always been a part of my life?"

Ellen blinked rapidly. She tucked her hands over his arms and rested her brow on his chest.

"Is it just need, Ellen? Do we want to be together because we're both overwrought and there's no one else? You do want to be with me, don't you?"

"Yes." Everything was so tough, so complicated. The effort it took not to cry again burned her throat. "But is that so wrong? I don't want to be alone, Hugh, but I wouldn't be with anyone else but you even if I could."

He put her gently away from him and threw down his jacket. "I was pretty rotten when you came to me last night."

"You don't have to talk about that now."

"Yes I do." He took her back into his arms and rocked her, kissed her temple. "Ellen, I haven't ever found it easy to let go with anyone else. I...I don't even know exactly how to explain this to you, but I'm going to try."

"I already know you're a reserved man, used to your own space. I won't ever intrude on that. I need it, too." She looked up at him, flushing. What she said already sounded like a declaration, and a claim. Was it the result of her confusion, her aloneness?

Hugh smoothed the collar of her blouse and let his arms fall to his sides. "I'd like to stay with you, Ellen. May I do that—stay with you, lie beside you?"

The welling up of so much she longed to say, so much she had no way of saying, made her weak. "Please," she told him and reached to kiss his rough jaw.

They walked, hand in hand, into Ellen's bedroom with its single narrow bed.

Ellen's limbs, every nerve and muscle in her body, trembled. He had to feel the trembling where he held her hand.

"No pressure, Ellen. Do you understand?"

She didn't. "Pressure?"

Hugh raised her hand to his mouth and kissed the backs of her fingers. "I want to be what you need tonight. If that's just someone to be with, I'm here."

He still wore the heavy sweater he'd had on when she'd gone to his flat. Ellen withdrew her hand from his and rubbed her palm over the rough wool. "I'm twenty-seven years old. I should be better at these things."

"Meaning?"

"Meaning I should be able to tell you, without feeling embarrassed, that I want us to make love."

He laughed softly and covered her hand on his chest. "Are there any 'shoulds' for times like this? I want it, too. I think I have from the moment I saw you."

Ellen laughed in response, and the sound was unnaturally high. "What I'm saying is that I'm not sure how to go about this with you. I feel...I'm not... Oh, Hugh, help me, please. Everything's so mixed up and—"

His mouth, coming down on hers, stopped her clumsy attempt to explain that although she wasn't totally inexperienced, there hadn't been a lot of men in her life—and never one she'd asked to make love to her.

He kissed her, first gently, then with a fierceness that left her breathless. Ellen pulled at the bottom of his sweater, desperate to feel his body naked against hers.

"Wait," he muttered and stripped the sweater over his head, unbuttoned the shirt he wore beneath and tossed them both to the floor.

Breath jammed in Ellen's throat. He was perfectly made, broad shouldered, his chest wide and heavily muscled.

When he dipped his head to kiss her again, she stopped him, leaned her cheek against the wide swath of hair on his chest and rubbed slowly, turning her face to kiss each flat nipple, standing on tiptoe to press her lips into the hollow places beneath his collarbones. She covered his shoulders and arms, the solid bands of muscle at his sides, with her kisses. Slowly, with her eyes closed, she lifted his hands and placed them over her breasts.

"Look at me," Hugh whispered.

She did and he brought his face closer until she saw into the clear, warm amber of his eyes, the darker ring that rimmed each iris. Her chest tightened. He smoothed back her hair and kissed her lips. She felt the prickle of beard and closed her eyes again. Hugh's mouth left hers but he continued to stroke her hair.

"Ellen, are you . . . do you . . . ?"

He was asking about protection. Heat rushed through her body. "There's nothing to worry about." Without knowing why, she knew she was right.

His hands shook. She looked at him again. He smiled, and she saw the feverish glow that had entered his eyes, the flush on his face.

"I want to . . . I want to look at you, Ellen."

Obediently, breathing shallowly through her mouth, she began twisting at the buttons on her blouse. The cuffs were stubborn, but she worked them loose and let the blouse fall. She knew she was too thin. Would she please him? She reached behind her back for the fastening of her bra.

Hugh stopped her. "Let me." He turned her around and freed the hook, slid narrow lace straps from her shoulders. Again he covered her breasts, naked now, stroked, rubbed her nipples. Searing heat shot through her and she turned.

He looked at her a moment. "You're so pale. Fragile. Perfect." When he bent to kiss her breasts she looked down at his curly dark hair, then held his moving head against her.

"Ellen, Ellen," he mumbled into the space between her breasts. "I do need you."

And she needed him, but didn't trust herself to speak. Jerkily he undid the button on her skirt, then the zipper. He worked her clothes down, slipping to his knees, brushing his mouth over her stomach, into the dips in front of her hipbones, down to the light patch of hair.

Ellen couldn't breathe. She held Hugh's shoulders, drove her fingertips into the raised tendons. A noise came from her yet seemed to come from somewhere far away. Ellen couldn't move. Electrically conscious of her skin, she felt transparent, as if all the elements of her body were exposed and raw.

Hugh finished undressing her and stood. He lifted her and placed her on the bed. She watched him take off his clothes, impatience clawing at her even as she savored the sight of him. The line of hair at his navel broadened over his belly, covered his long strong legs. Ellen half closed her eyes and studied him, her embarrassment gone. She dwelled on the urgent part of him. Man as man was intended to be with a woman he desired.

Their eyes met and Hugh lay beside her. Ellen shifted until they were both on their sides, facing, embracing. His hardness sought her softer flesh, probing her belly. She took him in her hand and saw him grit his teeth. Almost roughly he pulled her hand away and rolled over her, his tongue seeking hers. She met it, arching her hips and feeling his solidness nudging her again.

Hugh breathed rapidly, but he shifted back a little and propped his head on his hand to look down at her. He smiled, a strained little smile. "Let's take our time."

She wanted to protest. Eagerness to be joined with him shuddered underneath her skin. But she lay still. With the fingers of his free hand, he traced her, the side of her face, her neck and shoulder. At her breast he paused, cupped, and bent to take her nipple in his mouth. Ellen pressed closer but he lifted his head again and let his fingers trail on, down and to the inside of her legs.

"Hugh, come to me. I—"

"No," he murmured, "not yet. I want this to go on forever."

She was half-lost in the sensations he stirred. She wanted to tell him so many things, but all that formed coherently in her head was the sound of his name.

When she pushed on his chest he glanced into her eyes and let her roll him away a little. Again she stroked his belly and held him, felt his heat, his pulse within her hand. He let his head fall back and she kissed his neck, loving the way the lines in his face deepened, the intense drawing back of his lips.

Then Hugh moved, turned her on her back in one competent motion as if she weighed nothing. He rose over her, parting her thighs to kneel between. His entry, slow and gradual and driving deeper, hurt a little but she tilted up her chin, swallowing her indrawn breath.

"Okay?" she heard Hugh say, and she nodded.

"Relax, my love, let me do the work." He'd become still.

"Yes," she whispered. *My love*. Somewhere the thought came that the words meant nothing, but she banished the thought and tried to be calm. Her hips met his and she looked down at the tangle of their hair, blond with black, the length of him buried within her.

He began to move again, deeper, deeper, the slow strokes building sweet pain in her. Ellen matched Hugh's rhythm. Sensation mounted and her eyes flew open. She must wait for him. But she couldn't. "Hugh!" Fire, heavy white fire she couldn't douse. Her body convulsed and for seconds she forgot everything but the pulsating force.

Ellen opened her eyes, panting, slowly focusing on Hugh's face so close to hers. He was smiling.

"Oh, no," she said in a small voice, "I couldn't have done..."

"But you did," he said gently. "You looked so beautiful."

He was still inside her, still hard. His steady stroking within her began once more. She was filled with him. The throbbing that had scarcely abated began again, more fiercely. Hugh groaned. He was losing the control that must have cost him so much, but she understood what he'd done and she smiled. So, this was it, the way love could be made to be so much more, by giving and giving until the giving came back, as it was coming back to Hugh.

The thrusts became fierce and Ellen reached for each one. Hugh spoke incoherently, dropping his head beside hers. The sense that a white heat lapped at her started again and Ellen bit into her lip, desperate not to disappoint Hugh. But his cry, the last wild searchings, came seconds before she could hold on no more. Then he fell, heavy and damp onto her quivering body.

Their ragged breathing, the rattle of the window in the living room, were the only sounds in the shadowiness of early morning.

Hugh pushed himself to his elbows where he could look directly down into her face. He kissed her softly, slowly moving her face with his, and looked at her again. "Do you think we could sleep now?" He had about him the appearance of an exhausted handsome boy and she loved him.

Ellen closed her mind to the thought. As Hugh had suggested, they were two people brought together by need and loneliness. There didn't have to be love. Silently she helped him push back the covers. They settled, Ellen facing the wall and curled into Hugh's raised knees. He held her against him and the small space seemed all they needed.

Soon she thought he slept, one arm draped over her breasts. Ellen watched the wall. Filtered light from the hall slowly spread over the windowless room.

Hugh had gone to the police with her and he'd come back here and stayed. She couldn't have borne to be alone and he'd known that, so he stayed. He'd wanted to—she didn't fool herself that his motives were purely selfless—but what had happened was beautiful, and because of it she would never be the same.

Her thoughts sharpened. She worked for Hugh, would have to continue working for him as long as she was in England, and certainly until Fiona returned. But she wouldn't think about Fiona now. She feared that what she and Hugh had done tonight might make their working together almost impossible.

Ellen shifted a little against Hugh's body and he adjusted his position, enclosing one of her breasts in his hand. She held her breath. He *had* come to the police with her. That meant he knew nothing about Fiona's whereabouts, didn't it? A vague uneasiness sneaked in. He could have gone with her because he was familiar with the system and knew nothing could connect him . . .

She had to get rid of her doubts. Closing her eyes, she tried to doze. *Hugh thought the world of Fiona.* She rolled her face into the pillow. While he was making love to her, had he been thinking of Fiona? Could this man who still held her be a murderer?

No! her mind screamed back. He was gentle and sweet. He had given more than she'd dreamed any man could give of himself. Maybe this shouldn't have happened tonight, but it had and she would let it be. Fiona would return and then they'd all have to see what came next.

Hugh felt Ellen's restless movement, her shifting. Once he thought she muttered something, but he just held her, waiting, and eventually her steady breathing let him know she'd finally fallen asleep.

He would be for Ellen whatever she would allow him to be. The muscles beside his mouth jerked. How much would she let him be with her, for her, if she discovered that her sister had been at least partly responsible for his grandmother's death? How would he feel about her if and when the evidence finally fell into place? Was there still any possibility that he'd been duped by this mesmerizingly beautiful woman, that he'd been made more vulnerable by his increased involvement with her? It was inconceivable that Fiona should have gone to the trouble of getting Ellen a job in England while she herself was plotting murder with Macky—unless Ellen was to become a party to that plot.

Telling Ellen what he knew about Macky and the will was a possibility. He could let her know he was afraid for his own life and watch her reaction, see if he caught her off guard. His mouth dried. It would catch her off guard, all right. It would also terrify her if she was innocent. She would immediately become frantic for Fiona's safety.

Beneath his head, the pillow was hot. He lifted his cheek a little. Ellen's hair, spread and tangled between them, was fragrant. No, he was confused, that's all. She was guilty of nothing. He would hang on to that and pray for a way through all this that wouldn't break her heart.

He'd also pray that he could keep her safe, keep them both safe.

# Chapter Twelve

"Bulletins are out," the desk officer at the police station had told her the last time she called. Bulletins, in whatever form they took, passing along lines from one end of England to the other. Fiona's name, her age and description, copies of the photograph Ellen had given the authorities the previous day.

Being in the shop, trying to function effectively, became harder with each passing hour. She looked through the window, seeing, yet not seeing people on the sidewalk. Every day since the past Sunday had been like this, heavy with a waiting she could almost touch. Six days of jumping with every ring of the phone, six days of wondering about Hugh, of sensing a distance between them while she yearned to be with him. They were circling, wordlessly letting each other know that there was no going back from where they had arrived early Monday morning, and equally, no going on until the suffocating atmosphere of uncertainty dissipated.

"Ellen, Cecily said you wanted me." Jean-Claude, the skinny blond French student who worked part-time for Ed Butters in the wine bar and all day each Saturday in the bookshop, propped his elbows on the counter.

"Yes, Jean-Claude." She handed him a leather-bound copy of *Madame Bovary*. "Would you take this up to Hugh, please? Tell him it just arrived. He's been waiting for it."

Jean-Claude took the book in one hand and pushed wire-rimmed glasses back onto his thin-bridged nose with the other. He smiled and mumbled something before he shambled toward Hugh's flat.

Hugh had avoided her today. In the few minutes he had spent in the shop, Ellen felt as if she were enclosed in a vacuum. Nothing and no one existed but him. Every glance, a chance brushing of hands, transmitted their longing, but Ellen sensed, as Hugh must also sense, a barrier between them, a marking of time while they waited for news of Fiona.

Cecily Horton bustled by, talking to a customer. She gave Ellen's shoulder a motherly sympathetic pat. Everyone here knew what was happening now, that Fiona was missing. But nothing direct was said, even by Ed Butters, who usually blurted the first thing that came to mind.

Saturday again. Ellen flipped cards in a small file behind the counter but didn't read them. Almost a week since she and Hugh...

Last night, when the rest of the staff had gone home and she was about to leave the shop, Ellen told Hugh that she'd made fresh contact with the police. He hadn't asked what was happening, or how she felt. Nothing. He'd only held her hand quickly, as he had done several times during the week, then hugged her before he walked away and back up to his flat.

They'd parted early on that Monday morning without making plans, without talk of being together again. Ellen snapped the file shut. Had Hugh, in the light of day, seen her clearly as Ellen, not Fiona, and recoiled from what he had done? She refused to continue to entertain the possibility that he had killed her sister; that was, had to be, the sick product of her mind under stress. But the idea that Hugh might love Fiona persisted.

At six Ellen shooed Cecily and Jean-Claude out, insisting she would cash out the till and finish what few other tasks remained. She needed to talk to Hugh about what she saw as a need to raise prices, but not tonight.

An hour later, the last stray book in evidence shelved, she let herself out and locked the door behind her. The constant wind was at its worst, apparently intent on forcing her back the way she'd come. Ellen bent her head and struggled toward the High Street.

"Ellen."

Her heart made a gigantic leap and she stopped. Hugh stood beside her, hastily pulling on his leather jacket. A scarf trailed from one pocket, and he wound the garish red-and-white-striped wool around his neck.

"Hi," she said, hoping she sounded nonchalant. "Lousy night, huh?"

He placed a heavy hand on her shoulder and took the lapel of her coat between his fingers. "I quite like this kind of night. Brings out the wildness in me." His attempt at a devilish grin fell short, but his mellow gold eyes did their magic. "You need a warmer coat, Ellen. This is too light."

"I'm warm blooded. It's fine," she lied. He was right, but she couldn't afford new clothes, not while she didn't know how long she'd have an income.

"May I walk with you to the tube? I've got to catch a train, too."

Ellen suddenly realized she didn't want to go home yet. "I'm not taking the train this evening," she said, improvising, and starting forward with a rush. "It's time to get daring and try the top deck of those buses."

Hugh said nothing until they reached the High Street. "Which bus are you taking?"

"Um, I'm not sure," she said, then added hastily, "but I'll look it up on the chart." Her hands and feet might be icy, but her body throbbed with heat. Hugh had only to come close, in fact she had only to think of him, and the throbbing ache began.

"Maybe I'll take the bus with you," he said, looking straight ahead.

They'd turned onto the High Street. Dust and debris mixed with leaves scurried past their feet. Loud voices raised in song billowed from the lighted interior of a nearby pub.

Ellen had difficulty forming complete thoughts. "I'm probably not going the same way as you." But she wanted to be with him, how she wanted that.

He reached for her arm and pulled her to face him. "Wherever you're going, that's where I'm going. Okay? We need to talk. I want to hear everything that's happened in the last few days."

People hurried past. A man knocked Ellen's arm and she heard his muttered apology, but she saw no one but Hugh. "I tried to tell you last night," she said.

"I know. I'm sorry if I gave you the brush-off. Some of us are less comfortable with shared confidences than others. Do you understand that?"

"Yes." She understood very well that in temperament they were oil and water. "Hugh, I'm not going back to the flat right away, so tonight's probably not a good time to talk."

"Where are you going?" He pulled her to the curb, away from the stream of passersby.

*Anywhere,* she felt like telling him. *Anywhere I can be alone, yet with people, and still think.*

"Ellen, where are you going?" he repeated, slipping an arm around her shoulders and lowering his face closer to hers.

"Soho," she announced, not even sure where Soho was or how to get there.

Hugh looked puzzled. "You want to go to Soho alone? At night?"

"Yes. I haven't been there and I want to see the lights. It's busy, isn't it, with lots of people?"

He nodded slowly. "And lots of strip and porno joints. Hookers in every doorway. But it's busy all right."

"Good," Ellen said stubbornly. "That's exactly what I want to see tonight." She looked up the road. Red double-decker buses jostled with cars, bicycles and pedestrians. Nearby a bus schedule was attached to a pole. Ellen moved toward it and scanned numbers, destinations and times.

"Why Soho?"

She didn't look at Hugh. "I don't see it on here."

"We can go to Piccadilly Circus." He sounded weary. "Soho's off Piccadilly."

"You don't need to come with me," Ellen said, wishing she didn't want him to.

"This one will do." It was Hugh's turn to feign deafness. A bus pulled up, spewing forth passengers, and he grabbed a handrail and hauled Ellen aboard.

"Hugh . . ." She tried to look at him but he propelled her firmly up narrow steps onto the swaying upper deck.

"Sit in the front. You can see best there." He pushed her unceremoniously into the seat above the driver's cab and slid in beside her on slippery vinyl.

The motion surprised Ellen. At each turn, the bus leaned toward buildings, overhung people below, then it lurched forward again, tripping between other vehicles like a large yet mincing dancer amid less inspired performers.

Darkness was drawing in, flattening the scene outside. Ellen glanced down at the faces outside, most of them set and tired, bent on reaching home and peace. Would she ever feel at peace again?

"This is Maida Vale," Hugh said abruptly. They had sat in silence, each staring in a different direction through the bus's windows.

"I've heard of it," Ellen remarked. "I've seen it on the underground maps."

"I grew up here," Hugh went on as if she hadn't spoken. "My grandmother died here."

A lump rose in Ellen's throat. He was no more at peace than she was. "You miss her, don't you?" When they first met he'd told her he wasn't close to his grandmother. Ellen didn't believe him.

He looked at the shiny white paint overhead. "Not the way you would normally think. But she was good to me and I hate the way she died." His amber eyes met hers and narrowed. "No one should have to die like that, should they?"

Before she could stop herself, Ellen shuddered. Ed Butters had filled in the gory details of the fire and explosion that killed Millie Weston; how the experts figured that natural gas had been slowly seeping from a fractured main for days, that the explosion was heard for several miles. "You have to forget it," she said when she could speak, "or it'll eat you up."

He sat forward, looking straight down on the road. "I'll forget it. Takes time, that's all." Then he commented, "Edgware Road. Marble Arch ahead."

Ellen hardly cared what she saw anymore. The bus rolled on, jarring to a stop from time to time to disgorge and swallow more passengers. Marble Arch, like a mini Arc de Triomphe, stood in the middle of the intersection where they turned onto Oxford Street.

"Hyde Park." Hugh pointed right, evidently determined to be the perfect tour guide. "Speakers' Corner is over there." He pointed again. "Anyone with anything to say and a yen for an audience goes there on Sunday morning, complete with soapbox, and spouts."

"And people listen?"

"When they aren't shouting back."

Ellen laughed, unwinding slightly. "Sounds like fun."

Hugh shrugged. "If you like that kind of thing. I avoid confrontation. Peace at any price must have been designed as my motto."

How true, Ellen thought, not without rancor.

Great department stores lined Oxford Street, and when they made another right turn, Regent Street. Too soon, Hugh said, "Piccadilly Circus. Off we get."

On solid ground again, Ellen took in the scene. A vast Coca-Cola sign made of constantly flashing lights, more colored lights blinking everywhere, street vendors shouting, playbills flapping from the fronts of theater ticket offices. Bedlam. Why had she said she wanted to come here of all places?

"Right, here goes." Hugh gripped her elbow and steered her on an apparently suicidal path between snarled traffic.

Miraculously, they gained the other side of the street safely, but Hugh pressed on, moving quickly into a labyrinth of streets that all looked the same: narrow, dirty, tawdry. Women lounged in doorways, smiling, not at Ellen but at Hugh. Glancing up, she saw grim distaste in his face.

Up one street. Down another. Ellen noticed one street name, Wardour, but thought how all the others could have had the same name—just more pink lights, more women leaning on posts, in doorways, and proprietary men hovering nearby.

"Had enough?" Hugh said when Ellen had begun to feel anxious for escape but was unwilling to say so.

"I guess."

"Good. You aren't going to find her here, you know."

"What!" Ellen jerked her arm from his hand. "What do you mean by that?"

He shoved his hands into his pockets. "Isn't that what you're doing? Looking for Fiona?"

"N-no. I told you I hadn't been—"

"You haven't been here before. Yes, I know. And you intended to come down here and walk around this—" he spread his arms "—all on your own. Cecily told me she thought you went down by the river last night. Is that true?"

Ellen shifted her feet. "I don't want to stand here."

"Answer my question and we'll move on."

"Okay. Yes, I went down by the Thames last night. What's wrong with that? This is a new city for me and I want to see everything."

Hugh stuffed his hands in his pockets and started walking again. Ellen fell in beside him.

"Did you look along the shore by any chance? See if anything interesting had been washed up?"

Ellen recoiled. He knew her better than she knew herself. "I suppose I did. For a little way."

"So. Last night you went looking for Fiona dead. And tonight you decided you'd see if you could find her alive."

"I hadn't thought about it that way really. Most of all I didn't want to go home—and no one else seems to be doing anything."

"Didn't you tell me the police have finally taken notice?"

"Yes. But—"

"If they think it's appropriate, they'll drag the river."

"Don't!" Ellen choked on the word.

Hugh muttered under his breath and pulled her against him. He stroked her hair. "I shouldn't have said that, damn it. Forget I said that. I'm feeling helpless, too, but wandering the streets of a city like London isn't going to help find Fiona—and you could get hurt." He paused and tilted up her chin. Very gently he kissed her mouth. "I couldn't take it if something happened to you."

Ellen's heart was beating too fast and too hard. He was declaring how much he cared for her. Not how much he wanted her around because she was the closest he could get to Fiona while Fiona was gone, but that he cared for her, Ellen.

She stood on tiptoe and slid her hands behind his neck. "Thank you, Hugh. For worrying about me." She kissed him, a firmer, more insistent kiss than his, and the noise around them receded.

A hoot of laughter and a shouted obscenity broke into their private place, and Hugh rested his brow on hers a moment. "We'd better get out of here."

In a tiny Greek restaurant on Little Newport Street, Ellen picked at a too oily salad and watched Hugh do the same. He'd listened intently while she told him that the police had put out all-points bulletins for Fiona, that two officers had been assigned to investigate within the city and that she'd been told Fiona's disappearance was now considered a priority.

When she finished her story, Hugh was quiet for a long time before he put down his knife and fork and took a sip of strong espresso.

"They won't find her," he said at last.

Ellen swallowed too large a piece of spinach and coughed. "Hugh! Why would you say a thing like that? How could you?"

He stared somberly into his cup for a while, then hailed the waiter to ask for the bill.

"Hugh?"

"Take it from me," he said earnestly. "Fiona will show up when the time is right. Don't ask me how I know, or why it should be that way, because I can't tell you. I just know it here." He pressed a fist into his gut.

THE ACRID SMELL of the trains blasted up the escalator from deep tunnels. Hugh switched his briefcase from one hand to the other and moved to the left where he could hurry down past the line of people on the right.

He hated having to use the underground in the morning rush hour, but he had no real choice. At this time of day the streets were worse, and he had to be in Wimbledon by nine. The estate sale he'd been expecting had finally come up and he wanted to be among the first to preview the library offering.

Three days had passed since his difficult evening with Ellen. She had pressed him to explain why he was so sure Fiona was alive and well. He'd fenced, and cursed his loose tongue. How could he tell her he suspected her beloved sister of being an accomplice in murder?

Wimbledon was the last stop on the District Line. That meant he had to change from the Northern Line at the Embankment station. Hell, he detested this. The crush bore him along through yellow-tiled passages until he reached the right platform. He stood against the wall, watching destinations flash on a board hanging from the ceiling. The next train was no good, but the one after that would take him to Embankment.

Hugh edged forward, jostled on all sides. Guards stood by, ready to cram as many passengers as possible into each coach.

Grit swirled, stinging his eyes. The people around him kept one eye on their newspapers and one eye on the black hole from which the train would shoot. Hugh thought of Ellen. Without her to take over, and do it as efficiently as she did, he would have had to think twice about leaving the shop that morning.

The jostling crowd shoved him from behind and he shifted forward a step, gradually becoming jammed in on all sides. He couldn't ignore what he felt for Ellen. Every day increased his desire, both emotional and physical, for her. Love? He braced his feet wider apart. It could be that what he was feeling for Ellen was the start of love, something he realized now he'd never before felt for another woman.

A ripple of anticipation passed through the crowd. Hugh heard the surging roar of a train drawing closer.

Something solid and hard cracked into his spine between his shoulder blades. "Hey...!" He managed to twist partway around before a foot, thrust between his legs, smashed down on his instep. His knees buckled. Pain blurred his vision.

The foot came down again, a powerful blow in the middle of his back. He opened his mouth but no sound came. He dropped the briefcase and clutched ineffectually at sleeves and bodies around him, the same bodies whose crush stopped him from turning on his faceless attacker.

Again the mass pressed forward.

One more violent shove, and Hugh began to fall. The white line, a few inches from the edge of the platform, came up to meet him the instant before his cheek hit concrete and he looked down at the gleaming electric rails.

"Oh, my God! Get him! Get him!"

Hands grabbed. Clawed wildly at his hair. A moment later the silver flash of a train shot past and slowed.

Two men, their faces ashen, held him and he felt the quaking in their muscles. More people crowded closer, forgetting for an instant their previously urgent missions. A woman produced a handkerchief and pressed it to his face, wiping away blood.

"Makes you think," the woman said. "Dangerous down here, that's what it is, dangerous. Makes you think."

Hugh faced away from the tracks now, murmuring his thanks while he searched the shifting melee. One shape became a little clearer, standing motionless, removed from the concerned gathering around Hugh. Then it was gone, slipping aside to disappear into the cover of the crowd. A tall man, Hugh thought. The impression of blond hair was there, and dark clothes, but nothing distinct.

Carefully, murmuring thanks to his rescuers, Hugh disengaged himself, recovered his briefcase and made his way shakily toward the escalator and fresh air.

This morning was to have been the morning of his execution.

# Chapter Thirteen

He hadn't been wrong. He was marked to die.

Hugh sat at a window counter in a café where he could look down Flask Walk toward his place. When his nerves settled to something like an evenly spaced jumble, he'd go back. And when he did, in the first second he saw Ellen, he'd find out all he needed to know about her. When he'd said goodbye to her this morning, had she expected never to see him again? As they always did, her eyes would tell him everything.

If he had died on the electric rails beneath that train the verdict would have been accidental death. He warmed his cold hands around his coffee mug. Steam turned to watery rivulets as it touched the window, distorting the view outside. How many others had died from "accidents" hidden all too simply by inventive killers. His grandmother for one. Now more than ever he was positive her demise had been engineered.

The logical reaction to what happened this morning should have been an immediate report to the police. Even though he had no witnesses to call on or any definite evidence of a deliberate attempt on his life, they'd have had to listen to him and the complaint would have been logged, and referred to if... He swallowed. An overactive imagination was a curse.

For Ellen's sake, he had made the decision not to go to the police. If he did they would almost certainly want to talk to his staff, including her, and he wouldn't put her through that. Instead he would try the test on Ellen, watch for her reaction, though he expected nothing beyond shock at the battered condition of his face. And he already knew how he intended to explain the injury without telling the whole truth. She had enough pressure, enough potential trouble riding down the pike in her direction, without his adding the fear the facts about this morning would bring.

Fear? He was afraid, too, almost paralyzed by the certainty that this first attempt on his life wouldn't be the last, and that since Ellen might be perceived as a threat to someone's master plan, she, too, could be on a hit list.

Waiting another hour or so before returning to the shop, possibly even until the afternoon when he was expected, would be best. He'd be calmer and better able to minimize the impact of the way he looked. Also, Ellen would be less likely to suspect just how bad the incident had been if she thought he'd gone ahead to the sale preview.

Hugh paid for his coffee and left the café, heading away from the bookshop. He couldn't remember the last time he'd walked on the Hampstead Heath. Today it appealed. Maybe there, with the scrub grass rustling about him and no human intrusion, he could decide what to do next. Had Simon Macky, with Fiona's knowledge, paid an assassin to follow and wait for the perfect moment to make his move? Hugh didn't want to believe it, not of Fiona. Fiona was a woman he'd liked, a lot, and she was Ellen's sister.

Another thought came. Unwelcome because it set him further adrift. Fiona had definitely sought him out because of some connection with Millie Weston's estate, but could he be sure Simon and Fiona were responsible for trying to have him killed? Could he even be sure that Simon knew all the terms of the will? The answer, or likely answer, deeply disturbed him. No, he couldn't be sure. In fact, it was probable that Simon had yet to hear the details of his inheritance. At least from Lister. Hugh recalled that the solicitor, after he'd served tea to Hugh at the end of the interview, had said something about how slowly the wheels of the law turned and that the final accounting would take a long time.

The final accounting.

Hugh shuddered, leaning into the incline of the hill. Logically any effort to dispose of him should have been postponed until it was unlikely to be connected with his grandmother's death. Unless he was considered an immediate threat. As he would be if an interested party had discovered how much he knew. But who? And how? Was he completely missing the true danger lurking in the recesses of his world? Was there someone else, someone he didn't even know, who stood to benefit from his elimination, a person brighter and more subtle than Simon Macky?

As he walked Hugh found himself searching each face that passed, taking a long look at every man with light-colored hair.

Slowly, looking over his shoulder from time to time, Hugh climbed the hill. Who was the mysterious benefactor who had supplied his grandmother with such a generous allowance? Who had advised her on how to word her will to cover both the decent thing as far as he, Hugh, was concerned, while making sure Simon Macky would also benefit? And why Simon Macky? Where could he find these shadowy people? Later he'd take another crack at Lister.

At the corner he hailed the first cab he saw. "Bull and Bush," he told the driver. Being alone on the heath might not be such a good idea after all, but at least he could look at bits of it from the area's favorite old pub. And right now, the most appealing thing he could think of was a stiff Scotch drunk in the reassuring company of a few dozen nonthreatening and happy strangers.

"I'M GLAD YOU COULD COME."

Ellen looked sharply at Simon and sat in the chair he held for her. "You made it sound like a life-and-death command." Immediately, she regretted the comment.

"Maybe it is," he said intensely, taking his own seat again.

Refusing Simon's offer to pick her up for lunch, Ellen had made her own way to the Spaniards Inn by bus. Simon had called her at work, insisting they had to meet, and since Cecily said she was comfortable being in charge at Experienced Books, Ellen had agreed.

"I don't have a lot of time," Ellen commented, glancing at the pub's food menu. "Hugh's away for the day and I'm in charge."

"This is important."

"We already established that." She felt snippy, but his lack of decisiveness in pressure situations made her angry.

Simon took off his glasses and ground the heels of his hands into his eyes. "If I could just understand why Fiona didn't tell me all the things she must have been worried about."

Ellen sat back in her chair. A waiter came and she ordered coffee and poached eggs on toast. Simon's glass already looked well used, but he asked for a pint of bitter with a whisky chaser.

"Aren't you eating?" Ellen asked.

"Yes," he said, sitting straighter and signaling for the waiter to return. "I'll have the same as the lady."

He was already half-drunk, Ellen decided with a mixture of irritation and sympathy.

"Simon," she began as if speaking to a child. He was no help. She had to be the strength for both of them. "The good thing, what we have to hold on to, is that there's no reason to think anything awful has happened to Fiona. Also, we both know she can be flighty." She made herself laugh. "That's going to be your problem in future."

When he looked at her, his eyes were glazed. "What did she tell you?"

Ellen stared a moment. "Tell me? I'm sorry. I guess I don't understand. What did she tell me when?"

He bowed his head, flapping an ineffectual hand. "No, no. Didn't put that right. I mean, didn't she give you a hint that she was...that... Ellen, why did she go to work for Weston?"

The coffee was set before her and Ellen picked up the spoon from the saucer. "You really didn't know Fiona was working for Hugh?"

"Well..." Simon tore small pieces from a beer mat and mashed them into balls. "Of course, I knew she was doing some sort of little job, but not exactly what. But I assumed she probably told you all about it. After all, twins are close, aren't they? So, what did she tell you about it, the job I mean, and why she went there rather than somewhere else? She did tell you all about it, didn't she?"

A slow revolution left her heart hanging not quite in the right place. Simon was probing, looking for answers he either had and hoped she didn't, or answers he really didn't have at all.

"Ellen," he persisted, "why did Fiona choose Weston? If she needed money she could have come to me. Surely you can see that?" His beer and whisky arrived. He downed half the beer and tipped back the whisky.

She opened her mouth to speak, but her two anemic slices of toast, topped with two eggs, less well done than she would have preferred, arrived, and she waited until Simon's plate was also set down and they were alone again. "Look," she said, leaning forward, "Fiona told me nothing. I didn't even know you existed until she put on the pressure to get me over here. Even then she didn't tell me your name. I did know about Hugh because he was to be my sponsor for a work permit in England." Looking for respite from the tension, she took a mouthful of egg and toast. It was good, much better than she'd expected. A brainwave struck. "Maybe that's why she went after a job with him. My area of expertise is pretty specialized—narrow, in fact. I bet she looked for a job where she could find an outlet for me and he was the only possibility she found."

Simon looked skeptical, but her explanation gave Ellen some relief and she sank back in her chair, slightly relaxed for the first time in days. No final questions were answered, but any small insight helped.

At first she hardly heard Simon's next question. When she did register the words, she frowned and shot forward in her chair. "Don't," she implored. "Don't even suggest that."

Simon's glasses were still on the table. He picked up his napkin and held it over his eyes. "I mean it," he said. "Do you think she's all right, or do you think she's dead?"

His sobs were soft, inaudible to anyone but her. Ellen scooted her chair beside his and pulled his head on her shoulder. Simon Macky was falling apart, something his family would undoubtedly expect to happen under stress. Ellen wasn't ready to accept that the reaction was inevitable. She shook him. Tears welled in her own eyes, but she tipped up her head and blinked.

"Simon," she said very softly, "I refuse to think Fiona is dead. How can I? How can you? She's the most alive person I ever knew. But I do think something's happened, and she's going to need us more than she's ever needed anything or anybody before."

He sat up, his face bowed. "I want to be whatever she needs," he said.

"And you will be," Ellen responded without conviction. "We'll both be here for her. And who knows, maybe there's nothing to worry about."

"Right," Simon said. He sniffed, raised a hand to the waiter and ordered another drink.

IF HE COULD LOOK at her forever, forever would be too short. How had he ever thought her too thin, too tall? Ellen Shaw was the most gloriously feminine creature he'd ever encountered. He could close his eyes and see her naked body, feel it, her skin pressed to his, but just looking at her now was enough. She was a beautiful desirable woman.

Hugh leaned in the doorway between the wine bar and the bookshop, watching Ellen talk on the phone. There were no customers in sight, and Cecily Horton was perched on a ladder, her back to him, replacing books.

Ellen's voice was hushed. "We went over that already."

Her long slender fingers toyed with the cord. Hugh tilted his head. The lights in the shop were on and they turned the curves of her hair pale gold and white about her shoulders.

"No, Simon, I don't think so. Please be calm. For Fiona, as well as me—and you. Like I told you, the police are doing all they can and we have to trust them. We don't have the resources to do anything ourselves."

Hugh took the two steps down to the shop carefully, aware he was eavesdropping but not caring. These were exceptional times. Ellen reassuring Simon, or persuading him? It didn't matter which. So far the conversation underscored his decision that Ellen could have had no part in any plot already underway before her arrival in London.

"I'm glad Ross is still looking," Ellen said. "No, no, I'm not surprised he hasn't found her, either. That sister of mine is pretty inventive. You should have known her when she was a kid." For a while she was silent. "Please, don't cry, Simon. I do think, or at least I want to think she's all right.

Even as a little girl she could disappear when she felt like it and come back smiling like nothing had happened."

Hugh edged along the wall. Could it be that Fiona Shaw had simply pulled a stunt, that she had nothing to do with the vicious mesh closing on him?

"Yes," Ellen said. "I admit I feel helpless, too. But there's nothing either of us can do. Not now, anyway," she added.

Seconds later she hung up.

Hugh stood still, waiting. Ellen covered her face with her hands. Not going to her took superhuman effort.

He shoved his hands in his pockets and wished he could whistle, not one of his accomplishments. He took a few steps forward. "Hello, Ellen. How goes it?" This was the test, not that he believed it was necessary.

"Oh, fine." She lowered her hands and busied herself with a sheaf of invoices. "How was the sale?"

Obviously Ellen didn't know what had happened to him this morning. The rush of relief was ridiculous, but still it weakened his knees.

"Nothing interested me," he said, coming to her side. "All hype and no follow-through. You know how that goes sometimes?"

Ellen nodded.

"Did everything go all right here?" he asked.

"Yes." She glanced up at him and horror shot into her eyes. "Hugh! What happened to your face?"

He touched his cheek and at the same moment the phone rang.

"What have you done?" She came closer, peering at him.

The phone rang again. "It's nothing," he said. "One of us had better get that."

Ellen started and picked up the phone. "Experienced Books." She frowned. "Hello, Ross."

She covered the mouthpiece while she turned back to Hugh. "Were you in an accident?"

He shook his head. "It was ridiculous...embarrassing. I fell on my face on an underground platform."

Ellen raised her eyebrows, then lowered her head to resume her telephone conversation. "Violet? Why does she want to see me?" She tapped the counter and shifted her weight from foot to foot. "Today? This is the middle of a workweek for me. I have no easy means of getting to Stilton Hedges, and I'm needed here."

She listened to Ross's almost belligerent request, a relay of a message from Violet Macky suggesting that she, Ellen, come to Cadogan immediately, that they had important things to discuss that couldn't be postponed.

Ellen felt her hackles rise. She hadn't liked Ross the first time she'd seen him, and his arrogant manner now didn't help. "I don't think I can get away," she informed him. "Certainly not before the weekend."

"Violet's desperate." Ross's voice dropped dramatically. "The whole family's desperate. This was Violet's idea, but I would probably have suggested that you visit myself. You're needed, Ellen. I know you've seen Simon. What do you think?"

The sudden switch to a conspiratorial tone threw Ellen. "I...I'm worried about him." She might as well be honest.

"So am I. And he's very important to me." Ross waited a few seconds before he continued, "Simon means a great deal to his family, too. Fiona is—has been—exactly what he needs. The sooner we get all this straightened out, the better. I don't know what Violet wants to say, but I'm sure it's along the lines that we must face this problem head-on. Will you come?"

"Well..."

"I'll pick you up and drive you down tomorrow morning. You could probably be back at work by the afternoon if that's what you want."

She didn't know what to say. "Just a minute." Muzzling the phone against her neck, she turned to Hugh, "It's Simon Macky's assistant, Ross Ivers. He wants to take me to Cadogan—the Macky home—tomorrow."

"Go," Hugh said.

She loved his face, cared about nothing right now but looking after him. Deep scratches, grit and blood still embedded, covered his left cheekbone.

"I don't want to go," she murmured. "They scare the hell out of me." She wrinkled her nose and saw Hugh grin. One day, if fate also smiled, they would laugh a lot together. She banished the thought and asked impulsively, "Would you come with me?"

He frowned, chewing his lip, then nodded slowly. "Okay, love. If you like. Certainly, I'll come with you."

Ellen felt an overwhelming wave of gratitude. She said, "Fine, Ross. I'll be ready at nine," into the phone, listened to Ross's pleasant satisfied response and hung up.

When she turned to Hugh, reaching to touch the undamaged side of his face, he had to quell the urge to take her in his arms.

Whatever she intended to convey in her eyes, he knew what he read, knew what he felt. Love, and above all, trust.

## Chapter Fourteen

Ross Ivers was ever the gentleman. Although Ellen wondered how deep the act went, he insisted that she and Hugh sit together in the back seat of his pearl-gray Jaguar.

When Simon's assistant arrived at Fiona's flat, there had been no comment on Hugh's presence, and the conversation all the way from London had been relaxed: which horse each man favored in upcoming races, political issues, the Common Market.

From time to time Ross looked over his shoulder and Ellen saw no sign of a crack in his charming veneer. As soon as he met Hugh he had asked what happened to his face and offered a drawled "Rotten luck," before dismissing the subject.

The closer they drew to Cadogan, the more tense Ellen became. She ceased to hear what the two men were saying and jumped when Hugh covered her hand on the seat between them. Ross changed gears at a traffic light and Hugh leaned close, "Loosen up. Everything's going to be fine," he whispered. "I'll be there, okay?"

Ellen nodded at him, gratitude warming her slightly. At Cadogan, Ross parked, waited for Hugh and Ellen to join him on the steps and strode into the house without ringing the bell. The butler, untying a green apron as he hurried forward, was waved aside and Ellen felt sorry for the grizzled man. She smiled at him but pressure in the middle of her back, Ross's hand, urged her ahead and into the sitting room where she'd sat for her first talk with Violet.

"Make yourselves comfortable," Ross said. "I'll find Violet. Hello, Jo. Didn't see you there." And he was gone with the same sweeping air of authority he took everywhere he went.

"Hello, Ellen." Jo sat by the window. "Thank goodness you're here. Come and sit with me. I'm so worried about Fiona and Simon. Where can Fiona be? Simon's falling apart again, I know he is."

Ellen took a step toward her. "It's going to be okay," she said, wishing she believed her own words.

Jo fidgeted with the folds of her red tartan skirt. "I don't know, I just don't know. There are things going on here with them, Violet and Xavier, that is. I don't want to believe it of them, not after all they've done for us, but sometimes I wonder if they really care about Simon—other than worrying that he may muddy the family name. I want to talk to you about Violet before she gets here. She's really—" She stopped and cocked her head as if listening. "Who's with you?"

Ellen hurried forward, pulling Hugh. "Jo, Hugh Weston's with me. He's—" She snapped her mouth shut, darting a glance at Hugh. Not only had she failed to tell him all about Jo, or that Simon didn't want his family to know Fiona worked at the bar, but she herself had just been about to let out the whole truth about Fiona.

"How do you do, Jo?" Hugh said, shaking the hand the woman held out. He aimed a questioning look at Ellen.

She recovered enough to say, "I work for Hugh in his bookstore. And he knows Fiona," she added, narrowing her eyes significantly at Hugh and praying he'd pick up her message.

Jo continued to hold Hugh's hand, her face upturned, no trace of a smile on her lovely mouth. She took a deep breath, frowning, then withdrew her fingers quickly with a slight shake of her head. "It's nice to meet you, Mr. Weston."

The formality, so unlike Jo, startled Ellen.

"Hugh, please," Hugh said, apparently unconcerned. "You aren't a bit like your brother." He laughed self-consciously, giving Ellen a helpless shrug.

Now Jo did smile. "Okay, Hugh. I like that name. And don't be embarrassed about my appearance and comments about seeing. They always happen and I'm immune, I assure you." She patted the window seat on each side of her now and Hugh and Ellen both sat down. "Why do you say Simon and I aren't alike?" Jo turned to Hugh.

He studied her and Ellen felt his sadness. "I was thinking more of personality than looks. He's not as outgoing as you. Not that he isn't likable," he amended quickly. "But, on the looks side, God certainly gave the beautiful hair and mouth to a member of the right sex. Not that—"

"Not that Simon isn't nice looking?" Jo broke in, chuckling. "Thank you for the compliments. You're a very diplomatic man, Hugh." An almost imperceptible hesitation followed. "You've got a nice voice, a nice way of saying things. And Ellen likes you. That's nice, too."

Ellen and Hugh looked wordlessly at each other. Between them sat living proof that the loss of one faculty could sharpen others.

Hugh, a wide grin deepening the lines on his face, inclined his head toward Ellen. "She does, does she? Did she tell you that?"

"She didn't have to," Jo said.

"Well, however you know, thanks. I like her, too."

Ellen was relieved. In the first moments after their meeting she might have sworn Jo instinctively disliked Hugh, and for some reason Ellen wanted Jo to approve of him. That Simon mistrusted him was understandable and acceptable, even though it was a potential nuisance if they were all to work together in getting Fiona back and helping her through whatever had driven her away.

"About Violet," Jo began, then rested a hand on Ellen's, listening. "Later," she said urgently and went back to toying with her skirt.

"There you are. Oh, thank God you came." Violet, resplendent in an amethyst-colored satin peignoir that hugged a still spectacular figure and swirled around matching high-heeled slippers, tottered into the room. She held a handkerchief to her nose and looked around as if she didn't recognize her surroundings.

"Oh, Violet," Jo murmured in a voice only Ellen and Hugh could have heard. There was no sympathy in that voice.

"Hi," Ellen said, getting up. Hugh rose also, but made no attempt to approach the woman.

"It's all too much," Violet wailed. "You have to help us, Ellen. You simply have to or I don't know what will happen to our boy."

Bewildered, Ellen looked from Jo to Hugh and back to Violet.

Violet took a deep shuddering breath and fixed Ellen with a baleful stare. "We need to talk alone, Ellen." She cast a significant glance in the general area of Hugh. They had yet to be introduced.

"Violet," Ellen said, attempting an even tone, "this is my friend, Hugh Weston. He's also my—"

"Call Cummings," Violet cut in, waving her lace-trimmed handkerchief toward the door. "He's out there somewhere, has been since Xavier's father's time." The information was imparted as if Ellen ought to know these details. It was also given as an order for her to act.

"Why do you want Cummings?" Jo intervened calmly. "I hardly think a butler is what we need right now. Ellen was introducing Hugh."

"Oh, Jo." Violet sobbed with renewed vigor. "How can I meet new people at a time like this? I need to talk to Ellen and I want Cummings to take this, this..." She flapped the perfectly manicured fingers of one hand toward Hugh without once looking at him directly.

"This what?" Ellen said through gritted teeth. Who the hell did these people think they were?

Violet subsided in a graceful heap on a tufted velvet chair. "I'm not myself," she murmured. "Please excuse me." And she did glance quickly at Hugh before returning her attention to Ellen. "Ask Cummings to show your friend around the house, or get him a drink or something."

"I'd prefer not to do that," Ellen said. "Hugh is here because *I* need some support and because he's my friend. Whatever you can say in front of me you can say in front of him."

Violet played with a lapel on her robe. "Oh, well," she said faintly, "if you insist. I'm not important anyway. It's Simon we must think about."

From the corner of her eye, Ellen saw Hugh shift from foot to foot. He didn't want to be here. He wanted to be with her, of that she was fairly certain, but not here.

She turned to him, and at the same moment Jo got up. With the unconscious gesture she must have used so often since she was twelve, she found Hugh's hand. "This is a lovely house," she told him. "Perhaps you would like to see it?"

Hugh met Ellen's eyes and she nodded.

"Thank you," Hugh told Jo. "I would like that. Will you be okay?" He spoke to Ellen as if Violet weren't there.

"I'll be fine," Ellen assured him, not at all sure how fine she'd be but unwilling to subject him to any more of the scene Violet seemed determined to create.

Jo led Hugh from the room and Ellen retreated to the window seat, her favorite spot in this not-at-all favorite house. "Okay, Violet, we're alone. I want to get back to London by early afternoon at the latest, so if we could make this—"

"You have to help us." Violet's nose was now convincingly red. "Xavier and I are at our wits' end. We don't know what to do next."

"Why don't you explain exactly what you mean?" Ellen suggested, feeling like an uninvolved observer, wishing that she was.

"Mean?" Violet's already nasal voice rose to a piercing squeak. "You know what I mean."

Ellen took several calming breaths. "I take it we're talking about my sister's apparent disappearance. And I can assure you I'm doing everything I can about that."

"You really don't know, do you?" Great violet eyes, surprisingly clear, bored into Ellen. "Simon didn't have an easy childhood. He lost his parents when he was two. They were burned to death in this very house. That's how Jo was blinded."

"I know," Ellen said quietly. "Jo told me and I'm very sorry. It must have affected you all terribly."

"Jo told you?" Violet's beautiful eyes took on an almost wounded look as if only she had the right to discuss her family's problems. "I didn't realize she'd done that."

"She thought I ought to know," Ellen said, conciliatory, "because I'm probably going to become related to the family."

Violet released a fresh gust of sobs into the snowy handkerchief. "Simon's falling apart. Falling apart, I tell you.

And it's because of Fiona. If you have an ounce of compassion, you'll do what I ask."

Ellen crossed her arms tightly. She had begun to tremble. "You couldn't be more worried than I am. And I'm doing everything I can to find Fiona. Don't you think I'm out of my mind over this? The police are looking for her. Simon will have to hold himself together until she shows up, just like the rest of us must."

With a loud sniff, Violet clasped her hands in her lap and fixed her stare on her precious wallpaper. "All right," she said tightly. "I must appeal to you in simple terms and hope you'll see things the way they must be seen. For everyone's sake."

Ellen waited with an uncanny sense that she was witnessing an incredibly good dramatic performance. That, or this woman was in more emotional danger than her nephew.

"Simon," Violet said at last, and brokenly, "is probably having a nervous breakdown. It won't be the first."

"I'm sorry," Ellen said. Why couldn't she at least think of a different platitude?

"Ellen, I think you and I both know what's really happened here and what should be done."

The window creaked, momentarily distracting Ellen. Rain had started to fall and splattered on the panes.

"You do know what I'm suggesting?" Violet persisted.

"No," Ellen said hurriedly, "no, I'm afraid I don't."

Violet smiled as she might at someone of limited intelligence. "Come, come, Ellen. Of course you do. Fiona realized she didn't fit in here." She lowered her lashes. "I don't mean that to sound the way it does."

*Oh, but you do.* A piece of lint on the cushion caught Ellen's attention and she plucked at it venomously.

"In addition to that," Violet continued with cloying softness, "your sister is a very, shall we say, venturesome young woman. Simon's sweet but not as outgoing. She would have had a quiet life with him and I truly believe that although she thought at first that the, er, rewards would be worth the sacrifice, later she decided—sensibly—that she couldn't cope with what marriage to a Macky would mean."

Something close to hate entered Ellen's heart. "Go on," she said without inflection.

"I will. I think Fiona went away to let the relationship cool. She will return, and when she does, Simon will want her as badly as ever. That much is clear. And that's where you come in."

"Really?" Yes, hate was what she felt.

"In time, if he's left alone and taken care of by his family, Simon will get over Fiona and marry a nice girl who will be exactly what he needs. Someone secure and solid."

*And with the right connections and lots of money,* Ellen wanted to add. "Exactly what are you asking of me?" she said.

"Simply this. I can tell you're a sensible woman. You wouldn't want to be party to ruining a man's life. If Simon is to heal, Fiona must leave him alone. That's what I'm asking of you. When Fiona comes back, for me, but most of all for Simon, make sure he never sees her again or even knows she has returned."

HUGH LIKED JO MACKY, liked her very much, but he didn't like this house. He trailed along behind Jo, marvelling at the ease with which she found her way from room to room, up one staircase, down another.

"Out there," she was saying, and he went to stand beside her at a window, "that's where Simon and I . . . and our sister used to play when we were children."

An ornamental pool surrounded by topiary dominated the scene beyond the window. In the distance he could see great double gates. "It's beautiful." He glanced down at her slightly upturned face and frowned. What was it about her that struck a chord? The sympathy he was bound to feel because of her handicap? A feeling that she was like Simon? No, she wasn't at all like Simon, not in any way.

"What color were your eyes?" He instantly closed his own eyes, grimacing. What a damn fool thing to ask.

"Brown," Jo said lightly. "No one ever asked me that before. You're an unusual man."

He took a deep breath. "I'm a clumsy man. Speak first, think later."

"Nonsense. It's good for me to think of such things. In my mind, you see, I can only remember the way I looked before I was burned. And that's good, isn't it? I don't pretend I'm not ugly now, but there's no reason not to accept that and still remember that I was a pretty little girl with golden brown eyes. Ellen did explain about the fire, didn't she? How my parents were killed here in a fire and that's how I became blind?"

Hugh couldn't speak. The desire to cry clogged his throat.

"No," Jo continued serenely, "I can tell she didn't. Our sister died. Jenny. She was pretty, too."

"You're not ugly," Hugh said when his voice came back, and he meant it. "But we shouldn't be talking about this."

"I told Ellen all about it," she said. "She's special. I can feel that, just the way I can about Fiona. Simon needs Fiona, Hugh. I don't know what Violet's trying on with Ellen, but if it's what I think, please don't let Ellen do it."

"What...?"

"Ellen will tell you. I shouldn't say any more. My hearing's pretty exceptional, but even I can be crept up on sometimes." She laughed, paused and tapped his chest. "I know what I should show you—the portrait gallery. There are paintings of all the family there. My mother and father, Jenny and Simon and me when we were little. Then you can see just what a knockout I was." Her attempt at humor twisted his heart, but he didn't protest the idea.

Dead, he thought, trudging along endless gloomy passages past equally gloomy, slightly dusty-smelling rooms. The house felt dead. Even where light filtered through narrow windows it failed to dispel the suffocating shadows.

"In an older house, as in quite a few centuries older, we'd have had a wonderful long room—they were called long rooms because they were long. But you know that." Jo laughed in that marvelous free way that demanded an answering laugh. Hugh obliged.

"I think I've heard of them," he said. "What did they do with a long room?"

"That's where the portraits were hung and also where people took exercise in winter. They didn't have good clothing for cold weather so they built these enormously long rooms where they could march up and down, looking at paintings or playing games, and from what I've read, probably gossiping."

She was bright and interesting and fun to be with. And she enjoyed having someone to talk to. No wonder Ellen liked her.

"Here we are." Jo reached the top of a small flight of stairs opening into a square room lined with paintings. "We don't go back very far, so I've always thought a lot of these old fogies are probably borrowed relatives."

He couldn't help smiling. "Hmm. Well, how shall we do this?"

She put a hand through his arm. "You call out the inscription under a painting and I'll tell you the story, if I know it. Between you and me, from what Ned—our bailiff—tells me, there were a few additions made after Violet changed positions in the household. Portraits of a personage or two who were suddenly discovered to be long-lost relatives of the Mackys. Every family needs a duke and at least a marquis or two. To add to the effect, of course. Perfectly understandable.'' The corners of her mouth turned down in derisive contradiction to the words.

Hugh started down one side of the room, then stopped. "This one doesn't have an inscription."

"What does it look like?"

"A sickly skinny boy wearing a big hat with feathers, too many clothes and a lot of jewels. I don't know how a kid could move in that lot."

"Ah." Ellen nodded. "One of Violet's attic finds, I think. She did tell me who he was, and the connection with the Mackys. Prince something or other who died around 1800. I seem to have forgotten his name."

"Mmm." Hugh had already decided Violet Macky wasn't his kind of woman. That Jo couldn't stand her aunt didn't need to be said outright. "What position did Violet hold around here before she became lady of the manor?"

"Nursemaid," Jo said, no longer smiling. "Violet was Simon's nursemaid at the time of the fire. She was very good to all of us afterward, or so I'm told. According to Ned she cared for us exclusively until she was sure we were over the shock—if one is ever over that kind of shock. I don't remember too much about some of it. Most of all, she was good to Xavier."

Hugh didn't miss the bitter note. "She certainly seems to have adjusted well to her role."

"Doesn't she, though. But being left with two of his brother's children to bring up can't have been a picnic for Xavier. He's never been particularly good with children. He needed someone and Violet was there for him."

"Was she actually here at the time of the fire? Oh, it is all right to..."

"It's all right to talk about it. And yes, she was here. In fact, she's the one who saved Simon. For that I'll always be grateful. I just wish she wasn't such a bitch."

Hugh looked at her, taken aback. There was no sign of remorse in Jo for her blunt comment.

"Go to the end," Jo said abruptly, like a woman awaking from a dream. "To the right of the right window is the family picture of my parents and us."

He went, taking her with him and stood before a large piece showing a family ranged beneath the spreading branches of a vast oak. "I like it. It feels good," he said honestly.

"I never saw it," Jo said, "but Simon's described it to me hundreds of times. My parents were handsome, weren't they?"

Hugh leaned close. "Yes, very. Your mother had the same hair as you. Longer, but very dark and curly like yours. Your father had lighter hair, but you got his mouth, I think." The melancholy he felt took him by surprise. He wanted to walk away.

"And Jenny and Simon and me? We look pretty good, don't we? Simon always says so, but perhaps that's what he wants me to think."

"No, he's telling the truth. Jenny's hair was almost red, wasn't it? And she had blue eyes?"

"Yes. Like my mother. My eyes were the same light brown as my father's."

An insidious heaviness overtook Hugh, a weakness. He couldn't leave Jo here alone, but he didn't want to go on with this.

"How about Simon? He says he's become better looking with age."

"Hmm." Hugh edged away from the painting. "He's lost his curls if that's what he means."

For once, just as she'd predicted, Jo's acute hearing failed her. A man's voice, immediately behind them, came without warning. "Showing off the skeletons, Jo?"

Hugh felt her stiffen. "Xavier." By the time she turned around she was smiling. "Violet's in the drawing room with Ellen. This is Hugh Weston, Ellen's friend. I'm saving him from boredom, or I hope I am. I think Violet had some family things to discuss."

"Quite." The man looked not at Jo but at Hugh.

"How do you do, sir," Hugh said, extending a hand.

Xavier Macky looked him steadily in the face, a muscle moving rhythmically in one cheek. Several seconds passed before he noticed Hugh's hand and grasped it. "Have you met Simon?" he asked, ignoring pleasantries and maintaining his hold on Hugh's hand.

"Yes, sir."

"What do you think of him?" His appraisal didn't waver.

The question left Hugh nonplussed. He wished there were a graceful way to withdraw his hand from the other's tight grip.

"Like him, do you?" Xavier continued. "The boy needs all the liking he can get."

"He seems...likable." This was hardly the moment to inform Simon's preoccupied uncle that his nephew had appeared to despise Hugh on sight.

"Hmm. Good. And I suppose you met Violet?"

"We met when Ellen and I arrived." He looked at Jo. The fingers of one hand were splayed over her tight-lipped mouth.

"Well. That's good then."

One more long narrow-eyed stare, and Xavier dropped Hugh's hand. He walked quickly away, his footfalls soft on beautiful worn carpets.

"What was that all about?" Hugh asked.

He might as well have saved his breath. Jo wasn't listening. "We'd better get back," she stated, walking in Xavier's path.

Hugh followed slowly. What was going on here? He felt . . . threatened.

"Slow down, Jo," he called, jogging to catch up. "A man could get lost around here."

The sooner he and Ellen left, the better. The place was really getting to him.

# Chapter Fifteen

"I'm glad we understand each other."

Violet leaned back in her chair, the handkerchief pressed delicately to her lips. Ellen couldn't quite keep still. For more than an hour this woman had put forth her case, pressed her demands, and Ellen had agreed to nothing, stressing only her concern for Fiona, as well as Simon. Yet Violet chose to interpret what had passed between them as an acceptance of her wishes: Fiona was never to darken the Mackys's doors, or their darling nephew's life, again.

Already knowing the effort was useless, Ellen tried again. "I don't think you—"

"Hello, you two." Jo pushed open the door and preceded Hugh into the room. "Hugh's had the grand tour and is probably dying for some tea. I'll call."

"No." Ellen jumped up and reached for her purse. She cast Hugh a beseeching look. "Thank you anyway, Jo. We'd love to stay longer but we do have to get back to London."

"Right, we do." Hugh, frowning, had received her unspoken message. She was desperate to leave. So, in fact, was he.

"Are you sure?" Jo's disappointment was plain.

Impulsively Ellen hugged her. "We'll get together again, Jo. I promise. But I . . . we do need to go."

Jo returned the hug and Ellen felt as if the woman wanted to keep holding on. How awful, living in this house, dependent upon people like Xavier and Violet Macky. Ellen shot another pleading glance at Hugh, who nodded faintly.

Ignoring Violet, he went to Jo and put an arm around her shoulders. "Thanks for showing me the house. It's... impressive. I hope you and I meet again."

Jo stood still an instant, then quickly kissed Hugh's cheek. "I hope so, too." She moved away, smiling, and Ellen wished she could take her back to London with them.

"Get Cummings, would you, Jo?" Violet's plaintive voice was an unwelcome reminder of her presence.

Seconds later, the butler noiselessly entered the room and received instructions to find Mr. Ivers and Mr. Macky. The "guests" were leaving.

Ellen looked at Hugh in time to see him pulling his face into a parody of Violet's long-suffering expression. She caught his eye and swallowed a laugh.

By the time they were finally in the foyer, Ross Ivers in the lead, Violet and Xavier bringing up the rear with Jo, Ellen felt almost euphoric at the prospect of escape.

"Don't stay away long," Jo said while they put on their coats.

"We—" Ellen began.

"Call me from the office, Ross," Xavier cut in. "I need those figures this afternoon."

No mention of Simon. No "Have Simon call me." Ross Ivers definitely seemed far more the boss than the assistant at the Mackys's London operation.

"Shall we go?" Ross smiled benignly.

Cummings opened the great front door with a flourish and stood back—just in time to avoid being flattened by Ned Loder's solid body.

Ned stormed, puffing audibly, into the foyer. He brushed past everyone until he stood before Violet. "I've had it!" he yelled. "You can't expect me to go on with this."

Like Ellen, the other onlookers in the hall had become listening statues.

"Now, Ned—" Violet patted his chest and Ellen thought of an owner placating a faithful dog "—you're fine. Everything will be taken care of."

"Fine?" he roared. "She's driving me mad. Constant questions. Constant nagging. Where's this one? Where's that one? You've got to help me with that woman, Violet."

Ross was the first to move. He cleared his throat, gave a little laugh. "Well, folks. If all the goodbyes are said..." He let the sentence trail away.

"Yes, yes," Xavier said. "Have a nice journey."

As if they were going to the moon, Ellen thought, or at least to the other side of the world. "Thank you."

Ned turned. He looked at the others in the entrance as if seeing them for the first time, pulled off his hat, put it back on and walked out muttering to himself.

"Poor Ned," Violet said, not quite meeting Ellen's eyes. "He lost his wife when he was young. Now he's got her mother living with him because there's no one else left to have her. He's a good man, but a bit out of his depth with a female around."

"Ned never—"

"I know he didn't, Jo," Violet interrupted. "He never told you about it because he seems to feel helping look after you is his main mission in life. You know how protective he is."

Jo didn't respond.

The Mackys, their oppressive house and the petty intricacies of their day-to-day life held little interest for Ellen. Not saying as much was becoming a feat.

Several empty pleasantries later, she and Hugh made it to Ross's car. Safely inside, with Ross at the wheel, they held hands tightly. They were still holding hands when Ross dropped them off at the shop.

The door had barely closed behind them when Ed Butters poked his head in from the bar, his eyebrows raised, and beckoned with a jerk of his head.

Ellen frowned at Hugh, who shrugged and waved her into the bar. "What's up, Ed? You're in early aren't you?"

Ed scratched his stubbly chin. "I didn't want to give the message to Mrs. H. She gets upset and we don't need any more of that."

Tightness built around the inside of Ellen's head. The strong smell of beer and wine turned her stomach. She plopped down on the nearest chair. "It's Fiona, isn't it?" Pounding filled her chest.

Hugh dropped to one knee and grabbed her hands.

"No, no, no." Ed smacked a fist into the other palm. "What a fool I am. It's about Fiona, but not bad news—not that kind of bad news."

"Spit it out," Hugh snapped, and Ed's already ruddy complexion darkened. "I'm sorry," Hugh immediately added, "we're all on edge."

"It was the people from immigration," Ed said. "I got the call at home this morning and I tried to call Ellen but there was no reply. Then I came in here hoping I could soften it a bit by telling her in person."

"We were visiting Fiona's fiancé's family."

Ed looked surprised. "Fiancé?"

"Forget it for now." Hugh made a dismissive gesture. "Why did the immigration people call you? And what did they say, for God's sake?"

"Right, right." With a grunt, Ed hefted himself onto a stool. "When Fiona first came to work here, she asked if she could use the wife and me as references because she was applying to stay on in the country."

"I thought that was already settled by that time," Hugh said slowly.

"It was, just about, but immigration wanted proof that she had enough means of support, and the theater is a bit dodgy so she wanted another, er, good word, I suppose you'd call it. Anyway, she gave my address and phone number and they called me."

Hugh eased himself to sit on the floor and clasped his knees. "Why didn't she ask me?"

Ed looked awkward. "She said you'd already done so much for her and she didn't want to bother you anymore. And maybe since the two of you . . . well . . . maybe she just didn't want to put too much on your friendship."

Ellen stirred. Her skin hurt. Everything hurt. "What did immigration want?"

"Well, um." Discomfort showed in the hunching of Ed's shoulders. "Fiona is supposed to check in, er, sign a form or something from time to time and she should have done that a couple of weeks ago."

"But she didn't," Hugh stated flatly. "Not such a surprise really, if she's ducked out for a while."

Ed spread his hands on beefy thighs and rocked forward. "But it is a big deal. They said she's in a lot of trouble. When she does show she'll have to do some fast talking even to stay in the country."

"Are they looking for her?" Ellen grew warmer. The idea brought fresh hope. "Are they going to send out people to help track her down? I still don't think the police take the whole thing seriously enough. This could help."

"They didn't say anything about actively searching for her. They only said that anyone seeing her has a responsibility to inform them. And she could be imprisoned, then deported."

Hugh held up a hand. "Let's not worry about that now. We'll straighten things out on that front."

"There's something else." Ed looked miserably at Ellen. "The theater group has filled Fiona's place in the play cast permanently. Immigration told me that the director wouldn't vouch for her anymore and said she was as good as finished in London theater."

A cold hollow formed in Ellen's stomach. Steadily, definitely, Fiona was being closed out, erased. How long would it be before most people forgot her completely?

"I'd like to go back to the flat," she said abruptly to Hugh and stood up.

"I'll come with you. Ed, I'm sorry to put all this on you, but keep things together around here, will you?"

Ellen heard Ed agree and felt Hugh behind her as she walked through the shop. Cecily came forward, caught her eye, then retreated, a worried pucker between her brows.

Hugh walked silently beside Ellen up Flask Walk and hailed the first available taxi. "Come on." He urged Ellen gently inside and joined her.

"Don't worry about the immigration thing," he said. Her pale face showed no sign of emotion now. "As soon as possible I'll talk to them and let them know I'll vouch for her."

"Why should you?"

She sounded so lifeless she frightened him. "Because I care about . . . you."

"Everyone's forgetting Fiona." Her voice broke and he saw her chest expand. "The Mackys only want to get rid of her, pretend they never knew her. Violet Macky said that, you know." Ellen's lovely eyes held no light. "Whatever Ross Ivers suggested beforehand, the reason that woman wanted me down there was to ask me to make sure her beloved nephew wasn't endangered by my sister anymore."

"Forget them. Violet and Xavier, anyway. Jo's nice, but unfortunately she's part of their package. Concentrate on Fiona and think positively."

He looked through the window, organizing, or trying to organize his thoughts. More and more, his primary interest was in Simon Macky. The family seemed to be covering for him, insulating him. Why? Simon and Fiona were already involved with each other when Fiona came to Hugh for a job. Macky was the one who would soon be benefiting from Millie Weston's estate—although not as much as he might like, Hugh thought. He sank lower in the seat and settled his chin on his chest. Only the tip of a very explosive iceberg had been presented to him so far, and he hoped he could expose the rest without ending up in little pieces.

"This is it, sir."

The taxi driver pulled to a stop outside Fiona's flat, and Ellen got out while Hugh paid the fare.

On the sidewalk, they stood side by side watching the cab drive away.

"Rain's stopped," Hugh remarked. Tension stood between them, a solid barrier built of the intimacy they'd already shared and the knowledge that they were about to be alone together again.

Ellen turned up her collar. "It's still cold. We'd better go in."

"Yes. Lead the way." He glanced at her. He and she were different, but the differences intrigued him. Ellen didn't hide her feelings, or dodge touchy situations. He wished he could be more like her, but the best he could hope for at this stage of his life was to keep on enjoying her impetuousness.

She stopped halfway down the steps to the courtyard. "I wonder. I just wonder." When she faced him, color had returned to her cheeks. "Not doing anything is driving me nuts, Hugh. Why don't we at least see if we can find out something?"

He held the railings on each side of the steps, his elbows locked. "What did you have in mind?"

"Our charming landlady." She wrinkled her nose. "The solid gold witch with the heavy broom. I never have really pushed her for information. Will you come with me?"

Confronting anybody was low on his list of desirable activities right now. "Maybe. Why don't we make some tea first?"

"Oh, save me from you British." With an upward cast of her eyes, she clamped a hand over her heart. "What, Charles? You just found out you only have three days to live? Never mind. Why don't we make some tea?" Her phony English accent came pretty close.

His attempt at a scowl failed and he chuckled. "Low blow, Ellen. We've won wars on tea. It's the stuff a strong nation's made of."

"Aw, come on, Hugh. Let's live dangerously and try to win this battle without tea."

"You want to go and see the landlady right now?"

"Yup. You're quick."

"Don't be flip, old girl. Wait till I find your Achilles' heel."

"Less of the 'old' if you don't mind. I don't have an Achilles' heel. If I do it's something a bit more dramatic than needing tea every time the wind changes. Lead on."

He opened his mouth to protest, but she waved him on his way. Resigned, he returned to the sidewalk, looked up briefly at the peeling yellow paint on the front door of the house and climbed slowly to ring the bell.

Ellen came to stand beside him. "Ring again," she said impatiently.

"Maybe she's out," he responded hopefully. Luck hadn't been piling up on his rug lately, but there was a starting place for everything.

"Oh, I'll do it." Ellen leaned around him and punched the bell.

A scuffling sound preceded the loud crack of a bolt being drawn aside.

"I don't feel good about this," Hugh whispered.

Ellen ignored him. Her smile was firmly in place when the door opened.

"Yes?" They were confronted by a rangy woman as tall as Hugh, if not taller, and wearing a tasteful gray dress. Her pale hair was too short, too tightly curled, her lipstick too vivid, but she didn't fit Hugh's picture of the slovenly truculent landlady and he gained a little confidence.

"Good afternoon, Mrs. Thomas," Ellen said pleasantly. The narrowed-eyed glare she aimed in Hugh's direction clearly said, *chicken*. "Could you spare us a few minutes?"

"Why?"

Whether he liked conflict or not, it was time to take charge. "Because we'd like to talk to you, ma'am. You've already met Ellen. I'm Hugh Weston. Fiona Shaw works for me and so does Ellen. We're friends," he added hastily and felt unaccustomed heat in his cheeks.

"What do you want to talk about?"

Hugh took a deep breath.

Ellen stepped in front of him. "Fiona—"

"No, Ellen." He stopped her. "I'll handle this, please. Mrs. Thomas, you know that Ellen has been living in Fiona's flat for several weeks—and paying the rent. You also know Fiona hasn't been here since before Ellen arrived. We're worried about her. Could we ask you a few questions, just in case there's something you remember that might help?"

"No point in that."

Without looking, Ellen found his arm as if she'd felt the anger that had begun its slow rise.

"Mrs. Thomas," he said brusquely, "could we come in for a moment? I hardly think this is the place for a discussion."

A spark of defiance sharpened the woman's features, but her pale eyes slid quickly away and she made room for them to pass. The hall was as far as they got. Mrs. Thomas closed the door and crossed her arms. "The police have already been here," she stated, disapproval and annoyance at that event coloring each word. "I can't tell you anything I didn't tell them." She glanced at the circle of glass in the front door. "Nice thing, I must say, all the neighbors seeing the police coming."

Hugh didn't trust himself to speak at once. The Mrs. Thomases of this world epitomized the small-mindedness he abhorred.

"Not nice, not nice at all," Ellen almost crooned. When Hugh stared at her, startled, she kept her attention firmly and sympathetically trained on Mrs. Thomas. "You shouldn't have to put up with that kind of thing. And the sooner we can get these problems ironed out, the sooner you won't have to."

He leaned on the wall, a fist pressed against his mouth to hide a smile. So, Ellen could be devious after all. He was almost relieved to see another, mischievous side of her.

"Hrmph." The landlady smoothed her skirt and seemed to grow even taller. "That's what I say."

Ellen rocked onto her heels. "So why don't you tell us what you told the police? You know how they are—so much to do they never get to everything. Maybe we can clear all this up a bit faster."

"Nothing to tell." Mrs. Thomas gave an eloquent shrug. "Like I said to the officers. Fiona was quiet. No trouble. Always paid her rent on time." The testimonial was unctuously delivered and Hugh puffed out his cheeks. This was getting them nowhere.

"Thank you," Ellen said quietly. She was tenacious. So was he, but he didn't have her gift for diplomacy. "But what about anything different, Mrs. Thomas?"

"Different? I don't know what you mean."

"In the last few weeks. Did you notice anything unusual about Fiona, or any visitors you hadn't seen before? Did you hear anything?"

The woman shook her head slowly. "Like I told the police, Fiona had more than one visitor—only men, I think— but I don't have time to take a lot of notice of who comes and goes from my tenants' flats." She sniffed. "It's not my business."

"No," Ellen said blandly. "Let me ask you something else. Do you remember seeing Fiona with a blue suitcase at any time? About a week before I arrived, it would have been."

Mrs. Thomas frowned, pinching her bottom lip between finger and thumb. "Uh-uh, no. Nothing like that."

"She never suggested she might be going away for a while?"

"No."

"Not even a hint—"

"The lady doesn't know anything," Hugh broke in, exasperated. *And she probably wouldn't tell you if she did,* he felt like adding. "I suggest we don't take up any more of her valuable time."

"But—"

"Good afternoon, Mrs. Thomas," he said firmly, taking Ellen's arm. "Thank you for your help." Without waiting for a response, he opened the door, bracing himself against a blast from Ellen.

"Just a minute!"

He and Ellen were on the top step when Mrs. Thomas called out.

"I do remember a blue suitcase. Light blue, was it?"

"Yes," Ellen said eagerly, "sort of sky-blue."

"I remember." Mrs. Thomas smiled triumphantly. "It was that day."

Hugh let out a measured breath. "What day would that have been, Mrs. Thomas?"

"The first day Fiona didn't bring up my paper. She used to always bring up the paper when she got home from work in the afternoon, or she did until that day. She'd hand me my paper and take her mail. So thoughtful."

*Patience,* Hugh warned himself, *don't lose your temper now.* Ellen's voice appeared to have failed her.

"That sounds like Fiona," he said evenly, together with what he hoped was an approving smile. "Fiona is always thoughtful. But what's the connection with the suitcase? Did you see her with it?"

"I told you I didn't. But I did see a man coming up from her flat that night after I'd given up on her bringing the paper."

"A man you'd seen before?" Ellen put in breathlessly.

Mrs. Thomas appeared to consider. "Hmm, no, no, I don't think so. But he was wearing a hat, and one of those dark coats so many men wear and it was getting dark. I couldn't see him properly. Not that I was trying—"

"Not that you were trying to see him." The smile Hugh kept on his face made his jaws ache. "Of course you weren't. But never mind him. What about Fiona and the case?"

She flapped her hands impatiently. "Not Fiona. She wasn't there. I'm trying to tell you. It was the man who was carrying a blue suitcase."

# Chapter Sixteen

Any minute now he'd suggest they make more tea. Ellen studied Hugh's preoccupied expression and closed her eyes. She should be appreciating him instead of resenting his quirks. If it came to that, she kind of liked his quirks. She looked at him again and sighed. Being with him, even when her life seemed determined to fall apart, felt so right. Exciting but right.

"It's midnight," he said, shoving out his chin. "Something tells me we can forget reaching Simon tonight."

They'd tried unsuccessfully to phone Simon at his Mayfair rooms every half hour since leaving Mrs. Thomas and coming down to Fiona's flat.

"Where would he be?"

Hugh didn't answer, only slid farther down in his chair the way she'd seen him do so often when he had a lot on his mind.

"Probably out getting drunk, huh? Is that what you think?" she said.

"I don't know what I think."

"Yes, you do. The police said he was known for getting into trouble because of drinking. And I've seen him drunk a couple of times myself."

"You just answered your own question."

Ellen jerked to her feet. "You aren't helping."

"Calm down, love. And sit down. I was only making the point that, as you've just said, we both know Simon gets drunk. And you did tell me he's worried sick about Fiona. If booze is his pacifier, this is a time when he's likely to pour it in."

Logical. But she didn't want logical arguments anymore, only answers. They almost certainly had one. "I'm sure Simon was the man who came for her case. Who else could it have been?"

"Beats me." Hugh framed his nose and mouth in steepled fingers. "Although there was that mythical person who supposedly called the theater and said she was sick," he stated without conviction.

"I think she got someone she knew to do that. Some actor maybe." Ellen was tired. She couldn't go on with this uncertainty, this constant round of searching, asking and coming to blank walls. "Who knows? I think Simon got that case for her. I also think that's why he was so convinced she was going to France. She probably persuaded him to pick it up for her for some reason, then went somewhere else—somewhere in Britain."

"Whatever you say."

He sounded as exhausted as she felt. "It's not whatever I say, unfortunately, but we might as well let this go for now. We're not going to try Simon again tonight. But I bet he admits it when we do get him. Let's try first thing in the morning."

She watched Hugh stir and stretch. The wind had made an interesting tumble of his curly hair. He looked tired and vulnerable in the gray sweater that had worked above his belt and well-fitting gray pants, immaculate this morning but wrinkled about muscular legs now.

"Okay. I suppose that'll have to be it for tonight." Leaning forward, he dragged the sweater down. "Would you like me to leave now?"

His directness unnerved her. He was asking far more than the obvious. Ellen sat on the very edge of the couch, her knees pressed together.

Hugh stood up and looked at her. The tiredness had left his face. "Neither of us is a master at these situations, hmm, Ellen?"

"I guess not." She knew what she wanted to say.

"We would have...we were meant to be...close." He sat beside her, his tweed sport jacket draped over his thighs. "There was something there from the day we met. We'd have got together regardless. I know we would have. The other, the stuff with Fiona pushed us faster, but it's also standing between us, isn't it?"

She nodded. "Yeah, in a way. But I don't want you to go. I'd like to forget everything else for a while and just be with you."

One large hand cupped the back of her head. For a moment they simply looked at each other. Then he took her in his arms and held her close. Against her face, his sweater was rough and she rubbed her cheek slowly back and forth. The warmth of his body reached out to her.

"Thank you for saying that," he murmured. "What do you hope for?"

Ellen slipped her hands around his waist. "Between us?"

"Yes."

"I hope we'll stay together." Dangerous words. Words that could bring hurt. She took a breath and held it.

Hugh massaged her back. Then he spanned her neck and leaned away to look at her. "That's what I hope, too. Even if we do have a basic incompatibility."

He said it with no trace of humor and Ellen frowned. "We do?"

"The tea," he said on a long sigh.

They laughed and ducked their heads at the same time, knocked foreheads and laughed again.

Hugh pulled her close once more and she kissed the strong pulse in his neck above his open shirt collar. His embrace was fiercer this time, the pressure of his moving hands on her back more insistent.

There was no need to talk. Again and again they kissed, touched. Then they undressed each other, exposing skin for skin, caressing skin for skin.

Naked, kneeling on the jumbled pile of their clothes before the glow of the little living room fire, Ellen helped Hugh step out of his pants and wrapped her arms around his thighs. The pulsing inside her was near pain. She would never stop wanting this man. Her mouth, swollen from their kisses, tingled at every new contact with his flesh.

Hugh slowly knelt, too, his legs sliding down to press against hers. "You know what you do?" he said. He rolled her breasts against his chest and she moaned. "You make love as if you know what I want before *I* do." His voice was hoarse now, thick. His body probed her, solid and demanding.

"Maybe I do."

But it was Hugh who pulled her astride his lap, then stopped, clasping her hips, holding her inches from him, looking up into her face for unbearably exquisite moments before bringing her down.

Ellen shuddered and felt herself close around him, tight and hot, growing hotter with each stroking motion. Hugh hooked his hands under her arms, spreading wide his thumbs to incite her taut nipples.

Their breaths came, loud, mingled with little cries. She wasn't in control anymore. This body was hers yet not hers, and she rejoiced in giving it to Hugh. In return he made her a willing sacrifice of his own. Through half-closed eyes she saw sweat gleam on his shoulders and chest, saw the strained set of his features.

He lifted her almost apart from him again and she clung to his arms. But a second later she felt him fill her again, and with the filling came a bright searing arc that rocked her body and blanked her mind.

She throbbed on and on and tried to anchor herself close to him, to hold on. But Hugh shifted again and she opened her eyes. He parted his lips, tried to keep her gaze, but failed. His keening cry brought her heart hammering into her throat. She saw his eyes squeeze tightly shut, saw the final thrust of his hips into hers and a little exclamation of triumph broke free. Watching his climax was a beautiful thing. She was both powerful and vulnerable, server and served, and nothing could ever erase the moment.

"My God, Ellen," Hugh whispered. He swung his legs around and fell flat on the floor, pulling her on top of him. "Don't you ever go away from me."

When she tried to talk her teeth chattered with the release of tension. "I wish there wasn't a world out there," she muttered. "If this was all there was, it would be more than I deserve."

He opened his eyes and strained up his head until she looked at him. "Don't say that." He sounded angry. She couldn't bear to make him angry.

"I only meant—"

"You deserve the best. And you'll have it if I get my way." His mouth softened and he smiled. "Stick with me, kid, and we'll both have the best."

Ellen didn't have the energy to laugh.

When she awoke in the morning it was without recollection of leaving the living room. But she was in her bed, plastered to Hugh's warm body, his arms looped around her.

Cautiously she wiggled a little. The hair on his chest tickled her nose and her own hair was a wild mass in front of her eyes.

"I advise against that kind of activity if you ever want to get out of this bed."

Hugh's voice, wide awake and unconvincingly serious, took her by surprise. "Can't see," she mumbled, holding very still.

"So. Who needs to see?"

Ellen thought a moment, then smiled. "I do. And you do. I think we may both have seeing fetishes—when it comes to each other, that is."

"So true," he said, laughing. "Wise woman. Let's sort this out." He eased her up to his shoulder, pushed her hair back and kissed her soundly. Then, with a single sweeping motion that made her howl, he whipped the sheet and blankets back, letting cold air zap her skin into a million goose bumps.

"Sadist," she yelled, struggling to grab the covers.

Hugh held her down and kissed her languorously, her mouth, her neck, her breasts, her stomach and thighs, until she begged for mercy and pleaded that they *would* never get out of the bed if he didn't stop. He did stop and immediately she wished he hadn't. Her own body had begun to quicken.

"Hugh, maybe..."

"I've been thinking," he said with a knowing smile.

Ellen scowled. He knew exactly what he was doing at all times. And he wasn't above being a tease. "That can be a dangerous activity," she said.

"It can. But I'm serious about this. After you call Simon this morning, regardless of what he says, I'd like to go to the police and update them on what Mrs. Thomas told us."

Reality smashed Ellen's dreamy bubble. "Yes. That's a good idea. I'd better call Simon now."

"Wait a minute. Wait a minute. Calm down. The other thing I wanted to tell you was that from here on we work together, side by side. We'll put everything we've got into clearing up this whole thing. Then perhaps we can get on with the rest of our lives."

Ellen looked up at him. His gentle brown eyes were gazing softly on hers. "Thank you, Hugh," she said quietly. "I need you. And Fiona will be grateful you've helped me. I'm going to call Simon. Will you put the kettle on?"

Half an hour later she entered the kitchen. Hugh had made coffee for her, tea for himself, and toast was already heaped on a plate. She started to apologize for the sparse condition of her food supply but Hugh silenced her with a kiss.

"Sit down," he ordered, pushing her into a chair and leaning over her. "You look a bit grim. Did you get Simon?"

"Mmm."

"And?"

"He's no help, Hugh." Defeat sapped her energy. She put her hands atop his on her shoulders. "You should have heard him. So hung over he barely made sense, and when he did make sense all he did was rant about wanting Fiona back."

"Yes," Hugh said gently, "but what about the suitcase?"

Ellen looked up at him, shaking her head. "No go. He insists he didn't pick up the case. He has seen it, or one of the ones she has like it, because she's taken them with her to Cadogan, but he definitely didn't come here that day."

"And you believe him?"

"Don't you?"

Hugh straightened and stood, absently stroking her cheek with the backs of his fingers. "Yes, I suppose I do, damn it. It would make it a whole lot easier if we at least had that much that wasn't a mystery. Ellen, we're nowhere with this."

"I know." Utterly miserable, she wrapped her robe more tightly about her.

"That's it," Hugh said in a voice big enough to snap Ellen's head up. "I've had it with this. Action!" He grabbed his tea and drained the cup. "You take your time getting to the shop. I'm going to the police now and I'm going to demand some answers. I'll tell them as much as I can that they may not know. Not that it's much. But they've got to act."

Despite herself, Ellen smiled. She got up and hugged him before he pulled on his jacket and raincoat and forged, head down, into another wild fall morning.

She didn't bother with her coffee. If she hurried, she could get to the shop before Hugh was back from the police station. She wanted desperately to hear what he would have to report.

From what Ellen had been told, the shower in Fiona's tiny bathroom was unusual in inexpensive English flats. This morning the shower beckoned, luring Ellen with the promise of a few minutes of glorious warmth and oblivion.

Ellen laid navy woolen slacks, a cream silk blouse and an oversize navy-blue V-necked sweater on her bed. She picked up some underwear, found a clean towel and shut herself into the bathroom. Without heat in the room, taking a shower could be a major decision, but she'd discovered that running the water until she created some steam made getting undressed more bearable.

Within five minutes, shivering violently, she inched aside the pink plastic curtain on its curved rod and climbed into the tub. The water spurted erratically, sometimes blasting, sometimes trickling, sometimes deliciously hot, sometimes barely lukewarm. No wonder the British were a hardy breed. They lived under constant siege from the simple necessities Americans took for granted as tame allies.

She poured shampoo into her left palm and balanced the bottle in one corner of the tub.

As she lifted her head she felt as much as saw the suggestion of a shadow move across the sweating ceiling. Smiling, she slathered the shampoo into her hair. Hugh must have come back—he, too, had a key now—and she was supposed to be surprised. She wouldn't disappoint him.

Humming, she massaged her head, keeping one eye on the curtain. The shadow became a shape, rippling past the folds of plastic toward the end of the tub behind her.

Ellen hummed louder and kept her elbows angled up, hands rubbing, but with her face turned so that she'd see his face when he pulled back the curtain.

Soap ran into the corner of her eye and she rubbed it away. Another movement brought her eyes to the hand that slowly extended into the shower. A gloved hand.

*No!* She opened her mouth to scream but couldn't make a noise. In the leather-encased fingers was her hair dryer. Even above the sound of the water, Ellen could hear that the appliance was running.

Not knowing how she did it, Ellen continued to hum, continued to rub her hair, while she stood, waiting . . .

The man, and she knew it was a man, was inches from her, separated only by the flimsy plastic.

Then he dropped the dryer.

Her scream broke loose, a wild mad scream of terror. But while she screamed, she dropped to her haunches and caught the dryer against the wall.

Still screaming, she closed her eyes, bracing for the agony of electric shocks that might still come.

They didn't.

Outside the curtain, the shadow moved and one large hand, fingers splayed, pressed into the plastic.

Slowly, silently, holding the dryer away from the blessedly weak drizzle of water, Ellen slid down to lie on the bottom of the tub. Her predator was going to check his handiwork. She would die in the next few seconds anyway.

A sudden pounding on the ceiling jarred her teeth together. Mrs. Thomas. For the first time ever Ellen was glad of her presence.

Ellen's eyes had almost closed again. She opened them now and looked up.

The hand was gone. A breeze sent the curtain billowing inward. Then Ellen heard the bathroom door slam.

# *Chapter Seventeen*

Throwing on her clothes, dashing from Fiona's flat and flagging the first taxi to come into sight had taken less than fifteen minutes; the drive to Hampstead, another fifteen. Her hair was still wet. Ellen raked it back and surveyed Hugh's bedroom.

In the shop, Cecily had cast an amazed glance at Ellen, but then said the magic words: "Hugh isn't in."

Ellen had a chance to do what she must do—search Hugh's flat. What she didn't have was even a hint of how long he would be gone. He could walk in on her at any second.

Two closets were built into recesses on each side of a black iron fireplace. Ellen flung open one, rummaged in the bottom, slammed the door and ran to repeat the process with the second.

If he caught her, what would he do?

Ellen stood up, shaking, wiping damp palms on her slacks. What she must try desperately not to do was allow what she felt for Hugh, deep inside, to surface. Not until and unless she could disprove the obvious: Hugh might have tried to kill her. Who else would want to? Who else could so easily have got at her and have almost pulled off what was to have been her own "accidental" death? She'd considered and discarded Simon as a prospect. He hadn't had time since her call to dress, drive to St. John's Wood and be sober enough to own that steady gloved hand.

Today was probably the second time someone had set out to kill her. Ellen fought down a rush of panic. When she'd come back from Cadogan and discovered later that someone had been in the flat, she'd avoided facing the obvious—that her life might have been saved by Simon's appearance. She couldn't avoid the possibility anymore. When the time was right she'd thank Simon, even though he hadn't known what he was doing.

Oh, God. That night, after the break-in, she'd gone to Hugh. He'd taken ages to let her in and when he did he'd reminded her of the outdoors, the wind and rain. He'd smelled like wind and rain, like someone who had only just come home. From where? Her flat?

She fell to her knees and lifted the stark white bedspread. A man had taken Fiona's blue suitcase from her flat. That man, Ellen was still certain, had not been Simon. If her first horrible theory about Hugh's relationship with Fiona were correct, he could have been the visitor Mrs. Thomas saw the day Fiona disappeared.

Ellen looked under the bed and clamped a hand over her mouth to silence a scream. Two yellow lights glowed in the darkness. Her heart rammed into her throat. A mew sounded. Pushing her hair back again, she leaned on the bed, catching her breath, and Vladimir stalked past.

The suitcase wouldn't be here, not if Hugh were sane. He'd get rid of it. But murderers weren't sane. She'd read of instances where killers had kept mementos of their crimes.

Sweat heated her damp scalp and stung her eyes. What if Hugh had lured Fiona away on some pretext? He could have manufactured the whole story about the trip to France, having first persuaded Fiona to go somewhere with him. One last time alone together, maybe? Fiona had always been softhearted and unwilling to hurt. And it could have been

Hugh who called the theater with an excuse to make sure they didn't ask any awkward questions. She remembered something else, something Ed said when he'd talked about the call from immigration. The words wouldn't come to her exactly, but there had been another suggestion that Ed linked Hugh and Fiona together in more than a casual way.

There was no blue suitcase in Hugh's bedroom.

His office seemed the next obvious place to look. He could have decided to keep Fiona's red diary. Or a letter, a note, something to link the two of them together as more than boss and employee.

Ellen sat behind his desk and riffled through stacks of papers. Nothing. The drawers were stuffed with a hodge-podge of material. She searched through a file drawer, pulling out one folder after another, determined to find anything that would help confirm or allay her suspicions.

"Ellen?"

Without her firm grip on the file drawer, she might have slipped from the edge of the chair.

Slowly, very slowly, scarcely able to breathe, Ellen lifted her head.

Hugh, looking as he had when he left her earlier, stood on the other side of the desk, staring down at the gaping drawer, the disordered pile of documents.

"What are you doing?"

"What took you so long?"

He frowned. "Don't answer a question with a question. What the hell do you think you're doing going through my papers?"

Ellen tried to close the drawer. It was heavy and she gave up. She had two choices: confront him and risk ending up however Fiona might have ended, or lie and learn nothing.

"Talk to me, Ellen!"

Her stomach rolled. "Were you in love with Fiona?"

He stared at her for a long time. "In love with Fiona?"

"Just tell me the truth. Were you and Fiona having an affair? I'm sure Ed thinks you were. You must have given him some reason."

"I don't know what—"

"After Fiona met Simon Macky and they decided to get married, did you kill her? Were you the man who called the theater with some phony excuse about her being sick? Did you set up the story about her going to France? Hugh, was it you who took her suitcase, and her diary?"

For a second he appeared puzzled. His arched brows knitted together and he shook his head, turned as if he might walk out. Then he rounded on her, a hard white line around his pursed lips.

Ellen stood up. "I—"

"Shut up! Be quiet, you little fool."

She took a step backward.

Hugh skirted the desk until they stood toe to toe. "You really think things through, don't you? Maybe you'd like to hear a little idea I came up with. This—" he gestured to the disarray on his desk "—backs up what I'd prayed was all imagination on my part."

Ellen lifted her chin. "Go on." She hated the way her mouth trembled.

"This is crazy." Hugh bowed his head. "I don't believe you and I . . . It can't be."

"You had an idea you wanted to share with me." Her fear was where he couldn't see it. On the outside she cast an icy facade.

"Right, I will. Your beloved sister disappeared the day my grandmother died."

"She did?" Ellen frowned. "How can you be so sure?"

"Because she insisted on running an errand for me to Maida Vale that afternoon." He shouldn't have started this. The whole story sounded irrational even to him now. But after the accusations Ellen had just made he had to show her just how improbable her doubts about him were. And he did—how Fiona had shown up for a job that didn't exist and persuaded him he needed her, the way she'd befriended his grandmother and, after a brief hesitation, the details of the will.

When he'd finished he slumped into a chair and scrubbed at his eyes.

"You mean," Ellen said in a thin high voice unlike her own, "that you think Fiona helped Simon Macky get rid of your grandmother so that he could start getting those payments? You think they intend to kill you, too?"

He looked up at her. Her hair was a wild tangle about her pale face. She wore no makeup and her perfect skin shone slightly.

Dread ate at his gut. "Yes, that's exactly what I think."

"And I was supposed to be part of whatever plot they'd hatched against you?"

"Yes." He could hardly get the word out. "The closest I could come to a solid theory about your part in the scheme was that after the murder, Fiona intended to duck out until she felt absolutely safe and that you were supposed to keep an eye on me and report to her. I even thought I'd sponsored someone, given a job to someone, who was going to do me in."

"But you managed to put your reservations aside long enough to make love to me—if that's what we can call it now."

"Ellen, please—"

"Don't say any more." She stood up and turned to the window.

"Listen a minute." The way out of this wasn't clear, but there was a way and he'd find it. "Ellen, you came over here this morning believing I was some kind of maniac who'd killed your sister and was planning to kill you. I walked in here and found you going through my things..." He paused, remembering something she'd said. "What diary? You said something about a diary."

She lifted her shoulders. "Her diary was taken from beside her bed. She always kept it there."

"Oh." Why hadn't she mentioned it before? Of course, because he was supposed to be a homicidal maniac. "If you think I'm a murderer, why did you sleep with me last night? Why did you sleep with me at all?"

"I'd decided I was wrong. You seemed to want to help me find Fiona. You wouldn't have if you'd killed her."

"Listen to us, will you?" He gave a short laugh. "Doesn't anything strike you about this conversation?"

"I hate it. And I hate you for thinking Fiona could have... It's disgusting."

He didn't want to antagonize her. They'd both made wrong assumptions, but working together was essential. "Ellen. Please look at me."

Her crossed hands gripped her arms. She didn't turn around.

"What happened after I left you this morning to make you change your mind? You were fine. And I did exactly what I said I'd do and went to the police. It took as long as it did because I had to do the usual waiting around."

"You went straight to the police?"

He looked at his shoes and realized his feet were soggy. "What is it with you? Yes, I went straight to the police."

Then Ellen did face him. "I thought I'd ask, because this crazy woman who could have been involved in a plot to wipe out your family came pretty close to dying herself this morning. Of course, if I'm as crazy as you think, maybe I dropped the hair dryer into the shower myself. Crazy people do that—"

He caught her shoulders. "Ellen! What are you saying?" His stomach felt pretty close to where his heart should be.

Ellen shrugged free. "A man came into the bathroom and dropped a hair dryer—running—into the shower. I was in the shower. If I didn't have fantastic reflexes, I'd be barbecued meat."

"Stop it! My God, stop it!"

"Sorry if I'm indelicate. I'm kind of getting used to the idea."

"And you thought I did that?"

She held her bottom lip in her teeth. "How am I supposed to know what to think at this point? I didn't see who it was."

Then he did grab her and pull her close. "Do you think I could kill you?"

Her body went limp and she leaned against him. "No. I guess I don't. But who did, Hugh? Who did? And why?"

In his mind he saw the speeding silver sides of an underground train, gray concrete striped with white rising to meet him, sparks on deadly glistening rails.

"Someone wants to keep you quiet," he said. "And we've got to find out who. I didn't tell you this before because I didn't want to worry you, but—"

The jarring ring of the phone cut him off and he snatched up the receiver. "Hugh Weston," he barked.

The caller said nothing for a moment, then coughed and cleared his throat. "Is Ellen there?"

Hugh recognized the voice. He pursed his lips, struggling to let down a little. "Yes, here she is."

"It's Simon Macky." He handed over the phone.

Ellen raised a brow at Hugh, but he turned up his palms and sat down again.

She lifted the receiver to her ear. "Simon—"

"I've got to see you. Tomorrow evening at my place. About ten."

"Simon, I'm not sure—"

"Don't argue." The familiar break was in his voice. He gulped and Ellen heard an indrawn sob. "Just be there. I'll have it all worked out by then. Trust me."

"Simon—"

He'd hung up.

"Oh, Hugh." On legs that had ceased to feel she went to stand before him. "Simon's going to clear everything up, he says. I'm going to his place at ten tomorrow evening."

Hugh stood up so abruptly that Ellen clutched his sleeve. "After what I've told you, you'd still consider going anywhere near that man alone?" He shook his head emphatically. "You're not going."

She was afraid, but she wouldn't be told what to do, particularly when this could be her last, her only chance to find Fiona. Her eyes closed of their own volition.

Strong arms surrounded and squeezed her. "They tried to kill me, too," Hugh announced gruffly.

Minutes later she sat in the chair he'd vacated, trying to calm down. Terror, confusion and anger overwhelmed her. Someone had tried to push Hugh beneath an underground train?

"Ellen," he continued. "I want you where I can see you at all times. We have to pool our resources and look after each other. The police are at least interested now but they aren't exactly panicked, and I don't intend for us to be corpses before they get really interested. I'll come back to Fiona's with you and get your things. You'll stay here."

"I can't do that."

"You have to."

"I have to do what I think is right. And for now that means I'm staying where Fiona would expect to find me."

"No, Ellen—"

"Yes. We'll look out for each other, keep each other informed of where we are, but I'm not moving in with you. And I am going to Simon's tomorrow."

BOWLERS, PIN-STRIPED SUITS and furled umbrellas. Flanked by a sea of uniformed London businessmen, briefcases in hand, each with the mandatory copy of the *London Times* rolled beneath one arm, Hugh rode the escalator to the street at St. Paul's underground stop.

Once on the sidewalk, he turned left toward Gutter Lane. He'd told Ellen back at the shop, that he was visiting a fellow bookseller. Simon Macky was his real target. A little discussion today might be the way to head off the meeting Ellen planned for tomorrow night.

He had only a few blocks to walk. The lane was narrow, a chasm between towering buildings, and Macky Brothers' offices were easily located on the fifth floor of a concrete-and-glass monstrosity.

Ten minutes later Hugh was back in the street, frustrated and uncertain what to do next. Ross Ivers had been the closest he'd got to Simon who was "otherwise engaged," according to his assistant. And no, Ross had no idea when Hugh might be able to see Simon. Why not call later?

The only option was return to Hampstead and do just that. He started for the station, dodging pinstripes left and right.

A car turned the corner. Impossible to ignore, the dark green Rolls had gold striping and a gold bonnet emblem. Hugh glanced at the driver and immediately drew back into the nearest doorway.

Violet Macky, leaning slightly forward as if unaccustomed to driving the vehicle herself, peered over the steering wheel.

Hugh edged to the other side of the doorway and watched her draw the car to a stop outside Macky Brothers. She opened the door and at the same time he saw Ross Ivers stride onto the sidewalk, smiling broadly.

He went to Violet's side of the car and leaned down. His mouth moved and Violet dangled her keys over his outstretched palm. He took them. Then they kissed...and kissed.

# Chapter Eighteen

The doorman had been too busy helping a resident corral a runaway basset hound to give Ellen more than a cursory glance. Mr. Macky's rooms were on the second floor. No, no number. His name was beside his door.

As instructed, Ellen had taken the bronze-doored elevator and now stood before a plate marked S.J. Macky. His rooms were on the second floor—the entire floor.

She'd already rung the bell twice. By her watch, she was exactly on time. With every extra second of waiting her agitation mounted.

Uncertainly she turned the handle. The door swung open into a silent but brightly lighted entrance.

She took a few hesitant steps onto a deep blue Oriental rug. "Simon?" The atmosphere was cushioned, expensive, her small voice absorbed by Chinese screens lining walls in the square foyer, the name she softly called batted back from a gold foil-papered hall.

Ellen paused, drew the belt of her raincoat tighter. He must have forgotten, or been delayed.

The door could have been left open because he was afraid he might not be back in time for her arrival. She sniffed, lifted her face. The place reeked of alcohol.

Oh, God. Just what she needed tonight, a paralytic drunk looking for a convenient shoulder.

"Simon!" Ellen ventured into the hall, walked slowly past elegant rosewood cabinets, their illuminated glass shelves dotted with ivory and jade figurines. "Simon, where are you?"

Only one lamp cast its subdued glow over the drawing room. She moved on, hardly seeing her surroundings anymore. The stench was overpowering now. She went through a separate dining room, a small anteroom watched over by oppressive ebony tigers and into another, smaller hallway.

Light spilled from a crack between double doors at the end. Ellen halted for an instant, then pressed on, her jaw set.

She knocked, waited, knocked again. No response.

The doors swung easily over deep-piled white carpet—until the right one smacked against an overturned bottle. A pale amber stain marred the snowy perfection of the rug.

Ellen had automatically started to bend over when she saw the bed. And Simon.

The foul smell, her revulsion, receded and she hurried to his side. "Oh, Simon, how could you?"

Fully dressed, including shoes, his beautiful navy suit a crushed disaster, he lay spread-eagled. His face was turned away from her. An empty glass, wedged beneath one arm, had spilled more liquor over a black-and-gray-covered down comforter.

Exasperated, she shook him by the shoulder. "Wake up, Simon! Damn it, wake up."

He didn't move.

She leaned over him and something crunched beneath her foot. Looking down she saw the mangled remains of his glasses. Ellen glanced at the hand hanging close to her knees. Flaccid. A gripping rolling thing happened in her stomach, worked up into her chest and throat. Leaning over him, she took his chin between forefinger and thumb and turned his head. It was heavy.

"Oh, Simon, no. No!"

His partly open eyes focused on nothing, would never focus on anything again.

"Don't touch anything!"

Hugh's voice from the doorway thudded into her like a bullet. Ellen reeled away from the bed, banged into the nightstand. Her vision blurred for an instant.

"Hugh," she whispered, too shocked to move. "What are you doing here?"

He came to her side. "Following you. What else? You would come, regardless of what I said, so I had to come too. I had to be sure you'd be all right."

Ellen reached for his hand and squeezed tightly. "Thank you. Please look at Simon. Is he dead?"

Seconds that felt like a lifetime dragged by while she watched Hugh search for a pulse, a pulse she knew he wouldn't find. And in those seconds she saw what she hadn't noticed before—scattered pills, blue, green, and two empty containers on the bedside table with another almost empty bottle of whiskey.

"Alcohol and drugs," she said, as much to herself as to Hugh. "He killed himself. I'm so sorry. So sorry."

"Stop it, Ellen." Hugh straightened and framed her face with his hands. "You have nothing to be sorry about."

"If I'd got here sooner I might—"

"No! No, Ellen. He hasn't been dead long. But if he wanted to do this—and he obviously did—he would have anyway. I just resent the hell out of his giving in right when he must have known you'd be the one most likely to find him."

Ellen looked at Simon through a sea of tears. "He loved Fiona. He missed her. That's what did this. He thought she'd left him for good."

"Yeah. Hmm. Stay there and don't touch anything."

She crossed her arms and ground a fist against her mouth, watching Hugh. He circled the room, peering under tables, behind chairs. With his scarf wrapped over one hand, he lifted curtains and let them drop, opened drawers and cupboards.

"What are you...? Hugh, don't. We've got to call someone. The police. Get the police." He was searching, just as she had searched his flat, looking, she knew intuitively, for exactly what she had looked for. "Simon doesn't have Fiona's things. If he had known where she is, he'd still be alive, I'm sure he would."

"Maybe. I don't...I didn't know the man. But I want to be sure." He finished going through one last drawer and walked backward toward the door. "Come on, help me, but don't leave any fingerprints."

Ellen started after him. "Why? Hugh, let's call the police. I don't like this."

Hugh's laugh was derisive. "Don't like it? That's an understatement for the way I feel. But we can't run the risk of some member of his family getting in here and removing anything that could lead us to Fiona."

"I see," Ellen muttered, not wanting to see, to think, but Hugh was right and for Fiona she'd find the strength to do whatever must be done. She felt in her pockets for something to cover her fingers but found nothing. The hem of her raincoat would have to do.

Half an hour later she and Hugh faced each other back in Simon's bedroom. "I didn't expect to find anything," Hugh said, shrugging and lifting the phone.

"I'm relieved," Ellen responded. "Or I think I am."

The pulsing wail of sirens seemed to come almost as soon as Hugh hung up the phone. Then the police were there, polite but brusque. "Wait in the drawing room, please... Are you all right, miss...sir?" More men, police physician, photographer, sidelong glances—all business, the business they knew, one more body, one more job.

Another hour and the questions were over. For now. Ellen heard, "Is this where you two can be found?" The policeman read Hugh's address aloud and she didn't bother to say she might not be there.

"You haven't contacted the family?" she asked suddenly. A pause followed. "If you haven't, I'd like to do that."

"Very well, miss. Go ahead." And she was forgotten. There was more work for these men to do tonight.

"You're going to call Cadogan?"

Ellen nodded at Hugh. For Fiona, she'd do it. Fiona. Her fiancé was dead and she didn't even know. When she did come back, how could she cope?

Cummings answered the phone at the Mackys's house, and Ellen had to wait too long before she heard Violet's pinched voice. "Yes, Ellen."

Ellen bowed her head, visualizing the woman who undoubtedly resented having to bother with one of those tacky Shaw sisters.

"Violet," she began evenly while her heart jumped in her chest, "I'm afraid I have some bad news." Not that Violet was likely to sacrifice much sleep over the loss of Simon.

After Ellen had let the damp receiver slip back into its cradle she sat with her eyes closed at the black lacquered desk in a corner of the drawing room.

A firm hand on her shoulder reminded her that Hugh was standing behind her. "She really took it badly, didn't she?"

Ellen tapped her mouth with tented fingertips. "She fell apart. The woman cared about him, really cared. How could I have been so wrong? I thought she only tolerated him because he was Xavier Macky's nephew." She stood up and Hugh eased her into his arms. Against his shoulder she said, "She couldn't talk anymore. Xavier came on and he sounded almost human."

"Let's get out of here," Hugh said.

When they reached the street, the night air was incredibly sweet and clean. Misty rain drifted against Ellen's face in gentle gusts. Side by side, arms around each other's waists, she and Hugh walked awhile, not speaking. Then he hailed a cab and, without consulting her, gave his address to the driver.

There was nowhere else she wanted to go. No one else she wanted to be with. Peace of mind was a memory, but at least with Hugh she felt safe.

At six in the morning the phone rang. Ellen opened her eyes, blinking into the light Hugh switched on beside the bed. He looked down at her and stroked her naked shoulders.

The phone rang again and he picked it up, listened, said, "Yes, yes," and "Yes, yes," and "Goodbye."

"The police."

Ellen scooted to a sitting position, wrapping sheet and blankets around her.

"They'll definitely want to question us today." Hugh leaned forward, grasping his knees, and Ellen smoothed a hand over his broad back. "This is getting more sordid by the minute," he added distantly.

"They said last night that they'd want to talk to us again." She was sleepy, and she loved the feel of his back.

"He didn't kill himself."

The words sank in slowly. Ellen took her hand from Hugh's back and shoved at her hair. "He took pills with booze. We both saw that."

"We saw what we were supposed to see and thought what we were supposed to think. He'd had a lot to drink and some pills, but not enough to do him in."

"Then why did he die if it wasn't enough?"

Hugh hugged her fiercely. "We're into something rotten and dangerous, love. Simon was suffocated. With the pillow that was under his head when we arrived, they think. He must have been drunk enough and high enough on whatever he took to make an easy target. Couldn't even put up a fight."

His chest rose and fell rapidly against her cheek. "Why Simon, Hugh? I can't see any pattern to this, unless your theory was right and he expected to inherit your grandmother's estate completely, and soon. His next of kin will get everything now that Simon's dead. Whoever that is could want him out of the way."

"That's probably Xavier Macky. But he was at Cadogan when you called, and I doubt if he would have had time to get there. I also doubt if he would bump off his nephew, even if he didn't particularly like him."

"No," Ellen agreed. "So what's the answer? Will the police sort everything out?"

"They may. We can hope so." His fingers threaded through her hair. "Simon didn't give you any hints about exactly what he intended to say, did he?"

"No."

She felt his body become very still, tense. "Do you think he intended to tell you the whole truth about everything?" He paused and Ellen had the sensation he was voicing his own thoughts aloud. "If I was anywhere near the truth, there would have been others involved. Someone must have known about my grandmother's estate and her will. That someone undoubtedly told Simon, and whoever it was probably had a lot at stake in the whole thing. He wouldn't have wanted Simon spilling the beans to you."

Ellen felt very, very cold. "You mean Simon was murdered to stop him from keeping his appointment with me?"

"Makes sense, doesn't it?"

It made the best sense she'd heard for days, but she didn't like admitting as much.

"Ellen," Hugh said, leaning away but not releasing her, "don't get angry at what I'm going to say. Please just listen and think about it."

She didn't respond.

"Saying this takes all the guts I've got. But we can't afford to back off from honesty at this point." A pale ridge formed each side of his tight mouth. "It could be that Fiona had the best reason to keep Simon quiet."

ELLEN LET HERSELF into Fiona's flat. Anger with Hugh would have taken more energy than she had left. Besides, she was too confused to be angry. She was too confused to be sure what she believed about anything or anyone—except Fiona. She refused even to consider that the sweet impish maverick who was her sister could willingly hurt another human being. For Fiona to have killed was out of the question.

She saw the envelope when she closed the coat closet.

Someone must have pushed it under the door. All mail was delivered to Mrs. Thomas upstairs and picked up later.

When Ellen pulled the airline ticket out, a small square of paper fluttered to the floor.

She picked it up, read and reread, excitement speeding through her until her cheeks throbbed. An unfamiliar sensation of faintness came. She lowered herself until she sat on the floor.

The note was typewritten. Not exactly what she most wanted to read, but still the best news she'd had since she arrived in England: "It would be better for both of us if you went home. Love F."

The ticket was for a one-way flight to New York.

## Chapter Nineteen

"Why? Why shouldn't I be overly optimistic?"

Hugh propped himself against the windowsill in his study and read the note again. "Because I don't think you should get too excited too soon. Okay?" Please let me say and do the right things, he prayed. Let me be able to keep Ellen's spirits up without allowing her to hope too much.

"No, it's not okay, Hugh. I came rushing over here because I'm excited and I expected you to be just as excited. This means Fiona's all right. I thought you'd be so happy." The smile she'd burst in with had gone, thanks to him. Her eyes were desperate again, damn it.

Easy, he must ease into this. "Well, for one thing, the note isn't signed and—"

"I realize that," Ellen interjected. "But Fiona always wrote like that."

"Okay, but why do you think Fiona wants you to go back to America?"

As she so often did when uncertain, Ellen dragged in the belt on her raincoat. She held her bottom lip in her teeth.

"Don't sidestep this, love. Of course you're excited to hear something from her." How could he admit that the note constituted nothing more to him than another warning that he and Ellen and Fiona were all in danger?

Ellen crossed to his side and took the note from him. "I believe she's worried about me. You're right to be skeptical. Too much has happened for either of us not to be skeptical. But I believe she's in very bad trouble and wants me out of it."

He couldn't bring himself to argue, to say that he agreed that someone wanted not just Ellen, but both of them out of the way—and that he no longer thought Fiona was that person. He'd give anything to know where Fiona was right now. Ellen, he was sure, was right when she said her sister must be in trouble, but with Simon out of the way, Hugh's tidy theory about the nature of her trouble had been blown away.

"You really do believe Fiona's behind everything, don't you? You think she caused your grandmother's death and that she killed Simon."

"I didn't say that."

"Yes, you did."

"No. I told you I've wondered about those things. And—"

"I want to go to Cadogan. You can come with me or stay here. Up to you."

"Why do you...?"

"Because I don't know where else to go. The answer is there, Hugh. The Mackys are my last chance. Simon's heir is the most likely suspect in his death and I intend to find out just who his heir is."

He caught her arm. When she tried to twist away, he pulled her close and tight. "Slow down, Ellen. What do you think you're going to do? March into Cadogan and say, 'Okay, which one of you knocked off Simon to get his money?'"

"Don't be ridiculous."

"I'm not the ridiculous one, but I am a very bewildered and worried man. And I happen to love you too much to let you run any more risks than you're already running by simply being in London."

She became quite still. "You love me?"

He was startled. "I . . . yes, of course I do."

Ellen laughed. "You English really earn your reputation." She rested her brow against his neck.

"Reputation?" Hadn't he told her he loved her before?

"As nondemonstrative."

"Nondemonstrative? Hey, madam, look at me." She did. "Am I nondemonstrative?"

She laughed again and kissed him quickly. "Physically, no. But you don't exactly shine in the verbally romantic department. You drop 'I love you' for the first time and carry on talking like I was supposed to know already."

"Didn't you?"

"More or less."

"But you wanted to hear it."

"You've got it. I wanted to hear you say it."

"Well I have, and I'll say it again. I love you, Ellen. When we get through what's going on all around us right now, I hope you'll be able to decide if you love me back."

"You don't already know?"

His turn to laugh. "Now who's shining in the verbally romantic department?"

"I love you, Hugh. I always will."

He kissed her and felt her lips tremble beneath his. One day, and he hoped it would be soon, he'd do this the way it should be done. Candlelight and wine. Roses and a ring. But not today.

When he lifted his head her eyes were wide open. "Tell me what you intend to do at Cadogan," he said.

"You'll come with me?"

"If you can persuade me it's the right thing to do. Otherwise neither of us goes."

She bristled. "What I do isn't your decision to make."

"Not entirely." He'd have to learn just how strong this ?man was.

"Hmm." She eyed him narrowly. "I want us to go down ?ere and offer condolences. Then I intend to ask a few ?emingly innocent questions, like do they have any idea ?o might have wanted Simon dead. And also there has to ? a way to find out who will inherit from Simon."

"I don't know..."

"Then stay here." She ducked out of his arms and picked ? her purse.

He dared not ask, *What if Fiona is the one to inherit?* ?oking after Ellen must be his immediate and top prior-?. "I'm coming with you. We'll call the police and let them ?ow where they can reach us. Then give me a minute to ?k Ed into lending me his car."

?E TREES LINING the curving drive to Cadogan's main en-?nce stretched almost naked limbs toward a gray sky. ?am oozed from beneath the hood of Ed Butters's '56 ?rd Anglia. Twice on the drive from London, Hugh had ?ded water to the black car's leaky radiator.

"Jeez," Ellen muttered. "I didn't think we were going to ?ke it."

Hugh, evidently untroubled by the temperamental vehi-?, sprinted around to her side of the car. Before he could ?ch her door, Ellen was standing on the gravel driveway.

Cummings, clearly upset and wearing a black mourning ?nd around the arm of his jacket, let them in. He led the ?y to the sitting room without announcing their arrival.

Ross Ivers stood facing the fire, staring into its flames. ?hen he heard someone enter he swung around, his face a ?rd mask. Violet sat crumpled in her velvet armchair.

No one spoke until Xavier, sitting almost behind the door, ?mbled, "What are you doing here?"

"Is that you, Ellen, Hugh?" Jo, stationed behind her uncle, came forward, both hands outstretched. "Thank you for coming." Her puffy face showed the ravages of grief.

Violet stood, straightening a severe black suit and smoothing tousled hair. "You should have called. We weren't expecting company."

Ellen felt Hugh move at her side and put a restraining hand beneath his elbow. She must be the one to deal with this situation.

"I felt I had to come and tell you how sorry I am about Simon." That much was absolutely true. "Hugh was kind enough to drive me down."

"I hardly think your presence here is appropriate." Ross Ivers planted himself between Violet and Ellen. "The family is suffering. They don't need outsiders at a time like this."

"Ross," Jo said, patently distressed, "Ellen has every right to be here. She's Fiona's sister."

"Fiona doesn't count in our lives anymore," Ross insisted stubbornly. "She deserted Simon anyway, and who knows if they'd have got back together."

"It was her fault," Violet cried. "We were fine until she came along. Giving Simon ideas. Upsetting him."

"What ideas would those be?" Hugh asked quietly.

Violet glared at Ellen a moment before bursting into tears and collapsing back in her chair. Ross bent over her, making consoling noises.

Ellen tried to summon all the questions she'd intended to ask. The hostility in this room, from everyone but Jo, fractured her composure. These people were so very foreign to her. Xavier, who should be the most concerned as Simon was his nephew, had said nothing more and was sitting motionless. The only people in control were Jo and Ross, Jo maintaining her composure and trying to help Ellen, Ross preoccupied only with Violet Macky.

Ross looked up. "Can't you see we need to be alone here? This is very, very hard on Violet."

*What about Jo,* Ellen almost asked, *and Xavier? And why are you the one in charge?*

"You must be tired," Jo said. "Please sit down and have some tea."

"I think it would be best if you went back to London immediately," Ross announced, ignoring Jo's offer.

"Yes, Ellen," Violet put in. "Be good enough to leave us alone."

"I think you might prefer to hear what we have to say, Mrs. Macky," Hugh stated. Violet hadn't as much as glanced at him since they arrived, and she still avoided looking at him. "Of course Ellen and I are sorry about Simon. You all have our sympathy. But our first concern is for Fiona."

"Fiona?" Violet snorted. "A troublemaker from the start. Who knows what she dragged my—Simon into." She got up again and took a poker to the fire, jabbing, probing.

Ellen opened her mouth to protest, but Hugh shook his head. "We'll ignore that comment for now, Mrs. Macky. The point is that Ellen and I believe Simon knew where Fiona is and that he and Fiona may have been involved in something illegal—"

"Not Simon!" Violet turned and almost screamed.

"Ssh," Ross murmured, "don't get upset."

"Quite," Xavier agreed, stirring slightly. "Don't get upset, my dear."

"We're not certain who's responsible for Fiona's disappearance," Hugh continued when the others were silent, "but it would appear that Simon must have known something about it. The police seem to be doing the best they can, but Ellen and I don't feel we should wait any longer to make our own attempt at locating Fiona. We thought you should know that we intend to hire a private investigator who will give the case his full attention.''

Ellen stared at him, caught off guard by his statement.

"Haven't we suffered enough?" Xavier leaped to his feet, animated for the first time since Ellen had met him. "Leave it alone, will you? All this fuss and we still have to look forward to endless prodding into Simon's murder."

"Prodding?" Ellen said, mystified. "Don't you want to know who killed Simon? Don't you want that more than anything?"

"Yes, we do," Jo said quickly. "We all want the truth. And we want it as soon as possible. Please forgive us, Ellen, and you, Hugh. None of us is thinking too straight today. I think the private investigator is a good idea, don't you, Uncle Xavier?"

"Well—"

"Mr. Macky." Red-faced and puffing, Cummings entered the room. "Mr. Macky, there's an important phone call for you. Will you take it here or in your study?"

"Study," Xavier said promptly.

Ross Ivers followed him from the room and returned a few minutes later to announce that Xavier would be involved in a business matter for a while. "However," he added, "I will be pleased to give you any help I can, Ellen. But not today and not here. On behalf of the family, I ask you to return to London and let us cope with this bereavement as best we can. I also ask that you wait before calling in an investigator. It may not be necessary if the police do their job, and I see no reason to draw more negative attention than we already have."

Ellen looked at Hugh, who raised his brows. He was letting her decide what to do next.

Before she could say anything the door opened again and Cummings came in. He stood on the edge of the rug wringing his hands. His earlier ruddiness was gone, replaced by a doughy pallor.

"What is it, Cummings?" Ross's pinched mouth showed his annoyance at the interruption.

"I . . . sir . . . madam." He swallowed and sent a beseeching glance in Violet's direction. "Mrs. Macky, it's Mr. Macky."

Violet shifted to the edge of her chair. "What about Mr. Macky?"

"He . . . he . . ."

"Speak up, man," Ross said.

Ellen found Hugh's hand and clung.

"There's been an accident," Cummings mumbled.

"Oh, my God." Ross swept the man from his path and ran into the hall.

Hugh, still holding Ellen's hand, dashed after him. Ellen heard Violet's gasping breaths as she followed them upstairs.

A heavy paneled door stood open onto a book-lined room—Xavier's study. Ross crossed to an enormous leather-topped desk. The chair behind it was empty. The room was empty. A steady buzzing brought everyone's attention to the telephone receiver. It hung from the desk and swung gently at the end of its cord.

Cummings joined them, still wringing his hands.

"Where is he?" Ross demanded, turning to him.

Slowly, following the direction of Cummings's nod, they all looked toward an open casement. Chill air slithered past leaded panes and moved thick plum-colored draperies.

Ross replaced the telephone receiver and went, like a man in a dream, to the window.

Ellen, evading Hugh's attempt to hold her back, pulled free and joined Ivers.

Below the window, on merciless concrete, lay the broken heap of a man's body. Xavier Macky.

# Chapter Twenty

Hugh bent so that his ear was close to her mouth, and Ellen whispered, "Ross was the only one who had any chance to push Xavier and I don't believe he did. Look at him. He's in shock." She hoped her own shock wasn't as visible as it felt.

"Mmm, I'm with you on that," Hugh said. "And I bet it was that phone message that sent Xavier out the window."

Hugh and Ellen had returned with Ross, Violet and Jo to wait in the sitting room. The police had been called.

When the first of two officers was ushered in by Cummings, Ellen drew a quick comparison between these village constabulary officials and the abrupt and businesslike manner of their city counterparts. These men looked human, approachable.

"I'm Sergeant Wall," the first man stated, tucking his peaked cap under his arm. "This is Constable Stroud." He went directly to Violet, once more ensconced in her velvet throne. The policeman held out his hand. "We met at the police benefit, Mrs. Macky. Last Christmas that would be."

Violet sniffed and took his hand limply, briefly.

"We understand from your butler—" Wall checked a notebook he held, "—Cummings, is it? Yes, Cummings. We understand Mr. Macky was called away to the phone, then found where he is now." He coughed into a fist. "We've called for the appropriate help there. But Constable Stroud here thinks he himself was the one talking to Mr. Macky when er, er, when it happened."

"Ross," Violet implored, "I can't deal with this now."

"We'll try to make things as easy as possible on you, Mrs. Macky," Sergeant Wall said. "But we do need to confirm what we were told by a woman who came into the station at Stilton Hedges an hour or so ago. That's what Constable Stroud called Mr. Macky about. The woman is in the hall now with a policewoman. She told us a pretty crazy story and we thought it best to contact you and Mr. Macky. If you don't mind, we'd like your help in the matter."

"Now?" Violet wailed.

"It could have some bearing, ma'am."

Constable Stroud approached the door, but before he could open it, Ned Loder burst in. He stood on the threshold, his eyes wild. "Vi, you've got to help me," he gasped, then appeared to notice the police for the first time. He gestured at them. "They've got her. She'll tell them everything. You've got to let me be now. What happened all those years ago is over. Let me be."

He babbled on, going to stand over Violet, who cringed and seemed to grow smaller.

Ellen didn't notice the woman who had come into the sitting room until she heard Hugh's explosive, "Oh, my God!"

Plump, nondescript, thin white hair coiled at her nape, she resembled thousands of other elderly women.

Violet's muffled scream made Ned lean still further over her, clenching his fists and muttering. She was staring at the old woman.

"Violet!" Ross strode to her side. "Get hold of yourself. And you, Ned. Get out. We'll talk later when Mrs. Macky's calmer."

Ross might not have existed. Violet continued to sob and choke and Ned kept on talking.

Hugh felt the room recede, the people in it become like marionettes jiggled on invisible strings, their mouths moved by a puppeteer who forgot to make the sounds.

Only the white-haired woman had solid form. But she was dead. He'd bought a plaque in a cemetery for the little casket of ashes that contained fragments of her blasted remains.

She wasn't dead, though. Millie Weston, his grandmother, the only family he'd ever known, stood a few feet away. But she showed no sign of knowing he was there. Instead her bright blue eyes were fixed on Ellen.

"What's the matter, Hugh?" Ellen, oblivious to Millie's concentration on her, shook him until he looked at her. "Are you ill? Do you want to sit down, or get some air. Hugh, what *is* it?" she finished in an urgent whisper.

"That woman is my grandmother," he told her unevenly. His body was cold now, his skin clammy.

Ellen blanched. "Your grandmother? Millie Weston?"

"You're going to hear me out!" Ned Loder's shout drowned out every other noise in the room. "I stood by you, Vi, and you kept on using me."

Violet, rigidly pale, clutched his sleeve. "Ned—"

"No." He plowed on, undeterred. "You wanted Xavier Macky and you wanted him to be master of this house. To do that you had to get John Macky and his family out of the way. I didn't want to do it. You tell them that." His wavering finger jabbed toward the police. "It's all going to come out now. But you tell them I didn't want any part of killing Mr. Xavier's brother. He was good to me and I wouldn't have done it. But you had it over me because of that bit of nonsense when I was young, that bit of poaching."

"Could I have your name, sir?" Sergeant Wall interrupted tonelessly, flipping to a fresh page in his notebook.

"I'm Ned Loder, estate bailiff. I've been here since I was a boy. If Mr. John was here he'd tell you all about me. Fine worker, he always called me. Fine worker." He was ranting now, his voice breaking on each word. "But she wanted what he had. And I've been paying for her wants for twenty-nine years."

"Stop it, Ned." Violet stood up. "Go on home. I'll take care of this. Don't I always take care of everything?"

Blood had rushed to Ned's face. Veins stood out in his neck. "The only way she could get all this was by doing away with John Macky and his family. But she wanted little Mr. Simon to live because she could use him to control Mr. Xavier—make sure she'd have what wasn't hers for good. It all worked. We started the fire and they...they died, leaving the little boy for her to get at Mr. Xavier with. That's how she got him to marry her. He wouldn't have looked at her otherwise and she knew it." He swept the room with feverish eyes until he found Jo. "Thank God the one little girl lived, too. But even she helped, didn't she Vi? She was blinded, and she accepted the boy as her real brother—she couldn't see him, could she? So, she helped make your story more believable."

"Where's Hugh? I want to see our Hugh, not . . ." Millie Weston's demand trailed off as she wandered to the center of the group. "Where is he, Violet? I've waited all these years to tell him what I did for him. That man you married shouldn't have kept me, your own mother, from seeing her grandson. Even Fiona said that." She leveled a bony finger at Ellen. "I didn't tell her anything. She already knew. Hugh told her the truth and she wanted him free of you."

"The woman's lost her mind," Ross snapped. "Get her out of here."

"I don't think so, sir," Sergeant Wall said. "I think we'd better hear her out. Go on, Mrs. Weston."

Millie Weston glanced about her as if uncertain. When she looked at Hugh her gaze clouded. "I looked after *him* like I was told. I did it for you, Violet, you and my grandson so he'd have a chance. But you did him out of what he should have had. Fiona told me that." She nodded at Ellen. "Fiona told me how you made our Hugh sign everything away to you and Xavier so you'd always have control. She told me how you threatened Hugh that he'd end up with nothing if he ever told the truth. He was still a boy really—twenty-one—and you waited that long to tell him you were his mother. Then you let him know you only wanted him for what he could give you.

"But I fooled you, daughter." Her gaze was fixed on Violet. "All that money you sent for me and the boy you made me look after—I never spent it. I gave it to my solicitor to save for me—told him it was compensation for your father's accident at the mill. And of course you know I made sure you signed the paper for the payments to go on even after I'm dead." She paused, grinning triumphantly. "Well, our Hugh doesn't know it yet, but he'll get those payments. He hasn't seen me since he was two, doesn't even know me, but one day he'll be getting something from his grandmother."

"Be quiet, mother," Violet ground out. She'd stopped crying.

"Yes, Mrs. Weston," Ross put in. "It would be better—"

"Better if I went with you?" Millie Weston sneered at him. "Like you made me go with you that night Fiona was visiting me and she telephoned for Violet to come and see her at my house? You took me away when I didn't want to go. Kidnapping's what that's called. You and her—" the bright eyes again found Violet "—you and her are in it together now, aren't you? You're like her. You want what's not yours. That's why you took me to that man Loder's cottage and had him shut me away."

"Mrs. Weston, I brought you here to be near Violet, your daughter," Ross said in a voice that shook. "But only because she was worried about you, and as her husband's employee I agreed to help out. You weren't able to look after yourself anymore, so Violet wanted to make sure you were in a safe place."

"Mrs. Weston," Sergeant Wall said soothingly, "is Violet Macky your daughter?"

"Yes."

"And what did you mean about her using the little boy Simon?"

Ellen tried to take a breath but couldn't. The evil she felt in this room pressed in on her chest. She slipped her hand into Hugh's, and he gripped it tightly. When Millie Weston looked at him fully and without emotion, the pressure on Ellen's hand increased.

"She brought *him*, the real Simon, to me," Millie said. "He's the same age as our Hugh—Violet's son, my grandson—and with the fire taking his family away, except for the blind sister, it was easy to leave the real Simon with me and have our Hugh take his place. I didn't approve of what she'd done—taking advantage of a terrible accident—"

"Accident!" Ned Loder retorted.

"Let the lady finish," Sergeant Wall said. He made notes in his book and so did the constable.

"She convinced me that she'd make sure Simon—who I was supposed to pretend was really Hugh—would be all right. She'd keep us in more money than we could use. And then, everyone would believe that our Hugh was Simon Macky, so he'd inherit this big house and all the land. She said it was the only way we could give our boy what he deserved. I'd cared for him from the time he was born till he was two. Violet never told me who his father was and I never asked, but there was no man's name on his birth certificate."

Ellen slid her arm around Hugh's waist. "What is she saying?" she whispered incredulously. "Is she saying you're Simon Macky and Simon was really Hugh Weston?"

He closed his eyes, gripping her shoulder so tightly it hurt.

"It wasn't until Fiona came along," Millie went on, "that I found out that our Hugh wasn't happy, how you'd taken everything for yourself, Violet. Once the boy was of age, the estate should have been his. But of course our Hugh wasn't the real heir, and you could threaten him that unless he signed everything over to Xavier and you, he'd be back where he started. He didn't like the truth, but he went along with what you wanted because he was afraid not to." Millie sighed. "He was a man, but he was still a boy, and not very strong-minded..." Her voice hardened again. She pointed her finger at Violet. "So you ended up with what you wanted, your high-and-mighty position as lady of the manor. That was what you'd planned from the start—to replace Simon Macky with another boy who could be blackmailed into giving up his heritage. You used your own son."

With only a brief pause to take a shaky breath, Millie said, "And then you couldn't stand him being in love with Fiona, could you? You were afraid she'd find out what you'd done and use it against you, so you tried to send her away. That's why she came to me. Our Hugh knew about the real Simon, the bookstore he owns and everything. He'd already told Fiona and she found me. She wanted me to help and I would have, but you took me away. I'll help you now." She moved closer to Ellen and stared at her. "Just tell me what I can do to help."

"She thinks I'm Fiona," Ellen breathed. "Fiona became friendly with her to try to get her to help...Simon..." She faltered.

"Shut up!" Violet swirled toward her mother until Ross blocked her path. She grabbed the lapels of his jacket. "This is your fault. You murdered my son and that's why it's all fallen apart. If you'd left him to me I'd have managed him. I could always manage him."

"Really?" Ross drew back his lips from his teeth and closed his hands on Violet's wrists. "Well, I didn't lay a finger on your precious boy. Xavier did. He killed your son because he'd found out just how well you *hadn't* managed him. Xavier found out you'd told winner-boy 'Simon' the truth about what happened to Fiona to try to keep him quiet. Then Xavier found out you'd failed to get him to agree to go along. So Simon was going to tell Ellen everything and then take the evidence you'd given him to the police. Xavier knew that would be the end, so he did what he thought he had to do. He killed Simon. But I had no part in it. I'm just the loyal employee around here."

Sergeant Wall gave a soft cough. "What evidence would that have been, Mr. Ivers?"

Ellen watched the play of muscle and nerves in Ross Ivers's face. Fear replaced bravado, in the angle of his head, the attitude of his big body.

"What evidence, Mr. Ivers?"

"Nothing," Ross muttered. "There was nothing. Xavier told me he'd had an argument with Simon and Simon wound up in bad shape. That's all."

Ellen wanted the horror to end. As if he heard her thought, Hugh rubbed the back of her head, her neck. His hand trembled.

"Are you saying you did not visit the man we know as Simon Macky on the night of his death?" The police officer's voice had hardened.

"I didn't," Ross blustered. "I never went in there. I waited in the car…"

"Yes," Sergeant Wall agreed slowly. "You waited in the car while Xavier Macky went to see his, er, nephew?"

"No!"

"Yes, sir. You already said so. According to a report we received from London shortly before we came here, a blue suitcase matching the description of one belonging to a Miss Fiona Shaw was found in your flat."

Ellen could see sweat on Ross Ivers's face. "I don't know anything about a suitcase."

"Sir. The man who called himself Simon Macky phoned his local police station last night, the night of his death, to say he had a suitcase belonging to Miss Shaw. He knew Miss Shaw, his fiancée he said she was, had been reported missing. He also stated that he was afraid of a Mr. Ross Ivers but that he wasn't ready to share all the information he had yet. Mr. Macky stated that he was simply filing the report in case he wasn't able to later.

"Mr. Macky sounded very drunk when he made the call. Since the police in his area had had one or two previous experiences with him, they discounted the report—until he was found dead. Unfortunate, but these things happen. When they searched your flat they found the suitcase. How did you get it?"

Ross made fists at his sides and turned to Violet. "Why didn't you get rid of the damned suitcase like you were supposed to? I only took it to back up the story that Fiona had gone on a trip—just in case someone got serious about looking for her. Why did you have to show it to Simon to make your point? Did you think letting him take the thing away and moon over it for a few hours would make him change his mind about blowing the whistle on us? You little fool." Then he swung toward Sergeant Wall. "Yes, I was outside while Xavier was with Simon and I took the case. But I didn't know he'd killed him. I had nothing to do with that. Xavier made me leave the case at my place and drive him back here fast. I didn't understand what the hurry was about until I heard the news. He was rushing home to try to create an alibi. He almost succeeded, because he was here when Ellen phoned. But when your man—'' he nodded toward Constable Stroud "—called about the old woman, Xavier must have decided it was the end as far as his beloved estate was concerned, so he jumped.''

"Violet Weston," Hugh said softly, then louder, "*Millicent* Violet Weston, perhaps?" He looked at Violet. "My birth certificate names my mother as Millicent Violet Weston. But you were . . . you were Simon's mother . . . the real Hugh Weston's mother. *My* mother . . . you murdered her, and my family . . .''

Ellen barely heard what he said. "Please," she murmured. Light-headedness made her hold on to Hugh's jacket. But he wasn't Hugh. And she wasn't Fiona. And Millie Weston wasn't dead. "Please listen to me, Mrs. Weston. Fiona was at your house the night you were supposed to have died. Is that right?"

The woman stared back, uncomprehending.

"You didn't die," Ellen continued. "But someone did." Still holding on to Hugh, she turned to face Ross squarely. "Were the remains they found in that house Fiona's? Did you kill my sister?"

Ross directed his response to Violet. "She knows. They all know. Tell them, Violet, how you worked out the explosion and set the fire. Like you set the fire all those years ago. They'll understand your thing about fire—it's common. Tell them Ned helped you like he did before, and how you both managed it so there wouldn't be enough left for a positive identification. I didn't kill anyone. I'll even admit to trying to shut Ellen up a couple of times—'' he turned to Hugh "—and you, too. But I didn't kill anyone.''

Ellen let Hugh enfold her in his arms, heard Jo murmur gentle words of sympathy close by and smiled absently at

# Epilogue

"Come and get warm, Mrs. Macky." Hugh had already hung their coats to dry in the bathroom and gone to light the fire.

Ellen shivered a little and knelt beside her husband, rubbing her hands together. "Nice weekend, wasn't it?"

"Mmm. Wonderful. Jo looks good, doesn't she? In many ways I think she's probably happier than she's been since we were children."

"That's because she's got you back." One day she'd be able to say how happy she was that Hugh had been reunited with his sister without longing desperately for Fiona.

"I think about Fiona, too," Hugh told her quietly.

He was like that, tuned in to what she was thinking and feeling.

"It still hurts," she admitted. "But you and Jo help because you don't avoid talking about her. That's the worst thing people do. They're afraid of upsetting me but they only make it seem like she never existed. Poor Cecily and Ed tiptoe around the subject as if they expect me to burst into tears at the sound of Fiona's name."

Hugh rubbed her cold cheek with the backs of his fingers. "Give them time. Maybe if *you* talk about her they'll loosen up a bit."

"Yeah, you're right. Hugh, the wise." She sat down, turning her legs sideways. Hugh joined her and looped an arm around her shoulders while they both stared into the electric fire's red-blue glow.

"Did I ever tell you what a rebel she was when she was younger?"

He looked at her. "Sort of."

Ellen laughed. "One of the reasons I hesitated about contacting the police when I first thought she might be missing was because I was afraid she might be in some legal scrape."

"You're kidding. Why didn't you say something at the time?"

"Habit, I guess. I was always used to covering for her. She had a boyfriend who was a thief once. He ended up in jail and she had to do some pretty fast talking not to be there with him."

"Was she guilty?"

"No. At least, not really. I think she knew he was up to something, but she also thought she was in love." She smiled at him. "And we both know what love can do, don't we?"

Hugh wrinkled his nose. "Yup. Great stuff, love. It's probably just as well I didn't know about Fiona's checkered criminal record. I'd have been even more sure she was the great mastermind behind the plot."

"Mmm." The plot was on her list of things to forget. She concentrated on the fireplace again.

January had settled an icy cloak on London and they often sat like this in the evening. Tonight they'd come back from Cadogan through driving snow that turned country hedgerows into puffy streamers and grimy city sidewalks to sparkling virgin paths. Slim fingers of snow clung to the rims of each diamond pane in the windows of the sitting room above the bookshop.

"Jo and I are lucky people," Hugh remarked. He lifted Ellen's damp hair from her shoulders and turned to concentrate on piling it on top of her head. "We both got you. Still glad you decided to make this a permanent thing with me?"

"What do you think?"

He let her hair fall and kissed her slowly. Ellen met the kiss and pulled him to lie with her on the rug. His weight felt good. The warm delicious ache began.

"Everything's working out okay, isn't it?" Hugh wasn't asking for an answer, he already knew how happy she was looking after the bookshop and the wine bar while he, with the help of some longtime employees, rapidly learned the intricacies of the estate that was his by right.

"Kiss me again," she demanded.

He did. To the people at the brewery operation and at Cadogan he'd quickly become Mr. Macky. Ellen was Mrs. Macky, but there had never been any question of Hugh reverting to his real first name. Simon Macky was gone. To Ellen, as well as to Jo, Hugh would always be Hugh. Jo had loved Simon and she missed him. Ellen remembered him as the man who had adored her sister, and for that she regretted the loss of him.

"You're miles away, Ellen." Hugh propped himself on his elbows and looked down at her. "Care to take me there?"

When he smiled like that, turned the ardent force of those amber eyes on her, concentration was almost impossible. Nevertheless Ellen tried. They'd been married a month and they still had so much to learn about each other and so much to help each other conquer.

"I was thinking about all that's happened," Ellen admitted. "I'll be glad when I don't do that so much."

"Give it time. When the trials are over it'll be a lot better."

"Mmm." The trials were a subject she tried to banish. "You don't like Cadogan much, do you?"

"No. I'd get rid of it if it weren't Jo's home. I can stand it on weekends to be with her. We've got a lot of catching up to do. But I knew from that first day when I went there with you that there was something ugly about the place. I kept feeling the house was familiar, but I didn't know why." He shook his head slowly. "The mind's wonderful. Mine has done a first-class job of blocking out what I don't want to remember. I've tried, you know—to remember something about the fire, the switch . . . but I don't."

"Don't try anymore."

"Easier said than done."

"I'll help you."

Hugh stood and pulled her up. "You do help, my love. And this is where we belong. I love knowing that the shop is here, and the books, and that I can come home to you and to them. When I get a strong grip on the Macky operation I intend to delegate as much of my responsibility there as I can and spend more time here."

"Will you hold me, Hugh? Hold me very tight?"

He frowned a little before he did as she asked, slipping his hands beneath her sweater to caress her back. "What's the matter? Sad?"

Against his neck she said, "Not really. Just greedy. I'll never get tired of being close to you."

"Never?"

"Never."

Holding her away a little, he smiled. "I guess that's it then."

"What's it?"

"For me. I'm just going to have to get used to having you around."

He pulled her head to his chest and Ellen felt the vibration of his laugh.

# Postscript

Violet Macky (née Weston) was convicted on four counts of murder: John, Clarisse and Jennifer Macky and, despite the impossibility of positive identification of remains, Fiona Shaw. She was also found guilty of kidnapping two-year-old Simon Macky and causing grievous bodily harm to Josephine Macky. Ross Ivers was convicted for complicity in the murder of Fiona Shaw and for the attempted murders of Hugh Weston (Simon Macky) and Ellen Macky (née Shaw), together with the abduction of Millie Weston. Ned Loder was found guilty of complicity in the four murders and of holding Millie Weston against her will. Millie Weston was judged mentally unfit to stand trial and committed to an institution. Xavier Macky did commit suicide after learning that his crime against his wife's son, together with his illegal hold on the Macky estate, might become public. In his summation at the trial of Violet Macky for the murder of Fiona Shaw, the judge remarked on the futility of the crime. "Murder is the most vicious of acts," he told the defendant, "and in this case as pointless for you as for the victim. Had you allowed Miss Shaw to live she would probably have posed no great threat to your plans. Dead she became your nemesis. Alive, she might never have revealed what she told in death."

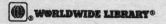